Johnny jerked the door open and dropped to a crouch

His Ingram SMG swept the room. A light burned brightly inside.

In the middle of the ten-foot-square room stood a metal table. Something was lying on it.

Mack Bolan also saw the table and rushed in front of Johnny, trying to block his view.

"Don't look, kid."

Johnny shook free and walked into the grisly room. Blood was splattered everywhere. Johnny trembled and dropped the Ingram on the floor as he stared at the bloody mass of bone and shredded flesh.

It was his girlfriend, Sandy Darlow.

She was the living dead.

MACK BOLAN
The Executioner

DON PENDLETON's

MACK *THE EXECUTIONER*

BOLAN

Resurrection Day

A GOLD EAGLE BOOK FROM

W RLDWIDE

TORONTO • NEW YORK • LONDON • PARIS
AMSTERDAM • STOCKHOLM • HAMBURG
ATHENS • MILAN • TOKYO • SYDNEY

First edition February 1985

ISBN 0-373-61403-9

Special thanks and acknowledgment to
Chet Cunningham for his contributions to this work.

Printed in Canada

I am marked for death. I am as
condemned as any man who ever sat in
death row. My chief determination is to
stretch that last mile to its highest yield,
to fight the war to my last gasp, to eat
their bowels even as they are trying to
digest me.

—*Mack Bolan*

MACK BOLAN

LEO TURRIN

JAY LUPO

JOHNNY BOLAN GRAY

ANGELA MARCELLO

SANDY DARLOW

MANNY MARCELLO

KARL DARLOW

"What do you hear from Johnny these days?" asked Turrin.

Bolan's eyes brightened as he answered Turrin. "I hear he's doing great. Growing like a weed in that Big Sky country."

"You're keeping wires on him, eh?"

"Very loosely," Bolan explained. "I don't want to jeopardize his cover. And, uh, it's better this way. Give him a chance for a normal—"

"Bull," said Turrin.

"That the way you see it?"

"Uh-huh. The kid idolizes you, Sarge. He'll never forget. And pretty soon he'll be at the age where he can make his own decisions. You'd better be thinking about that."

"I have," Bolan admitted. "Maybe...after we've interred the bones of Mack Bolan once and for all...well...it'll be a new life. If Johnny wants, uh, let's just say I'll be looking through different eyes. And we'll wait and see."

Executioner #37: *Friday's Feast*
by Don Pendleton

PROLOGUE

The valley was a natural grave.

Silence echoed across the warm Sicilian hills. Under the branches of an olive tree, a swarthy man in his forties finished setting up a small wooden folding table and two chairs. He motioned to his wife, young enough to be his daughter, to place the picnic basket on the table.

The air was heavy with the fragrance of wild thyme and myrtle in the late spring sunshine. The woman hoisted the basket onto the table and ran after the two-year-old boy who had started to wander off, chasing a butterfly.

By the time she returned with the toddler, the man had the contents of the hamper spread out on the white tablecloth: cheese, crusty bread, a bottle of red wine and a six-inch *prosciutti* roll.

The woman placed the child on her lap and watched adoringly as her husband began to slice the glazed pieces of preserved pork. The hard meat resisted the blade and the man leaned forward to exert more pressure into the cut.

Blood splattered the cloth and the woman's

mouth formed an O of concern, thinking her husband had chopped his finger with the knife.

She couldn't make the connection between the other small pieces of flesh that now scattered onto the table as her husband's stomach erupted, and the sharp *crack* that rolled across the valley only seconds later.

She screamed when her husband dropped onto the table, knocking the food and drink to the grass. In that instant she knew he was dead. She reached over to grab his shoulder, one hand still clutching the boy's arm, her eyes wildly seeking a place of refuge.

And that's when the second slug drilled into the back of her skull, sending her sprawling across her husband's body.

"Mama, mama," the child cried, uttering the only words he had ever learned, startled by the commotion. In his own innocent way, he sensed something was wrong.

The third bullet cut off the boy's cry and lifted him six inches above the ground, blood gushing from a crater in his neck, his head almost torn from his shoulders. The impact hurled him along the meadow grass, and his body came to rest in a clump of myrtle.

Then silence settled over the valley again, a faint gurgling from the tipped wine bottle the only sound.

High on a ridge overlooking the valley, the killer stroked the still-warm barrel of his high-powered rifle. Then he dismantled the weapon, placed the parts carefully in their preformed receptacles in the case and snapped the lock shut.

The usually white scar that ran down from his forehead dead center across his eye socket to his left cheek was splotched with red spots. As it always was when he was excited. Killing excited him.

He picked up the slender case and stepped over some rocks as he made his way back to the white Lancia parked on a turnout of the winding mountain road.

MACK BOLAN SWORE as he surveyed the scene in the valley through his binoculars. The growl of a car's engine fired him to action and he dashed toward the rented Alfa Romeo. In actual traveling time he reckoned he was at least ten minutes above the killer's spot on the road that spiraled tortuously down to the valley floor.

The Executioner slid behind the wheel and cranked the ignition of the small Italian sports car. The eager machine shuddered in a sideways skid as the rear wheels hit rubble from a mountainside rockfall.

Precious seconds slipped by and the Alfa seemed to stand still, then rubber bit the pavement and the little car shot forward on a straightaway, pebbles shooting out from below the tires into space over the sheer cliffs.

Bolan took his hand from the gear stick and

reached over to grab his binoculars. He had tossed them onto the passenger seat. He brought the glasses to his eyes after making sure there were no curves ahead.

To his left the road snaked across a spur on the mountain and he saw the white Lancia racing away from him. In a moment the car would round a sharp bend and disappear from view.

The vehicles were evenly matched in speed, the Executioner knew, and he hoped he could use some of his driving skills to gain on the killer who was eluding him once again.

For a second, Bolan's mind flashed back to the massacre in the valley and he cursed the poor phone connection between the States and Italy.

He'd been waiting for a call from Aaron Kurtzman, one of his last remaining links with Stony Man Farm, since early that morning, pacing the village hotel room and pounding a fist into his open palm.

The warrior hated sitting around, waiting, if even for an important phone call.

Bolan had flown to the Italian peninsula on the trail of Corrado Rienzone, the man assassinated with his wife and child only minutes before.

Rienzone had lived in the U.S. since he was twenty. He had worked his way up to being a "made" man in one of the Chicago crime families. Ambitious as ever, he saw a way to become chief capo. And that's where he ran into trouble.

Manny "The Mover" Marcello of San Diego

and other ruling slimebuckets of the international network learned of Rienzone's scheme and he fell into disfavor, to put it mildly. He realized that his star had begun to fall and he would be marked for execution. So he "sang" to the authorities and promptly slipped out of sight with a suitcase full of money.

By way of a circuitous route that took him to Venezuela and North Africa, Rienzone changed his appearance and bribed or paid his way to Italy—the last place he figured the Mafia would look for him—and settled in a remote mountain hamlet in Sicily.

He had left behind in the States a wife and two teenage children, hoping one day to somehow contact them and have them join him in Italy. But it was not to be.

Through secret sources that he had developed in the village, he learned that the heat was on more than ever. So he continued to lie low for two years.

But Rienzone needed a woman.

One day he spotted an attractive young girl, barely more than a teenager, walking in the piazza. Unfamiliar with traditional Italian courting customs, he approached the girl and she, impressed by this man with an American accent, shyly welcomed his attentions.

Rienzone found out where she lived and decided to talk to the girl's father.

She was the sixth of ten children in a poor

plasterer's family. At first, the girl's proud parent was reluctant to let his cherished Maria marry the older suitor, but when his eyes fell on the packet of lira notes that the stranger held, he agreed to the marriage.

Bolan had learned some of the dead man's recent history from Kurtzman and had tracked Rienzone to the remote mountain village.

In his probing of the evidence, the Executioner knew that vital links were missing from the information that Rienzone had spilled to the authorities; links that were vital to Bolan in his everlasting war against the Mafia, and that he felt he could extract from the informer.

But a new twist was added when Bolan discovered that an assassin, a top hit man from Chicago called Daga, because the scar on his face resembled a dagger, was sent to Italy to eliminate Rienzone.

The Executioner had followed Daga as far as the hillside ridge, but was too late to stop the killer from blowing away Rienzone. Bolan did not mind that the man had died. Violently. He had lived a violent life. But there was no reason to cut down the young woman and the child. As far as Bolan was concerned they were merely innocent bystanders.

As he drove, the Executioner was consumed by raw fury, made ever more acute by his frustration at being able to coax no more speed out of the racing Alfa Romeo.

"THANK YOU FOR FLYING ALITALIA," the stewardess said to the man with the dagger-shaped scar on his face who was about to enter the plane. He winked at her but did not reply as he made his way to the first-class cabin of the 747.

Daga took a window seat and positioned himself with his back to the bulkhead, looking anxiously at the top of the stairway that led down to the economy section of the airliner.

Someone had been following him on the mountain road, he was certain of it. On the hour-long drive downhill, he had caught three tiny flashes of sun on chrome in his rearview mirror. But he could not risk stopping to ambush the pursuer. He had timed his mission down to the final second; he had studied road maps of the region, speed limits and the schedule of flights out of Palermo.

The tension began to leave Daga when he felt the big aircraft shudder and begin to move forward. He could hear the powerful engines revving as the plane picked up speed on its run down the tarmac. He watched the terminal buildings flash by, then felt the nose of the aircraft lifting as the forward landing gear left the ground, the screaming turbines pulling tons of metal into the sky.

Minutes later Daga exhaled slowly and ordered a double whiskey, straight. No need to worry now. He'd be thousands of miles away in a few hours.

The attractive flight attendant smiled at the man with the scar who had ordered the liquor. She felt uncomfortable under his scrutiny and self-

consciously tugged at her skirt. Before she turned
away, she noticed that small red splotches had
begun to speckle the scar on the man's face.

MACK BOLAN had just pulled into the parking lot
of the international airport at Palermo when he
saw the Alitalia jet roaring across the runway past
the chain link fence.

The Executioner slammed the door of the Alfa
Romeo and dashed into the terminal building. He
looked up and down the corridor, searching for
the Italian air carrier's ticket counter. Finally he
spotted the desk and began to move, dodging suitcases and tourists.

He approached a young man fingering the key-
board of a computer terminal.

"What's the final destination of the Alitalia
flight that just left?"

"Chicago, *signore*, via Madrid and New
York."

Bolan inquired about the arrival time in Chicago, then purchased a ticket on a direct flight
there. It left an hour later and would arrive at
O'Hare well before the Alitalia flight.

He walked a few desks down the corridor to the
car rental agency, then chose a seat from a row of
chairs.

He settled down for the forty-five minute wait.

MACK BOLAN adjusted his photosensitive sunglasses and fingered the scratchy false mustache as

he waited behind a pillar outside the customs area at O'Hare Airport in Chicago.

He had passed through the immigration section with false papers an hour and a half before, having learned from a stewardess on the plane the precise exit Daga would use on his arrival at O'Hare. *If* Daga had continued on from New York to Chicago, which Bolan, knowing what was going down in Chicago, guessed he would.

From what Bolan could guess, half the passengers from the first Alitalia flight had cleared customs already. Still there was no sign of the killer. Could he have stopped off in Madrid?

Then the Executioner saw him. There was no mistaking the scar. The man carried a slender elongated suitcase.

The assassin looked up and saw a big man in dark clothes start to move toward him.

Bolan noticed a fleeting frown cross the killer's face. The guy pushed an elderly couple out of the way and scaled the stainless-steel railing, heading for the main exit door of the terminal building.

Bolan had made a quick recon of the area, prepared for such a move. The automatic sliding doors had just clicked shut when Bolan saw the man drag the driver of a waiting taxi from behind the wheel. Then Daga slipped into the cab and roared out of there, barely missing some pedestrians on a crosswalk.

Bolan flagged the next hack in line, ran around the car and wrenched open the driver's door.

"Slide over, buddy," Bolan growled to the young black man.

"Say what?" the cabby yelled.

"Enjoy the ride, no questions," Bolan said icily, and gave the guy a look that sent him cowering against the passenger door.

It was evening and Bolan could see the taillights of the receding taxi winking as Daga wove in and out of the heavy airport traffic. The Executioner realized the man would be in the downtown area in minutes. And it would be like hell to find him then.

The warrior looked at the black cabby.

"I need a shortcut, guy, with few lights. I need to intercept that car," Bolan said, pointing to Daga's taxi.

"Sure, man. Anything you say," the black replied, only too happy to help, so he could get his car back and save any explanations to the dispatcher later on.

He gave the Executioner the instructions and Bolan gunned the ponderous vehicle in a sharp left turn down a couple of alleys, then to the right, parallel to the main artery the fleeing killer was traveling on.

"Hang a right here, blood,' the black squeaked. "We'll catch him at the next intersection."

Bolan spared a glance at the youth next to him and couldn't help but smile as he realized the guy was caught up in the excitement of the chase. He was leaning forward now, both hands gripping the dashboard, his nose almost to the windshield. Bolan hoped he wouldn't have to stop too suddenly.

The Executioner trod on the gas and the car surged into the junction. Then he stood on the brake and the cab slid to a halt facing the oncoming traffic. Car horns started blaring, but Bolan ignored them as he spotted the lighted sign on the taxi coming toward them.

The big guy pulled a handful of bills from his pocket and dropped them on the seat next to the black taxi driver.

"Get out of here," he commanded, wrenching his door open and hitting the pavement in a shoulder roll.

Bolan heard the cab burn rubber as he came out of the roll in a wide-legged combat stance, dead center in the intersection. The Beretta 93-R had cleared leather and was now pointing straight at the oncoming taxi.

Pedestrians stopped to gawk at the imposing figure in black on the city street, aiming a handgun at something or someone.

The Executioner let them watch as he flicked the Beretta to 3-shot mode, triggering a burst, then another, emptying the weapon at the windshield of the approaching car.

After the first burst he saw the driver's hands fly off the steering wheel, but still the car kept coming toward him. It was almost upon him and he leaped out of the way in time, and as the vehicle swept past him, he caught a glimpse of the scar, harsh in the streetlight, the driver's head lolling lifelessly against the window.

The taxi continued on, sideswiping a line of parked vehicles before it came to a stop.

People were shouting and running toward the stricken taxi. Hardly anyone paid attention to the big man now and Bolan used the time to make a quick withdrawal, melding into the night.

The warrior walked away from there, pausing only once to look back, the babble of voices diminishing as he strode into the heart of the city.

The big man walked tall, in lockstep with Death as the reaper prowled the city this night. Grim and mean, it held its secrets secure, offering up nothing.

The nooks and crannies of the city writhed with menace, its denizens snapping out at innocents, sometimes going hungry. But no matter. Next time there'd be reward—perhaps a life.

Skeletal fingers beckon from the gloom, whispering promises of narcotic nirvana. Death's head grins when the weak submit but grimaces if the strong resist.

Shadows in motion on a wall play out a ghastly scene as upraised arm, clutching some instrument of death, plunges down between unsuspecting shoulder blades. A mercy cry echoes along the city's labyrinth, beseeching help, but the plea falls on deaf ears, ending in a gurgle, finally swallowed up by an unrelenting city.

An empty wine bottle clatters to the cold pavement and the sound is muffled by a paper bag. Its owner, sated by alcohol and warmed for a moment by the liquid's fire, pulls a shabby coat tighter, preparing for a dreamless sleep. But slumber is not without its perils and he will not last the night. Because he is weak and defenseless against the onslaught of the human demons that stalk the city's arteries. And his sleep will be dreamless—forever.

Wisps of steam rise in harsh fluorescence from a manhole. The metal cover shudders, then opens, the reaper gazing out to gauge the prospects, licking bony lips and baring fangs if passage is clear, recoiling and scurrying back to the depths of the sewer if danger threatens.

A human form hurtles downward past the unseeing gaze of a building to smash on the concrete below. But the cold visage of the monstrous glass-and-steel architecture will divulge nothing, its inscrutable countenance remaining cryptic about victim and perpetrator alike.

The city respects no one, chewing up the naive and the innocent year after year. Occasionally a merciful heaven unleashes a cleansing rain to wash the concrete corridors, but always indelible crimson stains remain.

Mack Bolan had seen it all, in cities everywhere. And it had also touched him personally.

From out of nowhere, Death had come swooping down, hunting for prey. And found it—in Mack Bolan's family.

For one heartbeat the soldier's world had crumbled about him. But an innate instinct surfaced in the microinstant before the heartbeat was complete. And Bolan knew what he had to do.

He was always aware of man's decay and degeneracy, but in tribute to the goodness he believed was inherent in all humans, he paid little attention.

Not all men were strong, he knew. And although he fancied himself no different from others, simply following the rules of right and wrong, an unidentified spark ignited the rage he felt at his family's cruel death. So he made his final peace at his parents' graveside

And declared war on Animal Man in all his forms.

Destiny had long ago decreed that Mack Bolan should travel a long and tortuous road. Along this route the soldier had questioned himself countless times about his motivations, his everlasting war. He had asked himself if what he was doing was worth it. Indeed, he had often thought that if he could have foreseen the future, would he have made the decisions that he had?

And the answer had always been yes. Because he knew there was no alternative. Just as he knew that as long as man walked the earth, there would always be a dark side to the creature

With every step the warrior took it struck him as amusing how man, being as insignificant as he was in a cosmic sense, perpetually flirted with the

natural order of the universe. But perhaps courting danger *was* part of the natural order.

Maybe.

Somehow Bolan could not fathom the infliction
of pain by the stronger upon the weaker as
"natural." No way. Not if he continued to hold
sacred the principles of right and wrong that he
was taught from childhood.

Sometimes the fight pulled him down, both
physically and emotionally. But Bolan, even in his
dispirited and weakened condition, resisted the
force, willing himself to take one more step. Because if he didn't, he would be cheating the
memory of his parents and all those trampled by
the savages.

Bolan had identified the savages very early in
his war. The first to come in Bolan's crosshairs
was the U.S. Mafia—*La Cosa Nostra*. After a
while it did not matter to the warrior that the Mob
had caused the death of his family. Because he felt
he had avenged their deaths long ago. To him the
Mafia represented Evil. Pure and simple.

They could not be allowed to flourish at soci-
ety's peril. And there was a chance, a small one,
granted, that they would one day find his only sur-
viving relative, his brother, Johnny, wherever he
was.

Bolan had always harbored a secret fear—bor-
dering on paranoia, and known only to a couple
of people—that Johnny might find himself the
target of Mafia guns. Because he was sure to re-

member the circumstances surrounding his family's death. And if he was a true Bolan, there would eventually be a desire to confront the Evil that made him an orphan.

For years Mack Bolan had stayed away from Johnny, keeping tabs on him through a friend. And through the years Bolan had often thought of Johnny, wishing he could see his brother, even for a brief instant.

The moment of truth was at hand.

1

Johnny Bolan Gray felt a tingle of apprehension as the LCVP—landing craft for vehicles and personnel—swung away from the U.S. Navy ship and turned toward shore. It was just past midnight as the LCVP's muffled 325 HP diesel engine powered it through a light Mediterranean chop toward the dark Lebanon shoreline two miles away.

This was only the second time Johnny had been in a landing craft. The boat was thirty-five feet long and ten feet wide, built like a steel coffin. He didn't like being in it any more than he had the first time.

Johnny rode the vessel toward the Beirut shore as a member of the twenty-man assault party. Ten were crack combat specialists from a SEAL team unit on the ship, the rest had been drawn from the deck force.

They would be disembarking north of the airport, near a demolished luxury hotel and a row of modest beach houses that had been the site of the previous landing. An intelligence team had infiltrated the area three nights before and had been due to flash a signal from shore over six hours ago. But no one had heard from them during the past twenty-four hours. Nothing had been seen.

Trouble.

The strike force's job was to find out what happened to the intelligence group and bring them out—if possible.

The night began warm and overcast, but now the cloud cover had dispersed, revealing the bright, nearly full moon.

The small force crouched behind the LCVP's ramp, getting ready for the short run to shore. There would be no air support, no big guns covering their landing zone.

Johnny was an E-5 petty officer, second class. He stood five feet ten and weighed one fifty-five. His big wish lately was for contact lenses, but for now he used GI glasses for far vision. He had dark brown hair, and soft blue eyes that women found fascinating, or at least that's what they told him.

Crouched beside Johnny on the steel deck of the vessel, gripping an M-16 rifle, was Randall Phillips, Johnny's closest buddy for the past two years. Neither one of them had ever fired a shot in anger, let alone aimed at another human being.

"Gray, you son of a bitch, how did we get into this stinking mess, anyway?" Phillips asked, raising his voice over the growl of the LCVP's engine.

"Volunteered, remember?" Johnny said, punching him in the shoulder. Johnny liked this rawboned hillbilly from Kentucky. They had hit it off well when they were assigned to their current

Navy bucket, and the two young men had shared an easy friendship ever since. They chased girls together, got drunk together and kept each other out of trouble.

Phillips was six feet two inches tall, gangly, with a mop of straw-blond hair and a wide grin that showed a row of slightly buck teeth.

Johnny shifted the Armbrust disposable anti-tank rocket launcher to his other shoulder. "Geez, this thing is getting heavier."

"I'm crying for you, Gray. I got to carry four rounds for that mother, and you get all the fun of firing it." He scowled. "What the hell are we doing out here, Gray? People could get hurt with all these damn guns and explosives."

"We're trying to save somebody's ass," Johnny said.

"Sure, but figure the odds," Phillips argued. "We go in with twenty swabbies to bring out four people Probably all of us will get wasted in there.'

Johnny remained silent as flashes of light from Beirut lit up the horizon. He hunkered down against the cold metal, looking at the crack SEAL team at the front of the craft. Hell, he and Randall had it made. All they had to do was stay behind the old pros with the hand-held M-60 machine guns and keep their heads down.

Johnny looked up at the moon again. The added light worried him. The success of this kind of strike depended on the darkness. This operation was shaping up like all the others he had been on: what you had to do was keep your mouth shut, do what you were told and never volunteer. So why the hell had he volunteered?

A sense of duty—to himself and for his country; indeed, for the free world.

But he had never expected anything like this when he joined the Navy fresh out of high school in Sheridan, Wyoming. He had asked for boot training in San Diego and the Navy approved. Sitting offshore and listening to the steady pounding as artillery and mortar fire devastated the city had been like looking at a movie. Now it was getting real, too damn real.

Johnny had qualified on the rifle during boot, but tonight when fired the M-16 it would not be at a bull's-eye or a man-size silhouette target. He would be shooting at another human being—trying to kill him!

Johnny wondered how he would perform. He had heard old hands talk about combat in Nam on the riverboats where the war had been up close and deadly for thousands of sailors. Johnny remembered the horror and confusion he had felt when he heard stories of hacking Vietnamese apart with a hatchet, blowing their brains out with a .45 round at point-blank range.

The engine on the LCVP hummed a note higher and Johnny felt a surge of power as the boat moved through the water faster. The coxswain must have picked out his landing site and was trying to match the waves to help them catch a building breaker so they could surf in. Johnny sensed a stirring among the SEAL members in the front. Most of them had seen action, been "blooded" as they said. Four of the men were new to the team.

"Thirty seconds to landing," Ensign Walters said.

The whisper came along the line of crouched, anxious men all wondering what to expect.

Thirty seconds, Johnny thought to himself. In two or three minutes he could be dead.

His hands began to sweat. Once more he shifted the 14-pound Armbrust to a new position on his back. He checked to make sure that he had a round in the chamber of his M-16.

Randall Phillips grinned and nudged Johnny. "Hey, Gray, you sign those papers they gave us? Last will and testament and all that crap?"

Last will and testament? Johnny frowned at the thought. He had in fact named his brother, Mack, as his beneficiary. Had Mack, on the eve of his first action in Vietnam, experienced the same apprehension that Johnny was now facing? Hell, yes. Johnny's face relaxed into a smile and he drew strength from that last thought as he answered Randall.

"Yeah. You?"

"No. I got nothing to leave anybody." Randall shrugged. "I found me a damn home in the Navy. What's to go back to?"

As he said it there was a slight shudder as the metal hull of the LCVP scraped against the sand.

Lebanon. . . .

Beirut. . . .

Invasion!

Johnny could see the SEAL men tensing. They rose to a standing position, still braced as the vessel rode a huge wave that lifted the craft off the sand and shoved it twenty feet farther up the shore. The landing ramp of the LCVP swung outward and fell with a splashing jolt into the Mediterranean Sea. The men began to spill across the metal walkway in ankle-deep water as they hit the hard Beirut beach.

Johnny felt his feet touch the sand and he kept running.

There had been no opposing fire so far. Maybe they had made an unobserved landing. Moonlight still bathed the beach and Johnny could see the small dunes and the row of modest beach houses in front of them.

The SEAL men dashed up the beach with the other ten sailors right behind them. According to plan, five of the sailors spread out on each side of the SEALs at five-yard intervals and continued running toward the row of residences.

Then it happened. Sudden machine-gun fire sliced into the center of the line like a scythe.

The instant he heard the gun-chatter, Johnny dived into the sand, still warm from the hot daytime sun. He rolled behind a small dune and pushed back his helmet, trying to catch his breath. To his right he saw three SEAL men writhing on the sand. A fourth lay perfectly still, the top of his head blown off.

A pair of grenades exploded ahead, then two more.

"Move it!" somebody shouted. "To the right! On the double!"

Johnny recognized the voice as Chief Swanson's, the only one of the SEAL men he knew. Johnny jumped up just as Randall pushed past him. They sprinted around the four bodies on the ground, and in the moonlight Johnny saw the shattered, bloody face of Ensign Walters That made Chief Swanson their leader.

Swanson had sent two of his combat veterans around the side to make sure the machine-gun position had been neutralized by the grenades. Now they were back and waving everyone forward.

"I wasn't cut out to be no damn infantryman!" Randall muttered. Swanson angled them forward to a trail that ran parallel to the beach and behind the first row of houses. Most of the structures had been damaged by shelling. Some had holes in the walls, many of the windows were shot out.

The men all knew the mission. They had to move about a quarter of a mile into the city from the landing zone, find the house that had two palm trees in the front yard and rescue the intelligence party.

Swanson ran up and down the line of his troops.

"We're home free right now, but the bastards heard the shooting and will get more troops here pronto. We need to be in and out of that house and back to the beach before they show up. Come on, move it!"

The men moved forward. The weight of the Armbrust rocket launcher on his back felt like a ton, but Johnny Bolan Gray kept up with the others. He was their heavy artillery if they needed it.

"Down!" Swanson roared, and the men hit the dirt along the side of the path. The building ahead of them and to the right erupted with small-arms fire. Johnny flattened himself on the ground.

"Who's got that bazooka?" Swanson roared again.

Johnny crawled on his elbows and knees until he was crouching beside the leader.

"Put one into that house, the first floor."

Johnny swung the Armbrust off his back and onto his shoulder.

Rifle fire sprayed the area and they all dived to the ground, ramming helmets into the dirt.

When the flurry of rounds died, Johnny repositioned the Armbrust on his shoulder, sighted on a first-floor window and fired the 2.2 pound warhead. There was no recoil because the countermass of plastic flakes in the weapon's firing tube eliminated it. Nor was there any flash, blast or smoke, as piston brakes at each end of the tube sealed in the gases.

The chief appeared surprised at the meager, pistollike sound, then turned a second later as the house ahead of them exploded with a stuttering roar, flames gushing out of the windows. A secondary explosion shook the residence and the roof fell in. The chatter of the SEAL machine guns and the M-16s all around Johnny was furious, and he flinched when the second explosion shattered the house.

"Let's go!" Swanson shouted.

Johnny slung the Armbrust across his back, grabbed his M-16 and ran ahead. In the moonlight he saw a man in a camouflage shirt and white pants stumble out of the house. The man aimed a rifle at them.

He's going to kill me, Johnny thought. The young man's knees wobbled for a second. Then he gritted his teeth, lifted the M-16 and triggered the weapon. It was set on full auto, and six slugs slammed into the Arab, knocking him backward.

Johnny watched the Shiite fall. For a fraction of a second he wanted to scream that he did not mean to kill the man, that it was a mistake.

He heard gunfire and felt a stinging in his arm. He sprayed more rounds at a window in the back of the house and ran past it, racing with the rest of the men deeper into the city. Passing another row of bombed-out buildings, they settled behind a long stone wall. Johnny checked his arm and found only a scratch.

The sounds of firing diminished. Soon there

were only the sporadic cracks of a few rifle rounds.

"The next house is our objective," Swanson said, breathing hard from the run. "Our people are supposed to be in there." He pointed at two of his SEALs. "Circle around back. If you draw any fire, get your asses back here quick. If you get all the way around, find a defensive position to protect the other side of the house. Go!"

The men moved out at once. Just like boot camp, Johnny thought. They command, you do it. That kind of discipline could save your life—or it could get you killed. As he sat behind the wall he unslang the Armbrust tube, got a live one from Randall and attached it to the triggering stock of the weapon. This was a special combat operational test for the weapon, to see if the military wanted to put it into regular issue. So far, Johnny was impressed by the Armbrust.

Johnny was breathing hard as he adjusted the weapon.

The unmistakable smell of rotting flesh came to him. For a moment it was overpowering. He turned to his right and saw a white goat that had been blown apart by a shell. Half of it was bloated. Even in the darkness a swarm of flies buzzed around the decaying flesh.

The sound of rifle fire came from a half mile away. A moment later the two men Swanson had sent came out on the far side of the house and waved them forward.

"Half of us will rush the house," Swanson said. "No firing. We hope friendlies are in there." He turned to Johnny. "Keep the bazooka thing back here as artillery. If we don't get in, we'll want you to put a round through a window, any window." He pointed to some of his men.

"Let's go, now!"

They darted toward the entrance. Swanson tried the handle, pushed open the door. Johnny heard some soft conversation inside. Then Swanson motioned the rest of them forward.

Johnny was the last one through. Someone slammed the door shut behind him and a wooden bar dropped into iron holders securing the door.

Johnny found himself in a modern furnished house, faintly lit by candles on the floor, and a sudden feeling of anxiety washed over him. People lived here! And he had been ready to blow the place into kindling.

Swanson yelled at a medic, who rushed over to a bleeding man lying on a cot at the far side of the room. Someone was holding a candle near the wounded man. The corpsman broke open a medical kit from his bag, pulled out some items and hurriedly worked over the man.

"He's dead, sir," the corpsman said.

"He's got to come with us, he's an American. We take out all of our people when we pull back. Dead or alive!"

The chief wiped sweat off his forehead. "Damn foul-up! There are two civilians and a captain in the other room. He says we were supposed to be here yesterday. Their radio got shot to pieces and they had to sit and wait for us. Some assholes got curious outside and they had a running firefight for the past six hours.''

A half-dozen rifle rounds slammed into the room and everyone hit the floor.

Johnny left the rocket weapon on the floor and crawled to a broken window. He triggered a burst with his M-16 through the window. It drained his magazine but sent two attackers stumbling into a death-sprawl in the sand outside.

"Nice shooting, kid. What's your name?" Swanson asked.

"Gray, Petty Officer Johnny Gray, sir."

"Keep them pinned down out there, Petty Officer. We've got to get the other three ready to travel so we can get back to the boat. The crew pulled it back into the sea, and they'll come back for us on three flashes of light, then three more."

Johnny looked over at Randall on the far window. Randall lifted up and fired three rounds, then dropped back out of sight. When he glanced at Johnny, they both made a thumbs-up sign and grinned.

Another cautious look by Johnny showed no movement outside his window. He had jammed in a new magazine and automatically charged a round into the chamber.

Chief Swanson slid down beside him.

"Gray, you been under fire before?"

Johnny shook his head.

"No sweat, just keep your head the way you've been doing and we'll all get out of this. We have three VIP types in the next room. As soon as we do a little more prep work on them, we'll start moving out of here.

"We lost some good men to that machine gun. I need a chain of command. You're it. If I go down, you've got to get this detail back to the landing zone. Everyone must be removed. This operation is highly classified. In fact it never took place—if we get out with all the people. Twenty-four is the number. If we can't get everyone off this rock, we don't go until we can."

Johnny looked up. "What's so secret?"

"Hell, nobody told me. We don't need to know. We just get twenty-four people into that LCVP."

A hand grenade crashed through part of the window glass still in the frame behind them. Without hesitation Johnny leaped for the explosive, scooped it up and tossed it outside in one continuous motion.

The grenade exploded as it cleared the sill, shattering the rest of the glass. A chunk of shrapnel tore through wooden molding and chewed a ragged, inch-deep hole in Johnny's shoulder.

"Keep the bastards back!" Swanson screamed. "We need another four or five minutes. Use some of those grenades. They don't do any good hanging on your webbing!"

The volume of rounds coming from the house increased. Johnny heard a stuttering machine gun in another room. Several of the candles were snuffed out. Johnny sent five rounds through his window and heard two more grenades discharge outside.

As Swanson talked he slapped a gauze pad over the bloody shoulder wound and wrapped Johnny's upper arm with a roller bandage over his torn shirt.

"Hell, I thought I was dead. I saw that grenade and I knew it was cooking and we had maybe two seconds to live. Thanks, kid."

Johnny flexed his arm and simply nodded.

Swanson ordered another man to take up Johnny's post. "Fire a few rounds to keep their heads down," the squadron leader instructed. "We leave here in two minutes."

Swanson motioned Johnny to follow him, and they crawled across the floor into the safe room. On a bed lay a girl who looked to Johnny to be about nineteen. She was beautiful, with deep brown eyes and glistening black hair. Her upper body was bare except for a new bandage that covered her right breast.

"We're almost ready to go," Swanson told her. She nodded. A younger boy, unmistakably her brother, moved to her side and helped her struggle into a white blouse. He buttoned it for her. She kept staring at Johnny, and at last she smiled. He knew the smile came despite her terrible pain. He nodded and smiled back. She looked away.

The third person in the room was Navy. He wore

a captain's silver eagles on his khaki shirt collar. He had a bandage on one arm and another on the side of his head. He appeared to be dazed.

Swanson knelt in front of the seated officer and indicated Johnny, who squatted beside him.

"Sir, this is Petty Officer Gray. He's next in command if I buy one. The most important people here are this young lady and her brother. Our orders are to get them back to our ship. And we must take out all of our dead and wounded. Now get ready, we'll move in one minute."

Johnny worked out of the room with Swanson, who pointed to the front. "Get around there and find our men and move them to the back of the house. We've got to haul ass out of this cracker box before the enemy bring up their big stuff."

Even as Swanson spoke, Johnny spotted a Russian tank lumbering toward the house where his assault force was hiding. In another twenty seconds the Soviet-built monster would be in a position to train its big cannon on them.

2

Johnny Gray dived across the living-room floor, grabbed the Armbrust and hoisted it onto his shoulder. Aiming through a broken window, he tracked on the tank past a tree, glued the cross-hairs on the side of the machine a foot above the churning treads and squeezed the trigger.

The pistol-crack of the weapon sounded louder inside the room, but of course there was no back blast. Johnny held his position so he could still peer over the sill. The round hit the tank and a second later the hatch blew off as the HE projectile set off the tank's magazine and blew it into an expensive piece of junk, smoking in the moonlight.

Chief Swanson nodded. "Now get the hell outside and bring those men around," he barked at Johnny, who spent a moment to detach the empty tube, take a live one from Randall and lock it in place. Then he shifted the weapon to his back, cinched it up and crawled to the far door. He slid through the opening on his belly and dropped quickly behind a low block wall.

A member of the SEAL team rose and motioned. Johnny rolled across a gap in the wall and fell behind another section of the concrete barricade.

"Pulling out," Johnny said. "Bring everybody else around back. Follow me."

There was no surprise. The combat specialist nodded, waved at two more men and they crawled along the side of the house, then began running in a crouch, heading for the rear of the residence.

In the dim light Johnny saw the girl appear at the rear exit and look out. Johnny ran to the door, took her hand. She wore sandals, a thin skirt and a white blouse. Her brother was ahead of them. Johnny urged her out the door.

"We must run," he said.

She nodded.

He tried to cover her from any danger. He saw the pale Navy captain lurch out the door toward the brush. They would use a safer route back to the landing zone.

They were halfway to the beach when the moon appeared again from behind shifting clouds, bathing the dry, dusty land in a kind of light that every combat veteran hates when he's moving, loves when the enemy is trying to advance. The brush helped.

Swanson motioned to Johnny as he ran into the thin growth.

"I've got a scout in front," the chief said. "He's a good man. Says there's a bunch of Arabs up there blocking our way. He's not sure how many. Do we have any antipersonnel rounds for that cannon of yours?"

"Three," Johnny said. "One is loaded now."

"Use one, see what happens."

Johnny moved quietly forward through the brush. He found the lookout twenty yards ahead standing behind a large palm. He pointed the weapon to the shadows fifty yards in front of them. There was an open area with nothing on it but sand, rocks and deadly moonlight.

The darkness under the brush beyond the clearing beckoned to them like a refuge. A hundred yards ahead and to their left, closer to the water, stood a gutted hotel. The top five stories were devastated by bombs and fire. No windows remained in the side of the structure that Johnny could see.

He sighted on the center of the black mass where the scout said the enemy troops lay. Through the light-gathering power of the sighting scope he could see men moving around. He checked from side to side. There had to be thirty soldiers there at least. Johnny knew the round would hit and spray hundreds of thousands of small wires and shrapnel forward in a 180-degree killzone. He acquired target on the closest moving blobs and fired.

The round exploded forty yards ahead of them almost at the same moment as the pistollike report of the weapon. Johnny kept his eye on the sight.

Bodies flew through the air, heads came unattached, arms sailed past. A torso with no appendàges slammed across his vision and was gone.

The screams began even before the rolling thunder of the explosion died.

Johnny took the empty Armbrust tube off the firing apparatus. Randall was suddenly behind him, handing him another antipersonnel round. Johnny stopped a shiver from sneaking down his back and locked the warhead in place. He saw that Randall had two M-16s. In the gloom their glances met and Johnny nodded his thanks.

Within a minute the others surrounded them in the brush, sufficiently spread out so a lucky grenade would not do to them what it had done to the untrained Shiite troops.

Swanson knelt beside Johnny.

"Look, Gray, I'm no damn ensign or lieutenant. I don't mind some suggestions."

Johnny looked at the shattered area ahead through the half-light. Clouds scudded over the moon. "Let's bypass those woods, bear left toward the beach and work through the fringe of trees behind those houses."

Swanson looked both ways, then nodded. "I want you to stay with the girl and her brother. They're the damn prize in this big hornets' nest we've disturbed. Keep them in the middle of our detail. Let's move!"

For five minutes they worked forward slowly through the dark line of trees, then came to another clearing. They were just past the burned-out hotel when a machine gun opened up behind them.

"Down!" Johnny shouted. They all flattened out. The girl reached over and held his arm as a volley of machine-gun slugs chopped up the brush over their heads.

"I'm afraid," she whispered, her face close to his.

"We're all afraid. But don't worry." He touched her cheek. "But don't worry, we'll make it."

He bellied toward the rear and found Randall. "How many grenades you got?"

"Two."

Johnny gave him two more. "Go back there and get that damn machine gun or he'll chop us up into pig feed. I'll take the two Armbrust rounds to lighten your load. Move fast!"

Randall Phillips ran to the nearest tree and peered around. The chatter gun had moved to the left. It spat out twenty rounds. Randall faded into the darkness toward the sound.

For the next three minutes they lay there waiting. A new sound came from the front. More troops moving up.

Johnny heard the first grenade go off, then a second. For a moment the echo trailed away, then he heard a scream as an M-16 chattered eight rounds.

A deadly silence closed around them like a shroud.

A minute later Johnny whirled at the sound of a rustling, his M-16 leveled at a figure behind him.

"It's me," Randall whispered. "I got the two bastards."

Johnny nodded and worked his way forward to where Swanson lay.

"They've got us bracketed, at least a company of troops out there," Swanson said. "They don't seem to be well trained and their firepower is low-grade. But we're cut off from the landing zone. We've got two more of your rounds. Time to try for the hotel before they beat us to it. We'll have some solid protection." He looked at his watch. "Damn, it's almost one-thirty. Be light again in four hours."

A scout returned, Swanson led the detail into the first floor of the hotel. They entered through a window and spread out in three rooms facing the landing zone. They were three hundred yards away from the closest point where the boat could touch shore. Escape to the sea was still that far away from them. Right then it looked a lot farther to Johnny.

An attack came almost at once, rifle and machine-gun fire riddling the hotel.

"Hold your fire!" Swanson snapped before anyone returned a shot. "Let them waste their lead upstairs. We don't want them to know we're all down here."

"A diversion," Johnny said. "We need a diversion." Swanson looked at him and nodded. The girl put her hand on Johnny's arm, then pulled away and shivered. She was too frightened to speak. She reached for her brother's hand.

"What's your plan?" Swanson asked.

"Send two men out the far end of the hotel at right angles to our route for about fifty yards. Down there they can throw a couple of grenades and shoot up a storm with the M-16s. That should distract the enemy for a while."

"Worth a try." Swanson looked at Randall, then changed his mind and pointed at two of his SEAL members. He briefed them on what to do and instructed them to haul ass fast back to the hotel. The pair slipped into the night.

The firestorm kept coming from the front, but at a reduced level. There had been no return shots. After some minutes the U.S. strike force heard the grenades exploding to the rear. Then the rifle fire from the enemy ahead of them stopped completely.

"No noise!" Swanson whispered.

Johnny craned his neck to look through the broken window. In the moonlight he could make out twenty men in ragged uniforms running through the night toward the firing. What did that leave in front of them?

A SEAL scout unsheathed a thin knife and went to find out. He returned just as the two men from the diversion checked in. The scout reported that there were still six men blocking their way. He suggested that he go back with four grenades and take them out. Swanson agreed and the man faded into the night.

"When the grenades go off, we get out of here

and move twenty yards south of the hit into the trees, then sprint for the damn beach,'' Swanson said.

"You want an antipersonnel round ahead of us?" Johnny asked.

"Save it, we might need it later."

They heard four explosions followed by screams and the group took off. Johnny was in the middle of the loose formation. The girl, now desperately clutching his hand, ran beside him. Her young brother grinned and sprinted ahead.

Just before the grenades had exploded she stood close to him. "My name is Astra. I am sorry I have caused all this pain, and the deaths of your men. I am Lebanese. My father works with the Americans hoping he can save our country. The Druse and Shiites have put a price on his head."

"I hope this works out well for all of us. My name is Johnny." She had said his name twice, the faint trace of a smile touching her drawn face. Then she put her hand to her breast and breathed slowly. He saw the pain, the new terror on her face.

They ran into the trees and stopped for a moment to regroup. Gulping air, they looked at the beach beckoning in the moonlight, and Johnny knew they were going to make it.

They were racing to the dunes when winking machine-gun fire opened up from a nest in almost the same position as the first one.

Johnny, Astra and her brother slid behind a

small dune as slugs geysered the sand above their heads. They lay side by side and she put her arm across Johnny's chest to stop herself from shaking. He touched her cheek and she looked at him.

"I'm going to get both of you out of here, Astra. I promise. I won't let anything happen to you. Stay here and keep down, I have to find the chief."

She nodded and he crawled along the base of the sandy hummock. He found Swanson behind a small dune, looking toward the still stuttering machine gun. Johnny dropped beside Swanson and touched his shoulder.

The mortal remains of Chief Petty Officer Swanson rolled on top of Johnny, and only then did he see in the moonlight that the chief's face had been blown away. Johnny bit back a scream. He gently pushed the body off him and tried to stifle the waves of nausea that were threatening to engulf him.

He unclipped the flashlight from Swanson's belt and found six men, forming them in a skirmish line facing the enemy. When the machine gun opened up again, Johnny ordered the troops to throw grenades in its direction. One of the small bombs rolled into the right spot and silenced the heavy machine gun.

Then Johnny pointed the flashlight seaward, clicking it on and off three times for five seconds. Two minutes later he repeated the signal, and this time he saw an answering flash from the sea. He hoped it was the LCVP and not some prowling Shiite patrol boat.

Johnny found Randall, made sure he was all right, then sent out two men to bring in the dead. They got the three who were hit by the machine gun, including Swanson, and the SEAL who had been shot in both legs. He was alive, but barely. The machine gun on its second attack had badly wounded one man and killed one more besides the chief.

Johnny asked Randall to help him and soon they had the bodies ready for transport to the landing craft. Two men were assigned to carry each of the two wounded. That left him with three fighting men, the captain and the two civilians. Not much of a defensive force.

They waited.

Twenty minutes passed with only the sound of groans from one of the wounded.

The attack came from the wrong side. Johnny guessed it would be another tank with a platoon behind it. But the assault came from the side he thought was safe. The .50-caliber cannon ripped through the silent night, chopping up the six dead men who lay in a row barely showing over the top of the dune.

Johnny felt no remorse for using the dead to protect his force. He changed rounds, ramming the antitank round on the Armbrust. The moment he had a clear shot at the rolling machine, he fired. The round hit the tank's treads, blowing them apart and tipping the heavy rig on its side.

His men pounded the stricken metal monster with rifle fire as the tankers ran and forced the infantry behind to scatter for protection.

When Johnny turned to Randall for the last rocket tube, he saw his buddy staring at him with a sly smile. It looked strange in the moonlight, and Johnny punched him in the shoulder.

"Hey, this is no time to be playing games. Got that last round?"

Randall nodded, then his eyes closed and a last gush of breath escaped from his lungs as he fell to one side. Then his eyes opened again and he rolled facedown in the sand.

"No, no!" Johnny screamed. Tears flooded his eyes. He turned Randall on his back and felt for the wound. One was low in his chest and another in his belly. He gently cupped his friend's face and looked toward the moonlit sky, his shoulders racked with dry sobs. He hadn't felt this way since he was fourteen, when he lost his parents.

As he sat there he heard the muffled sound of a motor at sea. The LCVP was coming in.

A fresh burst of firing razored in at them from the left.

"Come on kill the bastards!" Johnny screamed.

He worked his way along the dune. The boat came no closer; it seemed to be holding offshore. Johnny gave the signal again, three long dashes of light twice. The rifle fire increased. He had one more Armbrust round. One antipersonnel. Should he waste it? No, save it. He would use it to cover the loading of the casualties.

"Grenades!" he shouted, as he sensed the enemy creeping closer in the darkness. A cloud flitted over the moon and he heard the grenades exploding down the line. The boat was coming now, he could tell by the hum of the craft's engine. It would hit the beach almost in the middle of their haphazard formation. Then they would be able to load.

Did the landing craft have a machine gun on it? He could not remember. He hoped to God it had.

In a lull in the firing he moved the bodies almost to the waterline. He was brushing the wetness from his eyes, heading back to the safety of the dunes when a black form leaped up from their side of the dune and fired a 10-round burst at the Americans. Johnny wheeled and held the trigger back on the M-16 until the magazine emptied and the enemy trooper spun in a dance before he sprawled dead into the Mediterranean.

How did he get in that close?

"Watch them!" Johnny shouted. He ran along the line, then stopped when he spotted Astra, lying curled up on her side. She sat up when she saw him.

"Down, it's too dangerous to sit up," he said, and he took her shoulders in his hands to lay her down.

His hands and her shoulders were sticky with warm blood.

Oh, no, not again!

Her eyes flickered and she groaned softly.

"Hurts!" she said.

Johnny eased her down gently on her side, then jammed a fresh magazine in his M-16 and stood up, firing at the winking lights of the enemy gunners in the darkness ahead of him.

"Bastards!" he screamed. "Goddamned bastards!" He was running toward them when one of the SEALs tackled him and pinned him to the ground until he could talk coherently.

"Chief! Chief!" the SEAL said urgently.

Johnny shook his head

"Chief, the boat is just hitting the sand. We better haul ass out of here. We're ready to load the wounded first, right? Where is your rocket launcher?"

Johnny took a deep breath, looked at Astra's blood still on his hands.

"I'll get it," Johnny said. He shivered, then stared at the enemy fire. Most of it was concentrated in front of a wrecked house and to one side. He could take out most of them with the last round from the Armbrust. A minute later he found the weapon. He shouldered it and fired. The round sprayed the enemy with thousands of shards of metal, silencing the machine-gun nest.

He looked toward the sea. The LCVP's ramp hit the surf with a splash. Three men ran on board, each carrying one wounded, then they headed back for the dead.

Johnny threw down the Armbrust and picked up Astra, holding her bloodied body close to him. Her young brother was beside her now. Johnny ran through the dark sandy beach to the landing craft. He laid Astra on a stretcher and hurried back down the ramp. He found Randall Phillips and carried his dead buddy to the craft. The captain stepped on board and the last man came in.

Johnny counted. Twenty-four human beings: eight dead, three seriously wounded, one Navy captain not functioning to his full capacity, the Lebanese girl and her brother, and every man jack of the rest wounded in some way. He nodded at the coxswain and the ramp swung closed. The boat charged backward, then turned and headed for the mother ship, which had pulled in closer for the pickup.

Johnny Bolan Gray stumbled across the deck to the girl, who was lying on the stretcher with a Navy blanket over her. A corpsman was examining her wounds.

"Damn it to hell!" the medic said as he stood up, his eyes closed. He took a deep breath and let it out, then turned and looked at the man on the next stretcher. "Damn it all to hell!"

3

"What's the matter with Astra?" Johnny asked. The medic turned. He shook his head. He was the same corpsman who had been on the landing with them.

He motioned Johnny to one side and spoke softly. "She's hit bad. I don't know if there'll be time to get her to the ship. She needs blood and a surgeon, right now."

Johnny knelt beside her, brushed dark hair out of Astra's eyes, wiped sweat from her forehead. Her eyes fluttered open and she reached for him.

"Johnny?"

"Yes. I'm here. We're out of Lebanon, we're going to the ship. We'll soon have you in a hospital room and the Navy doctors will make you as good as new.'

"No, Johnny. I am badly hurt. I know I have lost too much blood." She stopped and gasped and a jolt of pain tore through her body. She trembled, her lips pressed tightly together. When the pain subsided she opened her eyes. He dried them of tears.

It was still dark. They would get to the ship

before daylight so there could be no more attacks on them of tears.

She clutched his hand. "Johnny?"

"Yes, Astra."

"Did my brother get on board?"

"Yes."

"Please take care of him. He wanted to fight like his fourteen-year-old friends have. We would not let him. Make sure he stays out of Lebanon. If he goes back he will be killed. My mother could never stand that."

"I'll make sure. Is that what your father wants, too?"

"Yes." She trembled again and the pain could not all be held inside this time. She groaned and then screamed. The medic was beside them.

"Astra, do you want some morphine? I could give you a shot and kill the pain."

"No. Then I would be drugged and not be myself. For the time left I want to be myself." She looked at Johnny. "How many men were killed trying to fetch us?"

"I...I don't know."

"How many Americans?"

"Eight, maybe nine."

Tears streamed down her cheeks.

Johnny bent and kissed her.

"Astra," he said, "you are a beautiful lady who will live to be eighty years old and have six children. You will lead your country out of the despair of revolution and into peace."

"You are nice, Johnny." She looked deep into his eyes.

Johnny could see the shape of the big ship looming over the small craft.

"You are nice but I know I am going to die. Sometimes a will to live is not enough." She smiled, then shivered. "I'm getting so cold."

Johnny grabbed another blanket and spread it over her.

Her sudden smile was radiant, but gradually he saw it relax. He realized she was dead. He touched the artery at her throat. There was no pulse. Slowly he lowered his head to her shoulder.

Johnny shuddered. He would never be the same. Never again could he look at evil and death and not want to do something to stop it!

He swallowed hard, then lifted his head and moved the top of the blanket upward and over the beautiful face now in repose.

The corpsman looked at him.

"Sorry, sir. There was too much damage, lots of internal injuries, internal bleeding. Nothing could have saved her."

"Yeah," Johnny said. He moved back toward the stern of the landing craft. There he knelt next to the body of the best friend he had in the world.

Randall Phillips stared at the dark sky. Johnny reached out and gently closed the eyelids, brushed the shock of fair hair off Randall's forehead.

Johnny's tears splashed onto his friend's face, and through the blur he saw the craft tie up to the cargo net on the side of the mother ship. The slings were flung overboard to lift the stretchers. The three wounded were still alive. They would go up first. Johnny was on his feet at once directing the operation.

The captain was hoisted up next in a bos'n's chair. He was too exhausted to climb the netting. In the end, Johnny was the only one left in the LCVP. He waited until the last of the detail was on board, then he shouldered his M-16 and climbed the netting.

Two naval intelligence officers met him on deck and requested that he accompany them for a debriefing.

An hour later Johnny Bolan Gray went down to sick bay where they dug the shrapnel from his shoulder, bandaged up his arm and found another wound in his thigh. Then they bundled him into bed where he would stay four days for observation.

IN THOSE FOUR DAYS Johnny worked out the plan for the rest of his life. He knew exactly what he was going to do, and how he would do it.

He thought once more about the raid to rescue the intel team. The intelligence men said that Johnny and every other member of the landing party were sworn to secrecy. The mission never happened. The dead would be listed as killed in accidents over the next several weeks.

Then they gave him two sheets of paper. The

Navy captain who had so nearly died had recommended Johnny for two awards for heroism and had promoted him to chief petty officer in a battlefield situation. The officers shook his hand when it was over, congratulated him on his new rating and for taking over and bringing back the living and the dead.

"Half a dozen U.S. Navy personnel found by the Shiites, dead after a firefight on the beach, would be political dynamite for United States foreign relations right now. You should have had the Congressional Medal of Honor, but that would have meant too many explanations." They shook hands again and left him.

The Navy did not figure in Johnny's new plans. He knew where he was going, and he was anxious to get on with it. He had been thinking a lot about his brother, Mack Bolan. All his life he had wanted to help Mack. Now maybe there was a way that he could. But first he had to become a civilian again.

Johnny thought about the last time he had seen Mack. He had been fourteen and wanted to go with Mack, to drive his War Wagon, to do the cooking and generally help him out. He just wanted to be with his big brother. That had been when Val said she would not marry Jack Gray unless Johnny came along in the deal. Jack had put it to her that way, he wanted both of them, so it was up to Johnny.

That was why he made Leo Turrin take him to

St. Louis to talk to Mack. Johnny had packed everything he owned in those two suitcases and lugged them all the way. He was ready to stay, forever.

But Mack had explained to him that it was impossible. The clincher came when Mack said that Johnny would be a gravestone around his neck, dragging him down, and they both would be dead within forty-eight hours. It had been hard to take then, a hero-worshipping kid and a smarter, older brother. But he had gone back to Val and she had married Jack Gray, and they adopted Johnny and added a new name to his old one.

Now it would be different. He had a plan that would not jeopardize either of them, and could be a big help to Mack.

Three more months in the Navy, then he would be out and ready to get his life in gear. He had been working on it a lot these past few days. He had enjoyed San Diego when he took his boot training there. Yes, he would go to San Diego and settle down.

Johnny Bolan leaned back in the hospital bed and closed his eyes. He was twenty-one years old. It was time he got on with his life.

4

Johnny Bolan Gray leaned back in the driver's seat of the battered Volkswagen and stared at the bay along the embarcadero. Beautiful. One leg was poking through the passenger window and his green Nike hung there in the soft breeze. It was springtime in San Diego. Johnny stared across the smooth blue water at Coronado on the far side where a huge U.S. Navy aircraft carrier had docked.

He should have taken the afternoon off and gone out on a half-day fishing trip on the *New Seaforth*. The bonito were biting, and while they were not much good to eat, the little five- and six-pounders put up a feisty scrap on ten-pound line.

Johnny sighed. It had been two years since he rescued that pretty girl, Astra, and her brother on the Beirut mission and then watched her die. The Navy never did tell him what it was all about. Absolutely nothing came on the news about it. He figured the kids had important parents, who were worried about getting them kidnapped and held for the ransom of a nation.

A lot had happened since that devastating six hours of death and violence on a foreign shore.

Johnny had landed in San Diego with his mustering-out pay and had used up half of it for three months' rent on a bare one-room apartment in the seedier part of town. It was above an empty store on Kettner Boulevard, and he still lived there.

This morning he had seen a news story on the inside page of the morning *San Diego Union*. The headline had leaped out at breakfast as he drank his orange juice.

"MAFIA NEMESIS STRIKES AGAIN. Is the Executioner back at work or have the reports of the Mafia fighter's style of attacks on underworld bosses been 'copycat' strikes? Police, and probably the Mafia as well, were wondering about that some months ago and again, recently, as two illegal gambling establishments in Miami, Florida, rumored to be run by the Mob, were leveled. The 'manager' of one place with a long criminal record was slain and an Army marksman's medal dropped on his chest.

"Police say the M.O. looks exactly like that of the Executioner, who stormed through the Mafia for several years before evidently being killed in New York's Central Park in a burning vehicle about two years ago.

"The man is described as being more than six feet tall, with dark hair, an olive complexion and icy blue eyes. He wears all black when he strikes and often uses the latest in military weapons.

"If he is the Executioner, there are more than

two thousand outstanding murder warrants waiting for him in practically every state in the nation,
as well as a dozen foreign countries. The police are
not the only ones searching for him. The word in
the underworld is that there is a $5,000,000 'con-
tract' out on the Executioner, also known as Mack
Bolan. The reward is rumored to be offered by his
old foes, the Mafia's *La Commissione*, the group
of 'Family' bosses who rule the nationwide Mob
with a 'reasoning together' approach backed up
by an iron fist.''

Johnny had had to put down the paper to calm
his beating heart.

Leo Turrin had told him years ago that Mack
had died in that War Wagon in New York City,
but Johnny had not believed it. Why would Leo lie
to him about something this important? He decided he would call Leo tonight and find out the
truth.

Johnny pulled his leg in from the window,
watched a sleek thirty-seven-foot sailboat slide by
on the noontime breeze and turned his bucket of
bolts toward Kettner. The old store below his
room had been taken over by the Free Legal Aid
Center. He had helped start it and sat on the board
of directors. He worked for pay as much as he
needed to stay alive; the rest of his time was spent
helping the underprivileged who came to the
center seeking legal assistance.

Armand Killinger was his boss. Killinger was
the best-known criminal lawyer in San Diego.

Johnny worked from 8:00 A.M. to 1:00 P.M. five days a week as a paralegal and legman. Anything Killinger needed doing, Johnny got done, whether it was checking out fake addresses or writing minor motions and other routine work.

He had come out of the Navy determined to be a lawyer. But the reality of seven years of college left him broke just thinking about it. He had used his schooling from the military and attended the University of San Diego, enrolling in their year-long, full-time, paralegal course. He had learned a lot and now could earn his living by working only part-time, and have energy left for the Free Legal Aid Center.

Maybe he was getting a start at really trying to do some good in the world, but he still thought about that big dream of helping Mack Bolan in his battle against the Mafia. Leo Turrin had tried to dash that dream with his report that Mack had burned to death in a New York explosion.

Now the newspaper stories.

Mack had always been special to Johnny. His brother had been a hero in Vietnam, and then he came home.

Johnny recalled the homecoming. He never forgot it, but it was not the sort of memory he wanted to dredge up all the time.

He remembered it precisely.

Johnny Bolan was fourteen at the time, on the edge of streetwise and a little brash but not real tough.

His father, Sam Bolan, had been sick with a bad heart for a while and was off work. Bills piled up and the elder Bolan borrowed some money. Then he returned to work but could not perform any of the strenuous duties he had before because of his heart, so they gave him an easier but lower-paying job.

The wages could not keep pace with the bills and the guys he got the loan from started giving him a bad time at work. Johnny had heard his father tell his wife, Elsa, the guys were bloodsuckers and he was going to tell them to go to hell.

The following night Sam Bolan came home with a dislocated arm. They said the next time he missed a payment they would break the arm. Johnny remembered that his mother wanted to call the police but his father told her the goons might take it out on her and the kids. Johnny heard his seventeen-year-old sister, Cindy, crying in her bedroom that night.

Then Johnny did not hear anything concerning the loan sharks for a while. His father said the goons were leaving him alone and he did not know why. But he sure was not going to ask them.

Johnny knew something about the outfit where his dad had borrowed the money—the Triangle Finance Company.

Everybody on the street knew about Triangle. It was one of the slimiest loan-sharking operations in that end of Pittsfield. Sam Bolan probably knew about Triangle too, but thought he could handle it. The loan at first was only for ninety days, and this guy Sam knew said he was a cinch for a job in another thirty days. It did not work out that way and when the first payment was due, Sam paid half, said he would have the rest soon.

The two big goons from Triangle had come to talk to Sam Bolan and Johnny heard some of it. The whole message had been pay up or else. It had been over a year and the interest was more than three times the amount of the loan.

Cindy Bolan knew enough about the system to realize how bad it was. One afternoon she visited Triangle Finance to try and persuade them to leave her father alone and let her repay the loan. She was working after school. She gave them everything she made, thirty-five dollars a week. It was not enough.

One day they suggested to her a way she could really help her old man. She could make good money and pay off the debt in three or four months. The seventeen-year-old girl knew at once what they meant. They said they would have to break her father's arm the next afternoon if she did not agree to their offer.

Johnny knew all about it a week later. News like that spreads quickly. Johnny had a fight with the kid who told him, and lost. To prove the talk was wrong, Johnny followed his sister that night.

When he broke into the cheap hotel room and found Cindy naked on the bed with a man, Johnny fled crying, furious and heartbroken.

The next day he did the only thing he could think of to make her stop: he told his father.

Sam Bolan was in the kitchen reading the help-wanted ads when Johnny told him. Sam roared in fury and punched Johnny in the mouth, knocking him down.

Cindy and Elsa heard the racket and hurried into the kitchen. He confronted Cindy and finally she admitted it.

"They said it was the only way we could pay back the loan," Cindy explained over and over. "It doesn't matter about me, I didn't want them breaking your arm. The next time they might kill you!"

Elsa put a cold cloth on Johnny's bleeding lip and hugged him.

Sam yelled at them all for five minutes, then fell silent and listened more calmly to Cindy's story. When she was through, he got up and left the room without a word. A minute or two later he came back.

Sam Bolan carried an old Smith & Wesson .45 he had owned for years. He calmly shot Johnny, who crashed to the floor. Johnny remained conscious long enough to see his father fire the big slugs into his wife and daughter, shooting them again and again.

When the gun was empty, Sam stared at them. He looked at Johnny. "Sorry I busted your lip, John-O," he said calmly, then went back to his bedroom.

Johnny huddled on the floor in more pain than he ever thought possible. He figured his father was reloading the gun. Before Johnny passed out he heard one final shot, and he knew that his father was dead.

Neighbors heard the shots and called the police. Johnny was rushed to the hospital. He would live, but had to remain under care for a month. Mack Bolan had come flying home from Vietnam on an emergency leave a few days after the shooting and declared war against the Mafia.

The opening gun spoke eight days after the interment of Bolans's dead relatives. Five messengers of merciless extinction from a big-game rifle found their mark and five officials of the Triangle Finance Company lay dead in the street outside the loan company office in Pittsfield, Massachusetts.

And so had started Mack Bolan's war everlasting.

When Johnny was released from hospital he went to stay with a woman called Val Querente. She had fallen in love with Mack and, since he was on the run, he had asked her to become Johnny's legal guardian.

At first Johnny felt strange in a new school, in a new town, but worst of all he was going under a different name, Johnny Bates. Val told him it had been her mother's maiden name. She explained to him why he must use the new name from then on. The Mafia was trying to kill Mack, and if they

knew where Johnny was they would grab him to
lure Mack into the open. The two of them had to
hide so they could help protect Mack. Johnny understood.

They had moved a lot that first year, and gradually he realized that his brother had declared war
on the Mob and was blasting them wherever he
found them. Slowly Johnny realized he should be
proud of his brother. Mack Bolan was paying
back the leeches who had drained a million poor
people of their last dollar. He was also punishing
the Mafia for causing the deaths of three members
of the Bolan family.

Soon Val met Jack Gray and wanted to marry
him. Johnny made Leo Turrin tell him where
Mack was and set up a meeting with his brother.
Johnny visited Mack in St. Louis and grew up a
hell of a lot in one afternoon. Mack hit him with
hard reality that day, and steered him toward his
true future. Johnny agreed to be adopted. Val
married Jack and they all went to live in Sheridan,
Wyoming. Johnny had his name changed officially through adoption to John Bolan Gray and
joined the Navy as soon as he graduated from
Sheridan High School.

And now it looked as if the Executioner was
alive and well and giving the Mob all kinds of hell.
Johnny grinned. He had not felt so good in weeks.
Maybe he could finally develop those ideas about
how he could help the Executioner. He would
think on it real hard.

He drove his VW into an off-street parking slot behind the narrow building that housed the Free Legal Aid Center. He entered and smiled at Vicki, their volunteer receptionist.

"Hi Johnny," Vicki said. "Here are a few messages." She gave him a sheaf of the pink phone-message slips and he went to his small desk against the back window. It was strictly a store-front operation: one big room with four desks, two benches and five phone lines. Everything in the room had been donated through lawyers they knew. A fund drive helped them to keep afloat.

They barely had money enough to pay their phone bill when it arrived. The rent was usually late, even after they got the rate reduced twice in two years. Electricity payments were a constant headache and there was no heat in the building.

He looked at the slip on top of the pile. Then for no apparent reason he thought of Val Querente and he put the slips on the desk, pushed his feet up on the first drawer and laced his hands behind his head.

Val Querente had been half mother, half pal to him those last three years. She was only twelve years older than he was, and he was in love with her that last year. Looking back on it he realized Val had been a good mother to him. He wondered if she knew that Mack Bolan was still alive. She confessed to him one day that she had fallen in love with Mack that first terrible week in Pittsfield when the Executioner began his Mafia payback. Mack had hidden in her house while he recovered from a gunshot wound.

But both Mack and Val knew there could be no lasting relationship, and they parted with sorrow. She had told Johnny that Mack had wanted her to marry Jack Gray and have some kind of a normal life.

Johnny still wrote letters to Val. She had written to him once a week while he was in the Navy. Now the letters came every couple of months. She had encouraged him to go to the paralegal school. His stepfather, Jack Gray, had sent him a bundle of material about how to set up a free legal aid center, and he and some friends had done it. Jack Gray sent them a hundred dollars every month for expenses.

Johnny still dreamed of being able to become a full-fledged lawyer, but that took time and money. He put his feet down and shook his head. No, he was kidding himself. If he had wanted to go to school more than anything else, he would have. He could have set up a schedule so he worked mornings, and have taken classes all afternoon and evening and finished his B.A. degree in three years. But he had not. He knew he could have borrowed the money he needed from Jack Gray, but he would not.

He loved doing the legal aid work. It was satisfying.

Johnny again studied the first slip on the pile. The time of the calls was carefully noted and he saw that the earliest call was on the bottom. He checked the phone number and dialed it.

Harry Chernin was the man's name, and he was having trouble with an insurance company not answering his letters about paying a claim. Johnny let the phone ring seven times, then hung up and called the second number in his stack of twelve. With luck he would be done by midnight.

When the second call resulted in no answer, Johnny reached into his desk and pulled out a small address book. He found Leo Turrin's number and dialed it. Should be no more than 4:45 P.M. in Washington, D.C.

He listened to the ring, then a voice came on.

"Good afternoon, this is a nonsecure line subject to federal monitoring. To whom did you wish to speak?"

"Leonard Justice."

"One moment, please."

He heard the usual clicks and relays, knew the line was on automatic record. He had given the code name that Leo Turrin used at his desk in the Justice Department. Leo had been an undercover agent for Justice working inside the Mob. He had met Mack Bolan on the first war against the Mafia in Pittsfield. Mack discovered Leo was a Justice Department agent, and then worked with him for several years. Now Leo was out of his spot in the Mafia, where he had progressed to be a trusted underboss. He had lived longer in such jobs than anyone before and now he was riding a desk in Washington under his real name. Whatever that was.

"Yes," said Leo's voice.

"Leo, it's Johnny. I have a simple question. We've been friends a long time, and I know you'll tell me straight."

"Right, Johnny," Leo said, but Johnny caught a touch of worry in his tone.

"Is Mack alive and fighting the Mafia again?"

"Johnny, this is not a secure line. . . . "

"Leo, the Mafia thinks he's back, they know. What could it hurt if they hear it from Justice?"

"Goddamn. You grew up too smart."

"Mack never died in New York, did he, Leo?"

"No, Johnny. That was faked. I had good reasons for telling you otherwise."

"Write me a letter about them. I want to know why you lied to me. I wanted to die, too, the day you told me."

"It was hard, Johnny. I've learned to lie well, working with the Family so long. I'm sorry."

"So Mack is alive, and he's back battling the Mafia."

"And you are still an Achilles' heel for him, Johnny. Remember what they did when they kidnapped you and Val to get at Mack? The same problem still exists."

"I've thought of that. I'm not going to make any big announcements, or change my name. I just had to know."

"Yeah, Johnny. I'm glad you know. I'll write you the whole long, involved story."

"Thanks, Leo. I forgive you. You still have some contact with him?"

"Now and then."

"Does he ask about me?"

"All the time. You know him. He cares."

"Thanks, Leo. I have some thinking to do."

They said goodbye and Johnny pushed back from the desk. The rest of the calls could wait. He left the office and drove up the hill to Presidio Park, where he sprawled out on the grass and looked out over Mission Bay and the Pacific Ocean. It was his thinking place. Everything seemed to come clear and plain and simple up here. His mind worked easier in the clean air.

Johnny stared out at the bay.

Mack was alive!

5

Johnny ran his fingers through his hair and sighed, a satisfied smile on his face. It was nine o'clock at night and he had managed to resolve most of the complaints over the phone, though there were still a few left for the next day.

Johnny was alone at the center. Two helpers, both law students, had left some hours before. He swung his leg to the floor and stood up. Quickly he strode to the front door, locked it and snapped off the lights. He went out the back way, down a few feet to the stairway and walked up to his one-room apartment.

Johnny unlocked the door and stepped inside. Soft music floated across the room, accompanied by sounds from the kitchen.

"It's me, Sandy."

The girl in the tiny cooking area looked up and smiled.

"You look tired, Tiger."

"A little." He watched her. She was six inches shorter than he, slender, pretty, a delight. He loved her long blond hair, which swept down to her waist.

Her brown eyes were set above high cheekbones, completing a beautiful face.

All afternoon he had been bursting to tell some-one about his news, but now he looked at Sandy and realized that he had to decide if he could en-trust Mack Bolan's life to her. He would trust his own life with Sandy, she was loyal and honest and dependable. But did he have the right to risk the Executioner's safety with her?

Johnny had met Sandy Darlow at a concert. She had come with a friend of a friend. That night he got her phone number, the next day he called and they had been together ever since. They seemed like a matched set, compatible, almost the same age and both a little conservative, deliberate, under-standing, and they liked the same things. Even their politics were close.

After they had been dating for two months, San-dy asked if she could move in with him. He had kissed her and they sat down on the sofa. That night they made love for the first time. He never did answer her question.

The next day when he returned home around nine-thirty at night, she was there with a steak dinner all cooked for him. She had brought everything she owned, including her sleeping bag. He never did tell her she could stay, she just did.

Yeah, he could trust her.

Now Johnny led Sandy to the shabby sofa and

told her the news about Mack. She listened quietly, then shivered.

He explained to her again how important it was that she never tell anyone about Mack Bolan. She nodded and kissed him.

"If he's your brother, I would never do anything to cause him harm."

She took his hand. "Now come and have some dinner."

As they ate, he told her about his phone call to Leo Turrin in Washington.

"How soon can we meet Mack?" she asked.

"Well, he's in rather a strange business. I may not be able to contact him for a month or two."

"What kind of strange business?"

"I think it's time you told me about your world of high finance."

Sandy always derived a kind of pleasure when Johnny showed interest in her work at a local bank.

"There's a management trainee spot up for grabs," she said cheerfully. "I'm going to apply for it. If I could get into that program it would be heaven. Of course then I would have to get to work finishing my B.A. in business at San Diego State."

"I didn't know you started."

"In a weak moment. I have about a year and a half to go."

"Easy," he said.

"Sure, about as easy as becoming a lawyer."

"Maybe I'll quit here and crew on your dad's ship."

She stared at him and scowled. "You do and I'll walk out. One fisherman in the family is enough."

"How's he doing this year?"

"Fine, as long as the game fish keep coming into the area. But some years they just vanish. Nobody knows where they go and that's a big ocean out there."

"Yellowtail should be biting about now. I'd like to go out with him one of these days."

"He said any time you want to get up that early. All you have to do is help clean up on the return trip, and fillet fish for the passengers."

"Deal. I like your old man."

"He likes you too, John."

Neither of them mentioned her mother, who had died three years before. They both knew Sandy would not be living there now if her mother were alive.

"So we can't see Mack, or even make arrangements to meet him until he calls this friend of yours in the Justice Department?"

"Right. His best security is a constant state of being out of touch with everyone."

Sandy knew nothing of Johnny's family history. Johnny changed the subject again and finished his meal. They did the dishes, then stood near the counter, leaning against the sink.

"Hey, handsome hunk," Sandy murmured. "Did I ever tell you that I am crazy about you?"

Johnny grinned. But suddenly her face became serious and she wrapped her arms around him.

"Oh, Johnny, please tell me that we'll always be like this and nothing will ever happen to us."

Johnny gently framed her face with both palms. He saw the tears welling up in her eyes.

"Hey, hey, what's brought this on? Nothing is going to happen to us," he assured her. He pulled Sandy tightly against him, looking over her head at the wall, making a silent plea to the universe that what he said was true.

6

Armand Killinger heard a knock on the door, then saw Johnny stride into the room to stand at ease in front of his desk. They had worked together for just over a year now, and the kid was the best at his job that the criminal lawyer had ever hired.

"Relax, Johnny. Have a seat. I called you in here because I've got a strange one I want you to start digging into right away. It could be a highly sensitive area. So give me a report every day."

Johnny pulled up a chair closer to his boss's desk and sat down.

"Our client blew away two loan sharks last night," Killinger said. "There is no way we can deny in court that our client pulled the trigger and killed the men. The prosecution has a dozen eye-witnesses. What we have to prove is that there was no preconceived intent, that he was suddenly over-come with a powerful urge to get even with these bloodsuckers. You with me so far?"

"Uh-huh."

"Good. That's the easy part. What I need is some way to connect this loan-sharking operation with the San Diego Mafia."

"Mafia? In San Diego?"

"Of course. But it won't be easy. If I can get the organized-crime cops behind us, I might be able to do some plea bargaining with the FBI. Instead of a first-degree murder rap we could be looking at one to two years for manslaughter.

"You'll have to dress casual. Nel will give you a list of places I want you to check out, listen to people talk, then move on. I'm looking for anything you hear about Willy the Peep and Joe Franarza. Both of these boys are honchos in the local Mafia. You can work twelve hours a day on this if you want to. We need the information, one way or the other, in two weeks."

"I'll get right on it, Mr. Killinger," Johnny said. "I never knew anything about a Mafia operation this in town."

"Most people don't hear about it. They planned it that way. They are deep into legitimate businesses here. You'd be surprised if I ran a list of names in front of you. But I want you a virgin out there. See what you can find for me."

Johnny nodded and left.

Killinger frowned as he watched Johnny walk out of the office. There was something unusual about this kid that he'd never figured out. He reminded Killinger a lot of himself when he was younger.

Hungry? No, not exactly. If Johnny had just been hungry he would have had his law degree well under way by now. It was more. A depth, a kind of knowing.

Johnny would not be a paralegal all his life, Killinger knew that. He would move up or out. Even with his fame and his wealth, Armand Killinger felt there was a lot Johnny Gray had that he wished he had. But he knew it was inside, it was born in you, and there was no way to learn it. He sighed and went back to work on the double murder case.

Outside the door, Johnny stopped at Nel's desk. The chunky blond woman in her forties handed Johnny a sheet of paper.

"Johnny, take it easy in these dives, okay," she said. "People can get hurt in them. If you drink one beer in each place you'll be drunk before noon. Concentrate on peanuts." She handed him sixty dollars expense money and told him to keep track of his spending.

"Yes, ma'am."

Johnny drove home and changed into a California T-shirt, jeans and his green Nike running shoes. Then he walked to the only bar on Nel's list on Kettner Boulevard, the one that was just around the corner from where he lived.

KARL DARLOW GRIPPED the wheel of his boat with callused and weathered hands. He had been a fisherman all his life, and at last had put together enough cash and credit to buy a used forty-five-footer called the *Flying Fool*. She had a solid hull, rebuilt diesel engines and a great heart. For the past twelve years he had made his living plowing through the U.S. and Mexican sportfishing waters.

Karl stood an inch over six feet and had been a power weight lifter in his younger days. He could still show some of the punks in the gym how to hoist iron even though he was a hair more than fifty.

His boat mainly worked the half-day, three-quarter-day and overnight runs for sportfishing, especially when the yellowtail came into the close waters and the albacore were running. Then he would jam forty-five tourists and locals on board and head for the hot spots with bodies lying all over the decks.

When the catch totals began to fall and the tourists went for the bigger boats with better galleys and more comfort, Karl dropped his sportfishing guise, bolted on the twenty-foot outriggers and repaired the winches. Then he went out as a commercial boat with one crewman, and they trolled for whatever they could get, usually yellowtail, sometimes some yellowfin. Now and then they would tie into a bunch of big-eye tuna and go at them with rod and reel.

Today he had the *Flying Fool* on a commercial run. They had worked the feeding grounds around the Mexican Coronado Islands, only sixteen miles off the coast, and had made a fair catch. He would be able to make the payment on the boat with no sweat this month.

It was a half hour to sunset. For the past hour

he had been watching the slow progress of a rusty freighter chugging along up the coast. Karl figured the old tub was not doing more than five knots. She appeared to be in no hurry to get to the next port. Maybe she was going to stop in San Diego and did not want to dock until the following morning.

He came up on her as he angled north toward the bay entrance, still six miles away. Poke, his only crewman when he went commercial, was below tinkering with the twin diesels. They had been running a little rough. Karl swung farther seaward to miss the freighter by a quarter of a mile. He had not noticed the small powerboat glide up to it, but now saw ropes passed, and the thirty-footer tied up to some lines dropped over the side.

Almost at once lines came down from pulleys overhead. They were off-loading something. Karl picked up his ten-power binoculars and focused on the scene.

Boxes, maybe forty pounds each and all double-wrapped with plastic and securely tied, were being passed down. Karl stood in the sun on the open bridge with the glasses, then shrugged and put them away, turned deeper toward the horizon and jigged the throttle up to twelve knots, his top speed. For a moment there he thought he recognized the powerboat, but he wasn't sure.

Poke came up and lifted his brows at their speed.

"You late for a date or something, Karl?"

"Yeah, late. You got something against getting the outriggers hoisted and this tub cleaned up before we get to the channel?"

Poke grinned. "That sounds more like the old sea-dog son of a bitch I work for. When the hell am I going to get shares on this rotten scow?"

"Forget it, Poke, let's get home. You take the wheel, I want to put up those outrigger arms before I forget how."

They were a mile off the first channel-marker buoy when the white-and-blue powerboat came past them. There was no name on the side of the thirty-footer. A pair of chilly-looking bikini-clad girls sat on the bow, just in front of the closed cabin. They waved, then vanished inside. On the small flying bridge a well-muscled man in white shorts and mirrored sunglasses stared back at Karl. He made no move to wave.

Karl caught the last four numbers on the craft, 7475, then the vessel was past. A crewman in white shorts moved to the stern and emptied the last of the live bait in the plastic tank that hung off the back.

Four sturdy sportfishing poles sprouted from holders along the sides and back of the craft, making it look like a typical privately owned sport boat back from a day of fishing. The more Karl thought about it, the more he decided it looked too damn much like a casual sportfisherman.

He throttled back a little for the channel and worked past Point Loma, along the side of North Island Naval Air Station and past Ballast Point.

He slid into his berth at the foot of Scott Street, near the Fisherman's Landing docks, and tied up. He had radioed in and there would be a truck in the parking lot from a small fresh-fish cooperative where he sold his catch. He was not big enough for a top price, but at least he had an outlet.

Together he and Poke pulled the fish out of the big bait tank and tossed them in a cart Poke had rolled alongside on the dock. The cart was a four-foot-long wooden box with one pair of wheels amidships and a push handle. Karl figured they had caught six hundred pounds of yellowtail.

They pushed the loaded cart up the steep ramp from the floating dock to the embarcadero and on to the parking lot.

They transferred the fish into a box in the truck, and the driver said he would mail Karl the weight receipt. As the extended van pulled away, Karl saw a big Cadillac sitting in a space reserved for the handicapped. A man was leaning against the fender of the limo. He wore mirrored sunglasses and white shorts, with a pale-blue knit shirt. For a moment Karl wondered if it was the same man he had seen on the powerboat coming in. He shrugged and rolled the cart back to its parking spot and went down to finish cleanup on the *Flying Fool*.

He was not naive. He knew damn well what was happening when those boxes were transferred from the freighter. Any time a small boat meets a big one off the coast, you can be damn sure it's for only one purpose—smuggling.

He had kept well away from that problem, and he sure wanted it to stay that way. If anyone asked, he had seen nothing, he knew nothing. He was just a fisherman trying to make a living. They would have to believe him.

But still Karl Darlow shivered.

7

There was going to be trouble. Johnny could feel it. Most of the clients who sought assistance from the Free Legal Aid Center came to the office on Kettner and were advised what to do, helped with forms, or sent to small-claims court. Sometimes the staff was able to exert pressure over the telephone. Now and then an in-person visit was in order as the best way to resolve a problem.

This was such a case, and Johnny knew it was going to be a tough one.

Landlords could be vicious. They almost always held the upper hand. He knew that the managers often had to use pressure to get rent when it was due. But lots of them went too far.

Like this one.

James Sylvester was the manager at the Alamo apartment building, a sixteen-unit in southeast San Diego. It was just off Logan Avenue and that meant a black neighborhood. Johnny knew that was a tough part of town no matter the color of your skin. A solitary white in there even in daylight was not the smartest move.

But Priscilla Monroe needed help.

She was twenty, black, single, had a baby and worked two jobs to stay off welfare. Johnny liked her spirit and the fact that she held down two jobs was reason enough for him to try and help her. A neighbor had told her about the center. She phoned and was advised to visit the clinic in person.

She had moved out of the apartment three months ago. There had been a two-hundred-dollar security deposit and cleaning fee. It was all spelled out clearly in the rental agreement she showed Johnny. If there was no damage, and if the apartment was left in reasonably clean condition, the money would be returned to the tenant two weeks after vacating. Otherwise the cost of repairs or cleaning would be deducted from the deposit.

Priscilla had a signed statement by Mr. Sylvester that the apartment was clean, there was no damage and the deposit would be refunded by check within two weeks and mailed to her new address.

She never got the money. She had phoned the manager four times and each time he said the check would go in the mail the next morning.

Johnny had phoned him once and said if the refund was not in the former tenant's hands the following day, they would take legal action. Sylvester had laughed at him over the phone.

Johnny followed the usual procedure. He filed a complaint with the Better Business Bureau against the apartment owners and registered another complaint with the Fair Housing Commission and the Better Renters' Forum. He had tried to call the owner of the building but was told by his answering service that the absentee proprietor resided in Palm Springs and would not be in his office for the next four weeks.

Priscilla Monroe needed the money. Johnny had arranged for her to meet him at the center that afternoon and they would go have a person-to-person talk with Sylvester.

Now, as they walked up to the sixteen-unit, Johnny saw that the building was not in good repair and showed no maintenance. They entered through a front door and found the first-floor manager's office.

Johnny rang the bell and a speaker blared at him.

"Yeah, whaddya want?"

"Mr. Sylvester. My name is John Gray and I represent Mrs. Priscilla Monroe. I think we should talk."

The door jerked open at once. The man was six-four, wide as a coal car and fat. His torso was bare and he wore only boxer shorts. Kinky black hair was cut short and his face was broad and sneering.

"Goddamn, you did come. Sheeeeeeet! I never thought you'd have guts enough. What's this all about?"

Priscilla stood behind Johnny and looked the other way.

"You know what it's about. You owe this lady two hundred dollars. You have promised six times to pay and you have not. We'd like to pick up the check now."

"Man, you are one crazy mutha, you know that?"

"We'll wait while you get dressed, if you like."

"Hell, don't bother me none, asshole. You ain't comin' in, you ain't gettin' no goddamn refund, and I'm gonna break off your arm and ram it down your throat you bother me one more time!"

"Fine with me. We'll sue you right back into jail. How much hard time have you done?"

"None of your damn business. Now get the hell out of here!"

Johnny stepped inside the apartment. "We're not leaving until you give us a check or cash for the refund."

Sylvester took a step toward Johnny, shaking one huge fist.

"Go ahead, hit me," Johnny said. "Just once is all I need with a witness and you and your boss will be on the stiff end of a half-million-dollar lawsuit for assault and battery. And with your record we'll get three times that much and you'll be back at Soledad for five to ten."

"How you know about that?"

"Just write the check, Sylvester. I know you have the authorization. Save yourself one hell of a lot of trouble, pain, court hassle and hard time."

"Bluff. Goddamn bluff!"

"Try me," Johnny said, his soft blue eyes quickly hard.

Sylvester looked around. He realized this young white dude wasn't going to back down, but Sylvester decided to continue his scare tactics. He growled and cocked his fist two inches in front of Johnny's nose.

"Now that, Mr. Sylvester, is assault, the threat or indication that force is going to be used. The battery comes when your knuckles touch my skin. Do you want to try for a million, or three million? And the thought of you back behind bars really makes me feel good."

"You little bastard!" Sylvester exploded. "Nobody hires a damn lawyer to collect two hundred. Lawyers cost more than that."

"Not this lawyer. I'm from the Free Legal Aid Center. We don't charge a thing. I suggest you get your checkbook and write the lady her refund."

The big black man belched, stared hard at Johnny, then turned. "Hell, be worth it to get you off my back!"

The manager moved out of sight and came back a few moments later with a check. Johnny looked at it, saw that it was properly filled in and signed.

"You are authorized to sign on this account?"

"Damn right! Now get out of here, both of you."

Johnny took a step back, Sylvester slammed the door and Priscilla Monroe kissed Johnny's cheek.

"Wonderful," she said. "I didn't think I would ever see that money again."

Johnny let the woman off at a bus stop, then drove back to the center. For just a minute he paused and relaxed. He had wanted to wade into that big baboon and punch his face in, but he had held his temper and he had won the fight. There was more than one way to beat the bastards out there who ground people down. It was not Mack Bolan's way, but this time it worked.

His brother was alive! Johnny jumped out, slammed the VW bug's door and ran into the office. He was going to call Leo Turrin again at Justice and demand to meet Mack.

KARL DARLOW DID NOT MAKE his regular half-day run to the Point Loma kelp beds that morning with the tourists. The roughness in the engine he had felt the day before had demanded attention, and he had spent most of the morning with Poke on it. He came out of the hold sweating and with grease all over his hands and shirt.

A man in a white suit and mirrored sunglasses stood on the dock. When he saw Karl come on deck he walked over next to the rail of the *Flying Fool*.

"You Karl Darlow?"

"Right, but I'm not going out this morning. Maybe this afternoon if I get this cleaned up, and if the fish report looks good on the morning boats."

"How did you do yesterday?"

"I was commercial yesterday with the outriggers down. Went straight west and then north a little. Ran into a school of yellowfin and did pretty good."

"I hear you went south."

"No way, fishing ain't good down there when we have a hot spell like this. You got to work north. South, maybe, if you want to try the albies, but them damn things might be anywhere out there and that's a mighty big ocean. Just luck if you run into them. I remember once I had a full load of passengers out looking for yellows. We were on an overnight and I put out the usual lures on the trolling lines—"

The man in the white suit shook his head. "Darlow, I'm not here to listen to fish stories. I'm with Star Insurance and we have a problem on a powerboat claim that was about six miles south of the bay entrance. Claim they saw a boat like yours, with the outriggers down, trolling. They say you can substantiate that they were in trouble and fired a flare gun just before they were carried onto the beach."

"No way, they got the wrong boat. I wouldn't have been close enough to the beach anyway. I'm usually about five miles out and working the north area. Lots of times on half days I run all the way to the La Jolla kelp. I go where the fish are, and yesterday they were north."

The man with the white suit stared at him.

"Our client may still want you to testify," he said at last. "By the way, it looks as if your boat name is getting a little faded on your bow. Our client said he had to use a pair of field glasses to read it. I'm sure we can expect your complete cooperation on this matter."

"Hell, I was north, and I didn't see anyone in trouble, or hear no Mayday call. Lots of folks know the name of my boat. Hundreds of folks been out fishing on her. Now, if you want to help me put a diesel engine back together again, you're welcome to come with me, because I got to get below."

"Mr. Darlow, I'm not a mechanic. But I am happy to hear that you saw absolutely nothing yesterday. I'm sure that everyone will be happy with that kind of response. Be sure that you keep thinking that way. Is all of this perfectly clear?"

"Told you, I was north. Didn't see a damn thing."

"Right." The man looked at Karl for a moment longer, then turned and walked away. As he turned, Karl saw the clear outline of a gun bulging under his left armpit.

Karl wiped new sweat from his forehead. He had been right. Somebody was smuggling yesterday and he had come too damn close. They got his boat name from that thirty-footer when she overtook him coming in.

Karl knew that from now on they'd keep their eyes on him, probably tap his phone, too.

He felt a cold menacing shadow moving toward him, and he knew there was no way to avoid it.

8

Johnny had to move his loan-sharking research to the afternoon and evening. There was simply no action mornings in the drinking spots and small markets that he had to cover.

It was past 9:00 P.M. when he slouched onto a stool at a small bar near the Tenth Avenue Marine Terminal. A lot of working men used the place to let off steam. Some of the stevedores were just off a long shift, relaxing with a beer. Their talk was raucous and reminded Johnny of his Navy days.

One voice came through to him. It was lower, more serious, and Johnny caught the tension creeping in. The man sat two stools down, talking with a friend.

"I told him I'd pay, but I didn't have that kind of money until payday. So on payday he showed up, grabbed my check and threatened to hurt my family unless we went to the bank. He waited for me and left me fifty bucks for two weeks. What can I do?"

The pair moved off the stools and headed for the door. Johnny heard two more complaints about the "instant money services" that made loans without collateral, but nowhere did he find any mention of a connection with the Mafia. It was a blind lead. He decided to call it quits for the evening because he had promised Sandy they'd visit her father. It was his birthday and she had baked a cake and arranged a small party.

Karl Darlow lived in a walk-up in North Park, an older neighborhood of San Diego. Johnny stopped in front of a small white house and they went to the side where a stairway led up to a self-contained apartment.

"Funny, the door's open," Sandy said. "Dad always locks his doors around here."

Johnny touched Sandy's shoulder and stepped in front of her. He opened the door outward and as he did a huge figure wearing a ski mask over his face came rushing past them. He slammed Johnny into Sandy and both of them stumbled and fell on the landing.

The masked man never looked back as he ran down the steps to the sidewalk. Johnny pushed Sandy off him, jumped up and charged after the fleeing man. But he had too much head start. When Johnny reached the sidewalk he saw the man turning the corner a half block ahead. Johnny put on a burst of speed but by the time he got to the corner, a car was laying rubber on the far side of the street, screeching away from him.

Johnny concentrated on the license plate but

could only make out four of the six letters and numbers. It was a light blue Pontiac, maybe two years old. He stood there panting a moment, then hurried back to the apartment.

He heard Sandy crying as he climbed the steps. Inside, he saw that the apartment was wrecked. The furniture was smashed, the TV picture tube shattered. The end table was broken, the sofa slashed. Family pictures were thrown on the floor.

Sandy's sobbing came from the bedroom. Johnny rushed through the rubble to the door.

Karl Darlow lay spread-eagled on the bed, hands and feet tied to the bed frame. He was on his back and naked to the waist. There were six long gashes across his chest and belly. One of his eyes was swollen shut and his nose was broken and bleeding.

Tears were streaming down Sandy's cheeks.

"Phone?" Johnny asked.

"Pulled out. Ruined."

Johnny looked at the slashes. They were still bleeding but not seriously. Who would do something like this?

"Cut him free, Sandy. Stop the blood flow if you can with compresses. I'll find a phone."

Downstairs he banged on the front door, but no one was home. Johnny raced to the house next door and rang the bell. A woman appeared and he asked her to call the police and an ambulance. A man was hurt next door. The woman looked skeptical, but after staring at Johnny for a few moments she nodded and turned indoors. Johnny followed her and waited to be sure she got through. Then he ran back to the apartment.

Sandy had cut the ropes on her father's hands and feet and was holding a folded sheet pressed to Karl's bare chest, trying to stop the bleeding. Karl was still unconscious.

Johnny was not sure what to do next. He applied a cold cloth to Karl's nose to stop the nosebleed. Then he heard feet pounding up the steps.

"Police," someone called from the front door.

"In here," Johnny said, and a young patrolman came in.

"What happened?" he asked.

Johnny told him what they had seen. The cop returned to his patrol car, made a report and came back.

"The paramedic unit should be here soon," he said."

Johnny went into the living room and began to pace the floor as if from the shambles he could gain some clue as to why the attack occurred. He was still walking when the medics arrived.

The two men in white brushed past him, examined Karl and called on the radio. A doctor somewhere told them what to do and Karl had regained consciousness by the time they got the temporary bandages on him and had moved him to the gurney.

Sandy sat on the floor by the bed. "Why?" she asked, looking at Johnny.

"I don't know. But I'm going to find out."

The patrolman introduced Johnny to a plain-clothes sergeant. The sergeant took Johnny and Sandy into the living room, where they sat on the slashed couch and answered his questions.

They could not determine why her father had been "disciplined," as the sergeant said.

When the officer was through with the interrogation, and the photographer he brought had taken pictures, Johnny took the detective to one side.

"You used the term 'disciplined.' What do you mean by that?"

"I'm from the Organized Crime Task Force, OCTF." My guess is that Mr. Darlow knew something, saw something or met someone that he shouldn't have. The Mob wants him to understand that if he doesn't keep quiet about it, the next time they'll kill him."

Johnny gave the cop a description of the intruder who escaped. The man was maybe an inch more than six feet, weighed about 190 pounds and was quick on his feet. Johnny had seen no weapon, but guessed a knife would be in his pocket.

The detective watched Johnny. "You remember anything else that I should know? Like where Karl has been the last few weeks, maybe special people he mentioned. Anything that might help?"

"I wish I did. Karl is a fisherman. Skippers the

Flying Fool out of the Point Loma sportfishing area. He hasn't been anywhere else. This is fishing season."

"Right," the sergeant said, and handed Johnny his card. "If you think of anything, let me know."

"Yeah, I'll do that." Johnny read the name on the card. "And thanks, Sergeant Hall. Oh, where did the paramedics take Karl?"

"Emergency at University Hospital."

Twenty minutes later Johnny and Sandy had closed up the apartment, turned out the lights and locked the front door. They drove to the hospital and found Karl in one of the ten curtained-off slots along one wall in the emergency treatment area. His wounds had been bandaged and he lay resting, his eyes closed.

A young doctor looked in.

"A little nasty, but nothing serious here. We set the cartilage in his nose so it shouldn't give him any trouble. The cuts on his torso were surprisingly shallow." The hurried medic shrugged. "At any rate we want to keep Mr. Darlow overnight and he should be able to go home tomorrow. We'd like to x-ray his head and do some scans to be sure there are no cranial problems."

A nurse entered, seemed irritated that they were still there. "We have to move him upstairs now. He's been given a sedative, that's why he's sleeping. He was conscious for a while when he got here. Don't worry, he's going to be fine." She managed a thin smile, then grabbed the narrow hospital bed and pulled it through the curtains.

Johnny took Sandy's hand and led her out to his VW.

That was when he remembered that he had not told Sergeant Hall the license plate number. It was not complete and he had almost forgotten about it. But he knew it, MWW--7. Should he call the sergeant?

Johnny decided he would do some detective work of his own. Mafia! Twice the same day the group had come into his life. He would have a talk with Armand Killinger in the morning. Then he would try to find out who owned that car and who the driver was.

He would also have a long talk with Karl Darlow. What could he be mixed up in that the Mafia thought was so important? Was it something to do with sport or commercial fishing or his boat?

Sandy curled up against the door as they drove home. Her face was wan and her voice shaky when she spoke.

"Why, Johnny? Why would anyone do something like this to daddy? He's never done anything wrong in his life. He's the only one of our family left. My mother dead in a car wreck, my older brother killed in Vietnam.... We Darlows are down to two."

"I'm going to help," Johnny said. "First thing

tomorrow I ask Mr. Killinger. He knows every-thing that goes on in this town. And I've got a small lead I didn't tell the sergeant about.''

Sandy glared at him. "Oh, Johnny, I've got one man I love in the hospital, I couldn't stand it if something happened to you, too."

"Don't worry, I'm just a coward at heart."

"You are not." She looked at him intently. "Johnny, you never did talk much about Lebanon and the fighting. But sometimes you have dreams about it. One night you cried out that your friend was killed. Then you screamed. I know you're not a coward. Just don't try to be a hero. Let the police take care of it, please."

"When I get something I will. I'm just a legman. I dig up facts. That's all I'm going to be doing."

"And it won't be dangerous?" she asked.

"I don't see how it could be." He smiled down at her as he parked behind the center. "Now relax, and smile. Your old man is as tough as shark hide. He'll be fine in a few days, a week at the most. Then he'll get mad. Before that we both have to have a good long talk with him."

Later that night as they lay in bed, Sandy wept and Johnny put his arms around her.

"He looked so helpless!" Sandy said. "Lying there with blood all over him."

"It's over, try to forget it. Think about the good times."

She was quiet for a while, then she reached up and kissed him.

Around midnight Johnny woke up and lay staring up at the ceiling in the darkness.

Would it? Would everything be all right?

Mafia! A cold fear had gripped his gut.

9

Johnny Bolan stifled a yawn as he strode into Armand Killinger's office the next morning. Johnny had not slept well, but awoke early because he felt it was imperative that he speak to his boss about the events surrounding the attack on Karl Darlow.

Armand Killinger had a nine-o'clock court appointment but he took time to listen to Johnny. When the story was told, Killinger pointed to a small item in the morning paper about Karl. The police called it an apparent robbery attempt interrupted when visitors came to the house. It gave Karl's name and address but not Johnny's and Sandy's names. Killinger peaked his fingers and leaned back in his big chair.

"Yes, Sergeant Hall was right, it certainly fits the M.O. of the Mafia types we have in town. They show a lot of fake class and polish, lots of money, but with morals and habits of alley fighters. My suggestion is to leave it alone. Talk to Mr. Darlow. Try to convince him that these men will kill him the next time without blinking an eye."

"He must know why they're after him," Johnny said.

"Hopefully, but he might not. I had a client like that once who witnessed a murder and didn't realize it. She was threatened and roughed up and told to forget something she didn't know. The police nailed the killers and she was called as a witness, but she hadn't really seen anything incriminating she could swear to."

"Great, so we just drop it?"

"Johnny, I know you're a fighter. I know of the work you do down at the Free Legal Aid Center. That's fine, down there. I've done the same thing now and then. But this isn't some self-important landlord, or some jerk trying to rip off a car. These people are *La Cosa Nostra*. These people are killers."

"I've heard."

"You know anything about the Mafia?"

"Not much."

"You know what 'making your bones' means?"

Johnny shook his head.

"Making your bones is the Mob's term for killing someone. Not even the lowest soldier can get a promotion in the Family until he's 'made his bones,' usually on a definite hit of someone who is presenting a problem. Like your friend Darlow could become."

Johnny was not satisfied with his boss's suggestion. He would not tell Armand about the license plate. Then he remembered somebody who he thought might be able to help. What was her name? He had dated her a few times just after he got out of the paralegal classes. Nancy! Yeah. He hoped she still worked in the San Diego Police Department.

Back at his desk he made the call.

"I'm sorry I'll need a last name, sir. We have more than one Nancy here."

He dug into his memory. "Carter, Nancy Carter."

The phone rang and a voice came on. "I.D. Lab, Carter."

"Nancy, this is Johnny Gray, remember me?"

There was a pause. "Oh, yes, the guy who said he wanted to date other girls and see how they compared to me. That was about a year ago. How did I compare?"

"Just fine, but I don't have much social life. I have a small favor I hope you can do for me."

"I guess. What is it?"

"Some guy banged into my car, hit and run, and I got part of his license but not all of it. I have the three letters in front and one number."

"That's work, John." She sighed. "Hell, I'll try. Things are slow here this morning. What do you have?"

Johnny told her.

"You still working for Killinger?"

"Yes, how did you know that?"

"I think I saw you behind him on TV once. Give me a half hour and I'll call you back. What's your number?"

He gave it to her and hung up. It was a long shot. Johnny looked over his stack of work and then dug into it.

The phone call from Nancy came twenty minutes later.

"We got lucky, Johnny," Nancy said. "That sequence of plates was sent to northern California for distribution, so most of them are up there. The computer came up with only six in the San Diego area. Got a pencil?"

She went through them, with the full plate number, last known name and address and year and make of car.

"Nancy, I owe you one. Lunch one of these days?"

"Sure, John. But I don't put much stock in those 'one of these days' kind of deals."

"I might surprise you."

"Hope so, Johnny. Give me a call, anytime."

Johnny said goodbye and stared at the information. Only one of the cars was a Pontiac. He looked at the name. Philmore Industries Inc. was the registered owner of the car. The address was 1200 Third Avenue. That was right downtown, one of the high rises, a big bank building.

Johnny finished his desk work, checked out with Nel and drove past the address. He had guessed right. The building was on the edge of the Civic Center complex, with about two hundred offices: the Security Pacific Bank Plaza. On a hunch he drove into the underground parking, took his ticket and spiraled down two levels. He parked in a slot and walked along the rows of cars looking at license numbers.

This was stupid. There must be two hundred cars down there. And what good would it do to find that car. He had the name of the outfit!

In the lobby he checked the directory and found Philmore Industries listed on the sixteenth floor, 1607. Easy.

Only it did not turn out to be that easy.

Johnny wore his three-piece suit the way Armand liked him to, and now he felt right in place with the junior executives rushing around. When he got off at the sixteenth floor he found not a typical office-building hallway but rather a soft, deep carpet, luxurious decor and a desk twenty feet in front of the elevators. The whole floor was taken up by Philmore Industries, with the name and company crest expensively displayed on the far wall.

Johnny hesitated, then walked over to the attractive blond sitting behind the reception desk. He was thinking fast. He knew no one here. He did not even know what the firm did. Just as the woman looked up at him with soft green eyes, he had his ploy.

"Hey, nice place. I thought this would be a little office. My name is Bill Johnson and I wanted to talk to somebody about sponsoring an advertisement in our college yearbook. It's really a very good advertising value because these books are kept for the life of the person. They are. . . ."

The woman was smiling and waving both hands in front of him.

"Wait a minute." She laughed. "You don't have to sell me. The people who decide those things are inside. Let me see, you said it was a college year-book. That would be corporate public relations, I would think. Oh, darn. Mr. Jabrowski is out to-day. He won't be back until Thursday. Could I set up an appointment with you for Thursday morning, say around nine-thirty?"

"I'm sorry, I can't. My deadline is this after-noon. Damn!"

The blonde smiled and put down her pencil. "Hmm, let's see. You could talk to Mr. Gates, but he can't sign an order, and I guess that's what you need."

A group of men were leaving an office down the carpeted hall. Johnny looked at the men as they walked toward him. Three of them looked like or-dinary businessmen, but the fourth evidently was a bodyguard. Only the thug looked at Johnny, dis-carded him visually and went on past.

Johnny glanced back at the woman and shrugged.

"Well, I wasn't going to win the prize for the most ads sold, anyway. Maybe next year. What type of business is this, anyway? We were sup-posed to get several categories of firms for balance."

"Actually we're a holding company here. We own at least fifty-one percent of a number of different kinds of businesses."

"Ah, well, thanks. I better get to my next prospect." Johnny turned and walked to the elevator. A woman came from a door down the hall, said hello to the receptionist and walked on to the elevator.

If Johnny thought the blonde was pretty, she paled into plainness compared to this brunette. He liked the smooth easy way she walked, almost a dancer's motion. She was taller than most women at maybe five-eight, and her silky black hair shimmered around her shoulders as she stopped beside him and pushed the down button.

She glanced at him and smiled. "You'll stand here all day unless you tell the little man in the small box on the roof where you want to go."

"Oh, right," Johnny replied, still staring at her. She was remarkable. Her voice was strong, yet had shadings of emotion and coloring. She was the most beautiful woman he had ever seen right up close. Not a blemish on creamy skin, soft brown eyes under arched brows and just a touch of mascara on her lashes. A natural, alluring face that sparked his immediate interest.

She stirred uneasily and laughed. "Well, how did I do?"

Johnny grinned, reached and pushed the down button again. "Sorry, you caught me. I've got to learn how to appreciate a beautiful woman without letting her know. I'm much too obvious."

"Hi, I'm Angela."

She held out her hand and he took it. "I'm Johnny." When he touched her fingers he tingled. That had never happened before. He looked at her and for a moment he thought she felt something, too. Then the elevator doors opened, spoiling the mood, and she dropped his hand.

The car was empty. They stepped inside and he pushed the first-floor button. "Oh, were you going down?"

She nodded.

He liked the way the stray black curl crept down on her forehead.

They had about twenty seconds to talk before reaching the lobby.

"What do you, do, Johnny?"

"I'm a paralegal. I work for a lawyer."

"How exciting. I always wanted to be a lawyer, but somehow I got sidetracked into business."

"It's a nice track, especially if you can work with the folks up there on the sixteenth floor. That Philmore Industries looks like a plush operation."

She nodded. "I guess it is. Are you in a hurry? Right now, I mean."

"No. Why?"

"I guess I'd like to talk to you some more. I have an instinct about people and I usually follow my instincts. It hasn't failed me yet. I...I like you."

"Have you had lunch? We could have a bite

somewhere," Johnny suggested, trying to sound calm.

"Wonderful!"

"There's a little place not far from here that sells pita bread sandwiches. Do you like them?"

Angela nodded as they crossed the lobby and headed for the entrance.

The automatic doors opened and she caught his arm and held on as they walked out into the sunlight.

Three blocks later, they entered the sandwich shop with a counter and wooden booths where hundreds of secretaries, clerks and junior executives had lunch every day.

"I've never been here," she said, looking around.

They ordered two pocket-bread sandwiches, found a vacant booth and talked as they ate. Quickly they covered the international situation, the political race for mayor of San Diego and at last the recreational choices for winter or summer.

Neither of them had said a word about themselves. It was as if that was not a permitted topic. They both finished the pocket sandwiches and had little paper cups of sherbet for dessert, then walked back toward the plaza.

He reached for her hand and put it through his arm, then smiled at her.

"I don't even know your last name."

She smiled. "Names, names. It's not that important."

"Suit yourself," he said, then added, "I'm parked in the garage downstairs."

"Me too. You can walk me to my car. That place gets kind of creepy sometimes."

"Glad to."

When they came to her car on the first level, he found with surprise that it was a brand-new Mercedes 380SL. But the expensive car was low on one side. He checked around the vehicle, then came back to Angela.

"Your left rear tire is flat."

"Damn!"

"No problem. I can change it in five minutes."

"Would you, please?"

He took her keys and opened the trunk. "And this really is your car?"

"Daddy owns it, I guess. But I drive it all the time. No, I think the pink slip is in my name this time."

He saw the Triple A sticker on her side window. She could have called the auto club to have the flat fixed. He did not mention the auto-club service. Neither did she.

Johnny went to work, changed the tire and stowed the flat one in the trunk.

"Have somebody fix that soon, you don't want to drive without a spare."

"Yes, sir." She smiled. Those sneaky brown eyes of hers could capture a person quickly.

"Since you won't tell me your last name, how about a phone number?"

"I don't give my number to people I haven't known for at least three hours."

"Good idea. I'm Johnny Gray."

"Let's compromise. I owe you a lunch already and I owe you a dinner for fixing my flat tire. You give me your number and I can call you. Deal?"

"Fair enough." He gave her his work phone.

"I've got to hurry away," Angela said. "I'm an hour late now."

Johnny nodded. "I'm glad I was lost on the sixteenth floor."

"You're nice, Johnny. I really do have to run." She kissed his cheek, then stepped into the Mercedes. Johnny closed the door.

He watched her drive down the lane of cars. When she was out of sight, he jogged to the next level where he found his VW. He looked at the blue Volkswagen with its faded, chipped paint job, creases in two fenders and one headlight sitting askew.

"Don't worry about it," he said, patting the car. "Being pretty isn't everything." He was halfway up to the pay booth when he thought about his problem again. So far he knew the Mafia car was owned by a big firm called Philmore Industries, who rented the whole sixteenth floor of the Security Plaza building. Not bad for a start.

Johnny realized he still had many more questions than answers. His next move was to go and see Karl Darlow and try for some information. Surely Karl would tell him what was going on.

Johnny paid the parking fee and headed for University Hospital.

As he drove, he had a lurking feeling that he was getting close to the solution of the puzzle. But a nagging dread crawled along his spine as he wondered if, when he finally found out what he was after, he'd be able to handle it.

10

Mack Bolan hovered like a lethal black shadow beside the rear door of the City Market. He was on a side street in Maywood, not far from the Chicago city limits. The market had been closed for two hours, but lights still showed in the back. For some it was "banking" time, midnight.

Bolan had waited in the darkness as a couple of runners came to the door, knocked twice, then paused and knocked two more times. The door opened and the errand boys passed inside. In only two or three minutes they were back in the alley and fading into the gloom.

No one had come for twenty minutes. Bolan moved silently and quickly to the doorway, his dark skintight suit making him a black on black apparition. He raised his big fist and used the same signal as the two messengers. The door opened a crack and when it did Bolan's size-eleven shoe smashed into it waist high, ripping the screws from the small night-chain latch, flinging the door inward.

The man who had been inches away from the door was hurled six feet across the room as he caught the full force of the wooden panel on the side of his head.

Four others sitting at a long green-topped table looked up in bewilderment. Nothing like this had ever happened before. The specter in black before them held a deadly looking pistol in one hand and his diamond-steel blue eyes glared at them.

"Enzio, you're a dead man," Bolan said. The silenced Beretta 93-R sneezed twice, and the boss of the Mafia numbers bank died where he sat at the table. The first round caught him just under his left eye and completed The Executioner's job before the second slug arrived. Enzio had been facing the door and pitched over backward as the 9mm parabellum rounds drilled into him.

"Lord have mercy!" one of the men wailed. Mercy is for the innocent, Bolan thought. He indicated that they should stand and the three men at the table stood in unison.

"Quaso, get the money from the safe," the Executioner growled. Quaso hesitated only for a moment, but it was all the time Bolan needed. Once more the 93-R coughed and Quaso fell backward on top of his former boss.

"The money. From the safe and off the table." Bolan motioned with his gun and the smaller of the two hoods knocked over his chair in his haste to get to the safe. The other thug began to gather up the stacks of currency on the green felt.

The fifth man, who had answered the door, groaned and started to sit up on the floor.

"Don't move!" Bolan barked at him. "Catch."
With his left hand Bolan pulled something from
his slit pocket and tossed it to the goon on the
floor. Still slightly dazed from his recent confron-
tation with the door, the man missed the metal
disk and it fell on his chest.

"Holy mother!" the terrified soldier whispered.

"Louder, Pete!" Bolan thundered.

"The marksman's medal. It's the Executioner!" Pete croaked.

At the sound of the name the man at the safe
made a desperate move. His hand clawed for iron
from an ankle holster. He whirled, firing as he
turned.

Bolan triggered the Beretta three times, the
force of the rounds pushing the gunner back into
the open vault. As the small man died he got off a
final shot, but it missed Bolan and ricocheted off a
metal filing cabinet, drilling a passage through
Pete's chest where he lay on the floor. He sighed
and died.

The third slug had not yet found its mark when
Bolan was tracking the 93-R to the fourth man at
the table.

"Rudolfo," Bolan snapped. "Drop your piece.
Then fill the sack, now!"

A minute later the money was all in a dark green
trash bag and sitting on the table in front of
Bolan. Four Mafia numbers soldiers lay dead on
the floor.

"Tell Louis Lavengelli that I'm in town, to keep

looking over his shoulder. Tell him Bolan the Bastard is back, and his head is on the line.''

Rudolfo was pale, his hands spread flat on the table, his arms trembling.

Bolan took another marksman's medal from his pocket, opened Enzio's mouth and forced the small disk between the dead man's teeth. Maybe the Chitown Family would get the connection.

Bolan grabbed the sack of money and retreated slowly. He watched Rudolfo's lips moving and Mack Bolan guessed the man was saying a prayer in celebration of the miracle that his life had been spared.

About an hour later, Bolan made another stop off Central Street, a few blocks from the Oak Park city limits sign. It was a little after 1:00 A.M. and the night people were out in force. The Executioner parked his car, then eased into an alley next to the Roxy Theater, and let his eyes get used to the darkness.

Socks was in her office as usual about fifty feet down the inky black alley. It was a half-basement stairway with a big landing at the bottom. At 1:00 A.M. every morning she took a folding chair down the steps, set up her kerosene heater, took out her flashlight and began her operation.

She was making a sale when Bolan arrived. He waited for the addicts to buy and leave. Then he walked down the steps.

Socks looked up quickly. The tread was too steady, too sure. Cops? She put one hand under her big coat and waited.

"Hear you got some good shit," Bolan said.

"Always good. You buying?"

"Not what you're selling, old woman. You want to sell out?"

"I don't sell out, I just deal."

"Not this time. It's your scrawny neck in exchange for the name of your supplier."

She laughed. Bolan watched her closely. He saw the slightest movement under the bulky coat near her waist. The Beretta leveled at his hip spat once in the darkness. The silenced round found its mark, Socks's right arm.

She screeched in pain and a .32 automatic clattered to the cement floor by her feet.

"Bastard!" she snarled at him.

"That was your only chance, Socks. You play the game my way, or you find out if there is life after death."

"Not this time, sucker," Socks shouted.

"You get half a point for guts, Socks. Now open the loose brick behind you and take out your stash."

She shook her head.

"How many teenagers have you killed with your PCP and horse? Five people died in a crash on the freeway yesterday. They were hit by a car with three seventeen-year-old girls in it, sky-high on drugs. They all died, too. The boyfriend of one of them told me you sold to all the kids. One choice, your supplier or your grave."

"Ha! You wouldn't shoot an old woman like

me. I'm a senior citizen. And I'll never tell you my connection.''

The Executioner shot her twice in the face. He felt no remorse even though she was a woman. She was part of the hydra that suffocated hope and honesty. Women held a special place in Bolan's heart. But on occasion, he had to execute a few, like now.

He walked up the steps, found a phone and called the police. He reported shots fired in an alley, then hung up and faded into the darkness after he gave the location.

There are nearly eight million people in the Chicago metropolitan area. Bolan had heard there were now four Mafia Families that had split up the territory and worked closely with *La Commissione*. They had a stable operation, with each Family holding to its territory. There had been no real intermob violence there for a year.

He had also been told that one drug czar held the franchise for the Chicago district. Since the most money was in drugs, the Families did not want the boss of each outfit trying to outbid and outfight the others for the best flow through the California pipeline. They were bringing modern business methods into the Mob operation.

Bolan had been in Chicago for a week working his sources, twisting arms, keeping a low profile and quietly gathering all the information he needed.

Now he had gone public and it was a hard hit all the way.

He was in his attack mode and when Bolan was through, the Chicago Mafia wouldn't know what hit them.

Bolan drove deeper into the heart of downtown Chicago, parked on a dimly lit street and jogged down an alley. He stopped in front of an abandoned building that showed lights on the fifth floor. Bolan entered through a cellar window and cautiously worked his way across the junk-filled basement toward the stairs.

"That you, Frisco?" a deep voice ahead of him in the dark asked.

"Uh-huh," Bolan grunted.

"Hell it is!" the deep voice boomed. A big flashlight came on and swept the basement. The Beretta whispered three times, with the single shots aimed in a pattern around the light source.

The silenced rounds had barely left the muzzle when the flashlight clattered to the floor and a strangled scream dropped to zero decibels as the basement guard died.

Bolan stepped over him and found the flashlight. It still worked. He pushed it in his belt and walked up to the first floor. There was no guard there. He continued to the second floor, treading softly on the sides of the wooden steps closest to the wall so they would not squeak.

On the third level Bolan heard voices and he slipped through a stairway door into the hall. It was dark, except for a flickering light three doors down. The hallway there was shadowed by the wavering flame, but Bolan could see spray-painted graffiti on the walls. He looked closer. It was all in Oriental characters, Chinese, Japanese, Vietnamese, he was not sure which. Sliding silently along the corridor with the Beretta out, the Executioner came to the doorway and looked in.

Dozens of candles lit the big room. Most of the floor area was covered with thin pallets and sleeping bags and prone human forms occupied more than fifty of the sleeping mats.

This was an opium den. Near the door of the room sat a wooden business desk. Behind it was a small Oriental man smoking a long-stemmed pipe. He chanted a few words in a singsong voice, then took a deep drag on the pipe and held the smoke in his lungs as long as he could. When he exhaled, a serene expression crossed his features and he relaxed in the chair.

Bolan shook his head. The scene had changed suddenly and he was sighting through a sniper scope at a headman in a Vietnamese village, his finger squeezing the trigger. Someone coughed in the back of the room, and the Executioner snapped back to the present.

He moved into the room with a firm, hard step and the languid eyes of the Oriental behind the desk turned toward him. There was no surprise or alarm there, only curiosity.

A Vietnamese in the first row of pallets rose up and fired a small-caliber handgun. Bolan felt the slug graze his side.

The Executioner spun and sent one silent round into the gunman, slamming him back lifelessly to the mat.

A second man in the front row sat up, swinging two short sticks held together by a six-inch chain. Bolan turned, acquired target and fired twice before the Oriental could hurl the weapon.

Two slugs caught the addict in the chest and the sticks flew out of his hand. With eyes glazed and spittle drooling from his lips, the mortally wounded man laughed and charged the Executioner, this time brandishing a long knife. The silenced 93-R spit flame again and three slugs cored the attacker's skull. The man finally went down, the blade skittering across the floor.

No more defenders rose from the front row.

The small Oriental behind the desk puffed unconcernedly on the pipe, nodding to himself. His drug-slowed eyes turned toward Bolan again.

"Can you pay?" the man asked.

"Only with lead," Bolan replied.

The Vietnamese blinked slowly, then shook his head.

"Lead has no value," he said.

"Sure it has. Right now it's worth its weight in gold." The Executioner put one silenced 9mm parabellum hornet into the man's mouth as he started to reply. It punched him off his stool to the floor.

No one else in the room even looked up.

The Executioner hurried to the desk. In the

drawers he found stacks of folded packets of co-caine. He took all the bundles and built a small fire on the desk top, feeding the packages into it one at a time until they were all eaten by the fire and only a sticky residue left on the desk.

In another drawer he found a quarter of a pound of white powder. He licked a finger and tasted it. Heroin.

The Executioner walked to the nearest window, ripped open the plastic bag and spilled the white powder into the night. It caught in the breeze, created a small cloud for a moment, then scattered in the Chicago wind.

Then Bolan dropped a marksman's medal on the desk, ran down the steps and exited through the basement window.

He had one more call planned before daylight. Bolan found the street he wanted a little after 3:00 A.M. He had no difficulty picking the locked outer door of the apartment house. The lobby was empty and Bolan took the elevator to the fourteenth floor.

He found apartment 1414 and tried the door. Locked. Again Bolan made short work of the twin locks and entered the residence.

The apartment's living room was luxuriously furnished with subdued lighting. A big-screen projection TV stood in one corner. He brushed past it and treaded down a short corridor toward two closed doors. The first one was a den. The second yielded the bedroom.

A bedside lamp glowed on low power, showing a king-size water bed with two figures on it. A nude black woman lay on her back, the sheets thrown off. Next to her, sleeping on his side, lay a black man.

Amos "Mo" Tabler was in his thirties. A Vietnam veteran and former Chicago Bears halfback, he was one of the drug suppliers to dealers in this area. Silently Bolan lifted a .45 auto from the nightstand. Showing under the edge of the pillow was a longer-barreled weapon, a Woodsman .22 with silencer attached. Bolan worked the weapon from the hiding place and checked the nightstand drawer. No more guns.

The Executioner took the Woodsman and using the silencer like a stick hit the underside of Tabler's bare feet.

"Please, no!" Tabler screamed, sitting upright at once. "No more. I'll tell you what you want to know!" His screech died as he looked around and realized where he was.

The girl sat up as well. "Damn it, Mo. Another one of your goddamn nightmares." It was then she turned and saw the big apparition in black. She stifled a scream and huddled against Tabler.

Tabler pulled himself together fast when he saw Bolan. The ex-football pro's hand snaked under the pillow but came out empty. He shrugged. "Hell, nothing but a two-bit burglar. Okay, how much you want? Toss me my pants."

The Executioner hit the exposed soles of Tabler's feet again with the Woodsman.

"Hell, mother! What you want?"

"I want your ass in hell, brother," Bolan said, his voice even, deadly, almost snarling as he uttered the last word. He shoved a copy of the newspaper in front of Tabler. It showed a picture of the head-on freeway crash that killed the three girls and five others.

"One dead big-shot heroin supplier like you isn't much to pay for the eight people you killed, but it's a start. Chicago is going to make good on the whole bill before I'm done." Bolan dropped a marksman's medal on Tabler's chest.

"Oh, shit!"

"Miss, you can get dressed if you want. Where Mo is going he won't need clothes."

Tabler came lunging off the bed faster than Bolan expected. Bolan sidestepped and swung the barrel of the Woodsman down hard on the back of Tabler's thick neck. Tabler continued to move as if he did not feel the stunning blow. He tumbled to the floor, somersaulted on the carpet and came up, his hands held wide, his face filled with hatred and fear mixed in equal parts. Tension rippled the muscles in the ex-pro's superb physique.

"Man to man, you mother! Put down the goods and take me on man to man."

"Who juiced up those high-school girls and sent them out on the freeway?"

"I never met them! They're not even in my territory. You're blowing wind, dude. Drop the hardware. Try me one on one!''

"I want your dealers. Now!"

The woman stood to one side, not trying to cover herself, watching her lover.

"Do it, Mo! Give him the names, then we can get out of here."

"You don't understand, woman. This is the damned Executioner. He don't play like the crooked cops. He thinks he's some kind of savior."

Tabler rushed Bolan again, his big hands reaching out for the Executioner.

The Beretta chugged out a silenced round. The weapon made almost the same sound as Mo Tabler did when the 9mm parabellum dug through his right shoulder and splintered a bone, lost its force and nestled deep in red tissue.

Tabler stopped his rush, grabbed his bleeding shoulder.

"Bastard!"

"Think how the parents of those three high-school girls feel."

"You get no names from me, man!"

"I'll get them, Mo. I got all night."

Tabler scowled. "Hell, experts worked on me in Nam. It was easier to talk than not to. What difference did it make? You'll get nothing from me."

Bolan turned and took one step toward the woman.

She gasped and backed against the wall.

"Hell, no sweat, girl. This dude is too straight to touch you. You're one of the innocents, not a bad ass like me. This mother won't even touch you. You lose, Bolan."

The Executioner swiveled and shot him in the right kneecap. Mo Tabler crumpled to the floor. He roared in agony, but Bolan stood unmoved, the Beretta ready.

"Think about it, Tabler. Your hands are dirty. You're shit and you don't deserve to live. Give me your dealers and your pipeline contact, and I might reconsider."

"No way!" Tabler screamed through his pain. "I owe you for this knee. You're a dead man."

"You've got sixty seconds to decide, Mo. Then I use your left kneecap for target practice."

"No!" He bared his teeth at Bolan and hugged his knee, then looked up. "Monique, go in the den and bring me the paper from the top right-hand drawer. Move it, baby."

Bolan quickly positioned himself in front of the bedroom door.

"No, Monique, we'll all go."

It took several minutes for Tabler to struggle into the next room even with his girlfriend supporting his weight. A lighted desk lamp cast a soft glow over the leather furniture in the den. Bolan ordered Tabler to sit in the swivel chair, and told Monique to wheel it next to the door.

Then the Executioner looked in the top right-hand desk drawer. Another .45 automatic lay there. Bolan took it and shoved it in his belt and began riffling through some papers in the desk.

Monique shivered, asked if she could get dressed. Bolan told her not yet, and kept looking for the names.

Tabler kept clutching his wounded knee, whimpering in pain.

Bolan found a piece of paper showing names, addresses and phone numbers. There were twenty-four names, with three crossed off.

Bolan folded the sheet and slipped it into a slit pocket.

Monique realized there was only one way she could help her man. She strutted toward Bolan, her shapely nude body moving gracefully in the subdued light.

"You want any of this, big daddy?" She thrust out her chest and wiggled her shoulders, making her big breasts dance delightfully. "Looks like my man is out of action and all this excitement has just turned me on. Mo won't be any good to me for a long time." She pressed her nipples against Bolan. She started to put her arms around him.

That was when Mo Tabler made a desperate move. Ignoring his pain, he rushed toward Bolan again, grabbing for the .44 AutoMag on Bolan's hip. The Executioner leaped back, pushed the woman away and felt Tabler's hands tugging at Big Thunder. The Executioner triggered the 93-R on full auto, the three slugs printing a tight triangle of death on Mo Tabler's chest. The black drug dealer jolted backward from the force of the rounds, tumbled to the floor and died as he reached out to his woman for help.

Monique sat on the floor where she had fallen, staring in surprise and wonder at Tabler's silent form. His eyes were open, gazing at the ceiling but seeing nothing. Then Monique screamed.

Mack Bolan quietly closed the den door, left the apartment and hurried to the elevator. He had some new ammunition, some new names. He would turn the Windy City into an inferno of dying drug dealers, pushers and suppliers. Fire would raze Chicago once more—Bolan fire.

11

At 4:00 A.M. the Executioner found a spot well away from the busy streets of Chicago. He locked the doors on the rented Ford Tempo, stretched out in the seat as best he could and closed his eyes. As a sniper in Vietnam the warrior had learned to condition his body to patrol sleep. In this mode he was not actually sleeping. He floated in a world of neither full consciousness nor deep slumber.

It was an efficient way to rest the body and let the mind take some R and R at the same time.

Trucks rumbled by on early-morning deliveries and a few cars sped past. Neither disturbed Bolan. A drunk staggering down the block touched the Tempo's rear fender for support, and the sudden movement of the car jolted Bolan alert. Quickly he found the source of the disturbance, and his hand relaxed on the Beretta resting in his lap. He watched as the drunk pushed himself off the car, straightened his grubby jacket and, stepping high, unsure how far away the ground was from his feet, careened on down the street. Bolan caught another two hours of patrol sleep.

It was nearly eight o'clock when he awoke. The

big city was humming. After breakfast Bolan prepared to zero in on the third name on his list. The drug dealer was also a corner grocery-store owner a block from a high school.

Bolan shuffled into the little store on the first floor of a four-story apartment house. He had a dirty handkerchief to his nose and kept sniffling. He wore a shabby overcoat he had found in the trash and had smeared dirt on his face. His eyes were red and watering because he had rubbed them hard a moment before he went in. By hunching over and shivering now and then, he gave the impression of an addict who needed a fix in a rush.

The store owner, in his forties and wearing a dirty, knee-length coverall, scowled when he saw Bolan holding a ten-dollar bill in his grimy hand.

"You got a twenty we can talk," Joseph Dabrowski said. "You ain't got the bread, get outa here."

"I need to score."

"Look, buddy, can't you keep it together when you come around here? I got regular customers too." Still the proprietor, never one to lose a sale, motioned with his head.

"In the back," he said.

Bolan licked his lips and nodded. They went through a curtain-covered doorway and the Executioner showed him another ten-spot. Dabrowski grabbed both and entered a second room. He was back a moment later with a package folded from a magazine page.

"Just what I need," Bolan said, the slurred speech gone, his eyes now angry, steel-blue and deadly. A six-inch stiletto in his hand lifted and touched Dabrowski's forehead.

"How many pushers do you have working, big man?" Bolan asked.

Dabrowski tried to pull back, but the tip of the thin knife punctured the skin on his forehead and he froze in place. His eyes were shifting wildly, seeking help, trying for an explanation.

"Who . . . ?"

"Some call me The Executioner."

The man's hand darted inside his coverall, digging for hardware. But he never made it.

Bolan drove the razor-sharp blade into the dealer's neck. A crimson fountain erupted, the drops making an irregular polka-dot pattern on the once-white coat.

Dabrowski grunted in surprise and his head sagged as Bolan stepped back, letting the body fall. He dropped a marksman's medal beside the corpse and continued out the back door into the alley and walked two blocks over to his car.

The big warrior was moving on, blowing a fresh breeze through the Windy City. By the time he was finished, every dealer and pusher in town would be looking over his shoulder, afraid he'd be the next on the Executioner's hit parade.

Bolan picked the next name on the list. It was a mile away in a fancier neighborhood, and the address was a health spa. He had discarded the dirty overcoat he used at the grocery, washed his face clean and now wore a light blue sport shirt over his black jersey. Most of the people who passed through the door were dressed in tights or jogging clothes.

He left the Beretta in the car and entered the workout center. There was a desk inside the door. He looked around at the facilities. About a dozen men, of all shapes and sizes, were in the weight room. An aerobics class was in session and the exercise machines were busy.

A girl in white tights came up and smiled. She was in her early twenties, with a trim figure that the form-fitting leotard and tights showed off perfectly. Every curve and muscle showed beneath the tightly stretched fabric.

"So what do you think? Like to sign up for a six-month membership? We're having a special, only $119 for six months. Can I sign you up?"

"Sure. But first I'm looking for someone. Liman Rogers."

She picked up the receiver and punched an extension number. She spoke a few words, then cradled the instrument. She pointed the way to Roger's office. Bolan went through swinging doors beyond the weight room into a hall and to the only office at the end. It was big, with a couch, a small refrigerator and a huge desk. Rogers looked up when the Executioner came in.

"Yes?"

"Mr. Rogers, I'm desperate. Got me about

twenty gung hos out there and my dealer gets himself smashed up in a car wreck. My people are in need! You're the only contact I know of who can help me fast."

"Who the hell said?" Rogers was big and had done his time on the weights. He looked solid, but it was all cold iron, not body-contact work.

Bolan shrugged. "Hell, it's around. Be in the business long enough and you hear things, get to know people. Can you help me? I got to move damn fast."

Rogers sat in his chair, took out a small package and tapped out three short rows of cocaine on his desk top. With a razor blade he pushed the coke into long thin lines. He used a drinking straw and snorted the coke up one side of his nose and then the other. He blinked away tears and wiped his eyes dry. They took on a new glint. Rogers shrugged.

"How much shit you talking?"

"For fifteen, sometimes seventeen people. All I can manage. You got the stuff right here?"

"You outa your mind? What's your name?"

"Mack."

"Okay, Mack, follow me out back."

They went through a side door into an alley. Parked behind the health club was a twenty-foot motor home. Liman unlocked it and swept an imaginary hat off, ushering Bolan inside.

"You do just coke or horse?" the guy asked.

"Anything you got. My people are hurting." Bolan laughed wildly, watching Rogers. The other man joined in the laugh, then pulled out the drawers of a cabinet. Bolan had never seen so huge a stash of illegal drugs before. A cold fury traveled through his gut when he realized what he was looking at.

The Executioner half-turned away from Rogers, then pivoted, his right hand swinging around flat and hard, the edge slamming into Roger's throat, crushing the man's windpipe. The hopped-up pusher stumbled backward, gurgling something unintelligible, his eyes glazed, bulging, as he clutched his throat.

Before Rogers could assess the damage, Bolan's right fist shot out in the narrow corridor of the motor home. The punch traveled only a short distance, Bolan's arm not fully extended, but the blow carried all his weight behind it. His knuckles impacted on Rogers's forehead, above the eyes, shattering bone and caving in his brow. He sagged to the floor, the massive damage to his brain slowly signaling a shutdown of the entire system. Twenty seconds later he was dead.

Bolan searched the rig quickly. He spotted a Coleman burner and a butane gas bottle. He found some matches and lit the portable stove, then laid the apparatus on the small couch so the fabric began to smolder. He piled some newspapers and other flammable material on top of it, then dumped out the drawers of drugs into the mess.

In a minute it was burning brightly. Bolan looked outside. No one was watching. He stepped out, closed the door and walked to his car before any smoke could escape from the camper.

Now he had a decision to make. There was one Mafia drug czar in Chicago, but various Families were still free to make separate deals on the side, as long as it did not upset the balance of power. This was not like the days when Bolan first brought his purge on the lakefront mobsters. The organization was more closely knit, the rebuilding had been better than he had expected.

One week before, when Bolan arrived in Chicago, he had tapped the syndicate underground and had learned of a meet that had been set up for today. He had phoned Carlo Genovese, special co-ordinator for the Chicago Mob's drug czar, and arranged an invitation to the "business" lunch being held at a local restaurant.

Bolan had also found out that the real reason for the meeting was to talk to free-lancers who might have "extra stuff" to get rid of, from a few pounds to a hundred kilos. As with any wholesaler, the drug bosses had to make sure they had a little more than they needed. When the California pipeline broke, as it did from time to time when the Feds got into action, there had to be an alternate supply available at once. Bolan would tell them that he could be the key to such a ready supply, if they were interested.

Bolan knew he was safe since none of the local Mafia members would know him by sight, because of the facial plastic-surgery operation he had undergone after the Central Park flameout some years before.

Now, as he entered Mario's, he was wearing a pair of gray slacks to go with his dark blue sport coat, an open-throated blue shirt and black loafers.

The restaurant was not full, and when Bolan told the hostess he was joining the Genovese party, he was ushered promptly to a room at the back. Two pistoleros lounged at the door. The girl pointed to the door and left quickly.

Bolan had expected a frisk and had left all his weapons in the car.

The Executioner stopped in front of the men and nodded.

"Boys, I'm Vito. I got special business with Mr. Genovese."

"Says who?" one of them asked.

"Says Carlo Genovese."

The one with the smart mouth vanished through the door. The other one kept his hand close to his waist until the spokesman returned. He looked at Bolan with more respect.

"Hardware? Ain't none permitted inside."

"Nothing but a nail file," Bolan said, holding his arms out so the Mafia hardman could search him. A minute later Mack walked through the door into a small room with a table set for four. All four at the table turned and watched him.

"Mr. Genovese, I'm Vito. We talked a few days ago on the phone."

"Yes," the smallest man in the room said. "Come in, we'll get another chair."

"Not necessary, Mr. Genovese. I know you're busy. I can double the quantity we talked about before. If it could be on a regular basis, monthly, that would be fine with me. I can show you samples by tomorrow. I understand the price is fixed by the Families, this is perfectly fine with me."

Carlo Genovese stood smiling. "Vito, you have answered all the questions I had." He paused and looked around the table. "We're businessmen and we must have the goods or we can't sell it. A lack of merchandise is always a problem. We're thinking of stockpiling. Call me tonight about seven and I'll give you our final decision."

Bolan nodded, turned and went out the door. He shouldered past the two hardmen and continued out of the restaurant. Mack Bolan realized he had just made visual contact with four of the top drug traffickers in Chicago: Mario Montessi, narcotics boss for the Dibartelo Family, Jack Spanno, drug man for the Spanno Family, Frank Mellini, top supplier to the syndicate in Chicago, and Carlo Genovese.

He stood outside the eatery for some minutes, then strolled up the sidewalk, looking for crew wagons. He found one of the black Cadillacs double-parked two doors down. A wheelman sat in the driver's seat. That would be one of the Mafia cars. The meal had been about over; they should be out soon.

Bolan returned to his rental vehicle in the pay lot where he had parked it and circled the block once. The black limo was still there. It should be worth the wait. The Executioner eased his car slowly along the busy street on his second circuit of the block and saw a Firebird pulling out from the curb three rigs ahead. He roared up and slid into the parking spot.

Bolan had a good position, four cars behind the crew wagon, and with time to look over his weapons case on the passenger's seat beside him.

He dug out Big Thunder and laid it between his legs, with the Beretta 93-R close to his right thigh. When he looked up at the Caddy, two men were walking rapidly toward it. One held the door and the Executioner saw Jake Spanno slide into the rear seat.

Spanno would be fine. The wheelman gunned the Caddy out of the slot and Bolan pushed the rented Tempo out after it.

Bolan had been following the limo for only three blocks when he saw a worried face in the rear window and a sudden burst of speed, as the quarry knew he was being followed. The Caddy took evasive action, but in the square-cut blocks the Tempo had no trouble riding the Caddy's tail.

The driver of the other rig knew it too, and soon the black car headed for a freeway on ramp. They passed through a light industrial section and Bolan pushed Big Thunder's snout out the window and triggered two rounds through the Caddy's rear windshield. The first 240-grain lead slug burned through the heavy rear window as if it was thin plastic, shattering the glass.

Bolan knew the second round had scored a direct hit when he saw the Caddy crew wagon begin to drift. The black limo slewed sideways, bounced off the guardrail and came to rest with two wheels off the edge of the soft shoulder, the car's nose pointing downward into the ditch.

Bolan stopped forty feet behind the Mafia wagon. The far side door opened and someone crawled out. A handgun blazed three times from the shattered rear window.

Another round from the .44 cannon thundered through the crew wagon's window, smashing into the neck of the hardman, severing the spinal column.

Bolan lunged out the passenger door of the Ford and peered over the fender. Someone moved beyond the Caddy. Then Jake Spanno jumped up and ran toward the ditch twenty feet away.

The Executioner bared his teeth as he gained target acquisition, squeezed off another round from the .44 and watched Spanno take the round in his back, heart high. The tremendous force of the riflelike round drove Spanno another dozen feet forward, dragging his bloody face along the concrete. Jake Spanno died instantly of massive heart damage.

Bolan saw no more movement in the car. From far off he heard the sound of a siren. He charged the crew wagon and looked through the driver's window. The wheelman slumped over the seat, blood streaming through his hand held to his head. He moaned. When he saw Bolan jerk open the door, he fumbled with the other hand for his .357 Magnum.

"Freeze, asshole, or you're dead!" the Executioner snapped.

The driver turned his eyes toward the big warrior.

"Tell Don Spanno he's next," Bolan growled.

The sirens came closer.

Bolan ran back to his car, gunned the engine and merged with the freeway traffic heading out of Chicago.

The Executioner knew there was no need to leave his metal calling card. The wheelman would make out as if he was a hero just to stay alive, but Don Spanno, one of the Chicago Godfathers, would get the message. His son, the drug boss, was dead and now he was targeted to die as well.

While the Spanno Family was going to the mattress, Bolan would make another hit. Mario Montessi, the drug boss who was part of the Dibartelo Family, would be a good target. Let them sweat a while, at least until tonight.

12

Angela Marcello stood in her bedroom clutching a robe and staring at her nude form in the full-length mirror. She turned from side to side, then sucked in her breath and patted her stomach. She threw her shoulders back and made a face at herself.

Not bad. But she was developing a tiny little belly. She decided she'd have to watch what she ate for a couple of weeks.

For a moment she thought about that guy today. Johnny, he said his name was. Something about him nagged at her. He was more cute than handsome, but he was so smooth, as if he understood what she was going to say or do before she did it. It gave her a little tingle even now, just thinking about him. She tried to picture herself in bed with him. What would it be like? She laughed and shook her head. She had more important projects right now.

Later she might call him and take him out to lunch. Maybe a picnic along the beach somewhere, a deserted stretch.... For a moment she let her imagination race, then laughed and put on the robe.

The bigger problem was her father. She had picked today for the showdown. She had been back from school for two months now, and still her father had not given her anything to do.

She flounced from her bedroom into her suite's sitting room. Angela had kicked and screamed five years ago until her father converted some of the rooms in his mansion on the slopes of La Jolla. Now she had a three-room apartment all her own. She could hole up here for days at a time if she wanted to, have her meals sent up or even do her own cooking in the tiny kitchen.

She sat at a small escritoire and frowned, drumming her fingers impatiently on the writing desk.

"Damn," she said, wondering when her father would begin to treat her as an adult. She was twenty-five and she had an M.B.A. from the Stanford School of Business. She knew more about running a business than ninety percent of her father's top management people in any of his firms.

He had to listen to her. She would give him a clear and concise business proposition.

She sighed. She had known since the fifth grade who her father was and what his "business" was. Another girl had spit the words out at her when she was still in public school. She had come home in tears. The next day she was enrolled in a private school.

Her father was Manny Marcello, or as he was known at first, Manny the Mover. Now everyone called him Don Marcello. He was the Godfather

of the San Diego Mafia. She had no argument
with that. Things were the way things were. She
could not change her father's spots. Nor did she
want to.

Angela moved to an easy chair so she could look
out the window at the green of La Jolla and the
bright blue of the Pacific Ocean in the distance.

She knew most of what her father did. She knew
as much about the Mob as anyone not actually in
day-to-day operations. Yes, people got killed.
Yes, men went to jail. Some of the happy, friendly
men she had known as a little girl were in prison
now.

Angela had never seen anyone killed, never even
seen a dead body, except at a funeral once.

She grinned. But she could learn, she would
learn all of it.

Angela walked to the kitchenette, opened the
door of the small refrigerator and took out a cold
bottle of Coors. She had decided to go to Stanford
to get her M.B.A. because her father wanted her
out from under his feet. Now she was considering
the economics of the situation.

Mafia Family organizations are often handed
down from father to son, if the kid has the guts
and the ability. Angela's older brother, Nick,
would have been in line, but he was killed in a car
wreck. The California Highway Patrol said they
chased him in his new Ferrari on the freeway at
130 miles per hour. They decided later that it was a
malfunction in the steering mechanism of the ex-

pensive Italian sports car that caused the crash on
the freeway along the U.S. Marine Corps' Camp
Pendleton.

Now there was just Angela left to inherit the
operation.

A few years ago her father was taking in, personally, over thirty million a year. Now it had to
be more with the price of cocaine the way it was.
Angela smiled. She had done her homework. San
Diego First Corporation alone controlled more
than twenty multimillion-dollar corporations.
There were other holding companies, the three
hundred highway tractors in Marcello Trucking, a
huge bowling alley, the luxury hotel in Mission
Valley, the shipbuilding firm in town that was the
largest on the West Coast, the international construction company and even a string of twenty-six
exclusive women's wear shops.

Manny Marcello controlled an empire, and it
could be all hers!

But she knew exactly what her father would say.

She should be ashamed of herself. A good Italian girl did not think about such things. She
should get married and have children. There
would be no need for her to work, daddy would
provide everything. Angela snorted. Sure, her father was wealthy, but he was a dinosaur, adhering
to old-fashioned values that were stifling her.

Angela had tried to get her father to take her
into one of the businesses when she first got out of
college at twenty-two. He had sent her to Europe

to play and learn about Italian men for a year. She talked to him again when she came home. He sent her off to New York to become a fashion model. She failed miserably because she did not attend any of her casting calls.

That's when she told him she wanted to go to Stanford for her M.B.A.

Now she had more than a simple argument to use on her father. She would work out a plan of action that would leave him angry and surprised. Direct action was all these Mafia Dons understood. So she would give him some.

She dressed in a tight T-shirt, no bra and short shorts, and then changed her mind and put on a blouse and pants. When her father came home to-day she would fire the first shot. She was tired of waiting. Today was the day!

Angela went to the first floor and checked the front door. A man was sitting there in a chair. Her mother always said he was the doorman, but long ago Angela realized he was a "soldier," the front guard. There were two more in the back, where their property behind the eight-foot fence dropped off into a sharp ravine. The man in the small gate house had two guns; she had seen them once.

These Mafia soldiers did not dress like the ones in the movies. They did not all wear suits. In fact none of them wore suits unless they were accompanying her father somewhere. Most of them around the house wore Hawaiian sport shirts, slacks and expensive shoes.

Angela's mother was out attending some kind of a committee meeting. Angela almost gagged at the thought. She did not want to wind up going the volunteer route, or the community betterment committees or even the social committees that her mother favored. Well, none of that for her. She wanted the Marcello empire!

Don Marcello came home at 4:30 P.M. He arrived at a different time every day so no one could establish a pattern on his movements. The dark blue Lincoln limo had been customized up the highway in Costa Mesa. It was bullet- and bomb-proof, with heavy plates under the engine and passenger compartments. More steel plates were in the side panels. The rear window had been reduced in size and two-inch thick bulletproof glass installed all around the vehicle.

It was a rolling tank with built-in TV set, bar, refrigerator and small microwave.

The rig came through the gate, down a drive and swung into a six-car garage at the rear of the house. There was no chance for a sniper to get a shot at Manny from the street.

Manny Marcello fell into a pattern once he got home. First he had a shower, then a massage, and finally he spent twenty minutes in the indoor pool. The swimming area had been fully considered before it was built. What use, Manny had said, was it to fortify the premises with high security, then fall prey to a marksman in a prowling chopper. After his swim, he had a martini and read the *New York Times*.

Manny was fifty-one years old and had built his power base on Marcello Trucking, which his father had started in 1939 and had developed into one of the largest in the nation. Manny stood an inch under six feet and kept himself trim in spite of his love for starchy food. He had a natural nervous drive that used up calories even when he sat still.

At that moment, he was sitting at his desk, reading. He looked up when Angela came in. At once he put down the paper and stood up, his arms held wide.

"How did I ever sire such a beautiful creature as you? Angie, *bambina*, you are a picture. Maybe I should buy a Hollywood studio and make you a movie star."

Angela hugged her father and stepped back. "No, daddy, I don't want to be a movie star. I'm a businesswoman and a damn good one. Right now we need to talk." She walked around and sat in the visitor's chair and faced her father.

"Don Marcello, I have a business proposition for you. Will you listen to it carefully?"

"Sweetheart...."

"No. I am here as any other of your associates would be. I want you to listen to my proposal and decide on its merits. Right now I am an outsider."

"Angelina...."

"No!" She stared at him until the boss of the whole San Diego area lost his smile, put on his business face and sat down in his big chair. He took out a cigar, lit it and nodded.

Angela frowned. She had seen him do this dozens of times, and that had been when she was quickly ushered out of the room.

"Okay, okay. I knew this was coming. Happens about once a year. What now?"

"I am twenty-five years old. I have had an extensive background of travel and education in several countries. I have just earned my M.B.A. from Stanford University. The degree is what any worthwhile company worth its salt is looking for these days.

"You have a big and complicated business empire. I am ready to join your organization. I can be of value to the Family."

"How? So I need somebody roughed up on the docks, I send you out to beat his head in or break an arm?"

"Of course not. My talents are in other areas. You don't send your bookkeepers to do those jobs. You don't send your business managers to be hoodlums. You use people's talents where they fit."

Manny chuckled. "Looks like you did learn something at that fancy school." He shot her a sudden questioning glance. "Just how much do you know about my, uh, business empire?"

"Almost everything. You were just coming up in the 1950s when Senator Kefauver had his big investigating committee, but you were brash enough to attract attention and get called to testify. It didn't hurt you any, but the way you stood up to them on the stand helped you with the Mob. Then you moved to San Diego and went in with grandpa in Marcello Trucking."

Manny held up his hand. "Save it. I know my own history." He paused and blew out a large smoke ring. "You have it all the way up to the present?"

"I know you have twenty or thirty large companies, that about half of them are entirely legitimate and some of them are used to launder money from loan sharking and prostitution, from the protection and drug business where most of the Family's profit is made. I also know you have a personal income of around thirty-five million a year.

"And I know your 'business' is worth between two and three hundred million dollars."

Manny shook his head. "And all these years I thought you figured I was just a trucking company owner."

"Hey, I'm not stupid. Look who my old man is!"

Don Marcello nodded. "Yeah. If you'd been a boy you'd be my right arm by now. Damn it, why in hell did that brother of yours have to go and get himself smashed up in a car?"

Manny stood and went to the window. It was shielded so there was no spot on the slope below where a triggerman could get a shot. Still he stepped back quickly.

"Baby girl. There is just no way I can do it. *La Cosa Nostra* is an organization of men. The Men of Honor. If I even try to bring you in on some small piece of work, I got a revolution in my own Family."

"Daddy, I'm not asking to be a boss! All I want is a piece of one of the legitimate companies. What about the Leisure Lady shops? Surely they aren't used in any other way. Let me take over the corporation that runs them!"

"I've got a good man doing that job, princess. He's been there ten years, and doing good work."

"Daddy, I know all the modern methods. I can move into that group and jump the profits by ten percent the first year. I need something to do! I can't sit home all day, or walk the streets or keep on going to school. And I'd go crazy in six months if I had to go to those damn committee meetings with mother. Give me a job!"

Don Marcello beat back tears as he went around the desk and put his arms around his only remaining child. He kissed both her cheeks and held her tenderly.

"*Cara mia*, you are so important to me. I will protect you from harm with my life. And I'll give you anything you ask. But this...this feminist thing. A good Italian woman does not go around wearing pants and being a boss in a business! A good Italian woman finds a good Italian man and gets pregnant the first month she's married and has ten grandsons for her father!''

Angela had expected it, but it was still a shock. She stiffened in his arms and pushed away. She knew her face was white with anger. Somehow she did not cry.

"Don Marcello. I am not a goddamn brood mare just panting to give you a dozen little Mafia soldiers! I hate that whole idea of thinking of a woman as a bitch in heat! I'm a person, but just because I don't have balls you kick me out of the fraternity and tell me to go get into bed with some slob and get knocked up!''

"Angie, Angie. I didn't mean all that. Every father wants to have some grandchildren. I don't see why you want to *work*. You have money, a car, clothes, travel. Most people work their entire lives and never own a thing.''

Don Marcello shook his head and sat down in his big chair. Slowly he looked up at his daughter. "I'm sorry, but I don't think the Family is ready for you yet. The guidelines are strictly drawn. There is nothing I can do. The commission would call me to task in a moment if they heard. . . .''

"Daddy, Leisure Lady is not a front. Let me run it. At least give me a chance!''

Don Marcello stood. "No. This talk is over. I don't want to hear anything more about it.''

Angela spun around and marched out the door.

Downstairs she had one of the guards bring her car around. She stepped into the brand-new blue Mercedes 380SL. It still had the "new car" smell in it.

She checked her purse to make sure she had some money, then she drove away. The gate opened automatically and she charged through, barely missing a car as she headed for the shore. She figured Sunset Cliffs would be the best spot.

Twenty minutes later she found the place. She smiled grimly, drove over the curb and onto the sandstone cliffs along the Ocean Beach section of San Diego. Angela left the car in neutral, stepped out and closed the door. Through the open window she pushed the gear lever into Drive and let off the hand brake.

The $45,000 car picked up speed as it rolled down the slight incline, nosed over the hundred-foot drop-off and then vanished over the side. Seconds later the car crashed onto the rocks and breaking waves at the bottom of the cliff.

Angela walked along the cliffs where no one could see her. After she had gone a half mile, she headed for the street and began looking for a cruising cab. Five minutes later she hailed one and watched as a San Diego police car tore past on Sunset Cliffs Boulevard with its red light on and its siren wailing. She smiled.

The police were never supposed to use sirens unless there was a life-in-danger situation. She told the taxi driver to take her to the Glass House

Square shopping center. There was a movie-theater complex where she could stay until midnight. By then her father would be crazy as the police and the fire department divers tried to figure out if she had died in the crash and was still somewhere in the surf.

She hoped her father worried himself sick. It would serve the mighty Marcello right!

13

Johnny Bolan sat down in the visitor's chair in Karl Darlow's hospital room. The weathered fisherman was propped up in his bed, looking frustrated and irritable.

"Johnny! Am I glad to see you! This place is driving me crazy! Think you can break me out of here? We'll have to use a window, they've got a guard nurse in the hall who is six-two and goes about a hundred and eighty. Couldn't land her with 60-pound mono, I'm damn sure."

Johnny held out his hand and Karl took it, wincing slightly as he leaned forward. A woman's jacket lay on a chair and a moment later Sandy came in with a fresh pitcher of water.

She kissed Johnny's cheek and they both turned toward Karl. He looked at the door. Johnny shut it quietly. There was no one else in the two-bed room.

"Karl, it's time to tell us about it," Johnny said. "We know it had to be the Mafia. Why are they mad at you?"

Karl Darlow took a long breath and let it out slowly. "At first I wasn't sure, then I figured it was something I saw at sea a few days back."

"What did you see?" Sandy asked.

"Nothing I could swear to, but close enough. A small boat was taking some boxes off a rusty old tanker."

"Smuggling," Johnny said softly.

"About the size of it. This one gent visited me yesterday morning. I was hip-deep in grease and diesel injectors, and he claimed his insurance company was interested in what I saw south of the harbor entrance the day before. He had a sinking-boat claim and the owner said I was in the area and could back up his story. I told him no. Said I went north and was trolling that day. But he had the name of my boat. He was warning me to keep my mouth shut. Then last night some goon comes through my front door without knocking. Picked the lock, I guess. He came in and knocked me down and half out, and when I came to I was spread out on my bed."

"He didn't say anything?" Sandy asked. "He just came in and hit you?"

"Right. Then he used that knife. Sharp as a razor and he was an old hand with it. He had just moved from my chest up to my face when he heard you kids coming up the steps."

"He was going to cut you some more?" Johnny asked.

"Hard to figure. He might have been going to warn me what to expect if I said anything. I've heard about this kind of attack from other captains."

"You have any idea what was in the packages you saw being offloaded?" Johnny asked.

"Search me. I was a quarter of a mile away. Used the glasses and saw the plastic-wrapped bundles. That was it. Could have been anchovies, diamonds or fish guts for all I know."

"Counterfeit money, gold bullion, hashish or any other kind of dope," Johnny said. "But best bet is dope. A lot of value in a little package and a booming market."

"So what do we do now?" Sandy asked.

"We keep our mouths shut," Karl said. "I don't want that son of a bitch coming to see me again!"

Sandy nodded. "Yes, that sounds like the best idea. We just say it was a burglar daddy caught in the house. Nobody else will know."

"The cops know," Johnny said. "Besides them, I know. And I don't like them pushing Karl around."

"Better a push than a grave," Karl said.

Johnny looked from one to the other, then finally he nodded. "Okay, Karl. You're right, it isn't worth it."

They talked for a while longer and then Johnny said he had to get back to work. Sandy was taking the day off from her job to be with her father.

Back at the Free Legal Aid Center Johnny found four people waiting for him. There was plenty of work to take his mind off his dilemma. He wanted to dig into the Mafia's attack on Karl, but how could he do it without getting Karl into even more trouble? He would think about it until he came up with an answer.

By the next morning he still had no idea. There was work for him piled up on his desk at the Killinger law office. Besides that he still had to try to connect the Mafia with the loan sharking for the double murderer Mr. Killinger was defending.

Johnny pounded a fist into his open palm and swore. So far he had absolutely no luck. He wrote the results of his investigation on a note to his boss and dug into the paperwork. He could get it done by noon, but still this afternoon he would have to check the bars, hunting for that Mafia loan-sharking link. He was afraid it looked like an impossible job.

Just after eleven his telephone extension buzzed and he picked it up.

"Johnny? This is Angela. You remember, from the elevator? How about lunch today?"

Twenty minutes later they were driving along U.S. Highway 5, moving north toward Del Mar. She drove another Mercedes Benz, same model but a different color. She cut across on Carmel Valley Road to Old Highway 101 and turned south again along the beach. Angela wheeled the car off the old highway, then parked facing the crashing Pacific surf.

"Last stop, everyone out!" Angela said. Johnny could tell she felt excited, as if this was going to be a day to remember.

"Let's take our picnic basket and walk down the

beach to Torey Piñes. We'll find some dry sand, catch some sun and just enjoy!''

"Sounds good to me. We could go all the way down to Black's Beach.''

"The nude beach?'' she said with a grin. Then she shrugged. "I've never been into allover sunbathing that much, at least in public.''

They walked along the damp sand because it was better footing. There were few people on the beach since it was a little early in the season and school was not out yet. They walked south for a half mile and Johnny kept his eyes peeled for a good spot.

"Those rocks up there,'' Angela said. "Let's get to the other side of them.''

It was like a private beach. The rock fall from the two-hundred-foot sandstone cliffs had made a false cove, shielding the spot from the north. The beach was only one hundred feet wide, the sand coming up against the towering cliffs. They could see only one lone walker to the south, and nobody to the north.

"Perfect!'' Angela said as she helped Johnny spread the blanket. He put the lunch basket down and sat on the blanket. The sun was shining, the temperature was in the high seventies and almost no breeze stirred the sand.

"A great time to come to the beach,'' Johnny said. "The sun isn't too warm yet, you can pick up a little tan, and the place isn't cluttered with herds of tourists from Kansas and Oklahoma.''

"True," Angela said. She wore shorts and a thin white blouse that she now unbuttoned. Under it was a blue bikini top. She folded the blouse, laid it to one side of the blanket and stretched out beside Johnny.

"Eat first, or swim?" she said.

"We didn't stop at my place for my suit."

"Suits are optional," she said, eyes flashing.

He laughed. "Shouldn't swim on a full stomach."

"Good." She unzipped the shorts and kicked out of them. The bikini bottom was as small as the top, string on the sides and just enough fabric to cover the pubic area. "Like my suit?" she asked.

"Mm-hmm."

"Thanks." She paused, then leaned toward him. Her lips touched his. For a moment neither of them moved. Then his arms came around her and she held him and the kiss went on and on. Her tongue traced his lips and she sighed.

They broke apart.

"Oh, Johnny, that was perfect. Once more?"

Johnny leaned back and rubbed his jaw with one hand. He laughed softly and shook his head.

"Hey, this is getting too serious. Secluded beach, the sun and surf, picnic lunch. Angela, you're irresistible, but in all fairness I should tell you I have a lady, and we have a commitment to each other."

"Fairness? Well, isn't all fair in love?" Angela said. She leaned forward, pressed her body tightly against his and kissed his cheek.

He felt her breasts thrusting against his chest. Gently he rested his hands on her shoulders and pushed her away.

"Johnny, I understand that, but this is just a friendly picnic. Who's to know if we mess around a little?"

"Me, Angela, I would know. I just don't go out and get laid every time I have the chance."

"But, Johnny!" Slowly she unsnapped the fastener at the middle of her bikini top and let it fall away from her breasts.

Johnny Bolan sucked in his breath at the view. She reached for him, but he caught her hands.

"Angela, don't do this. You're a beautiful girl, and evidently rich in your own right. You don't need to do this."

"I want you, Johnny! Don't make me beg. I want you right now!" She pulled the strings on the sides of her bikini and stripped the patches of cloth away.

"Oh, damn!" Johnny said softly. "Angela, don't do this. I haven't touched another woman since my lady and I got together."

Suddenly she pushed him down on his back and let one pink-tipped breast hang directly over his mouth, then lowered it so the nipple brushed his lips.

"Go ahead, Johnny! They're yours. Please, Johnny?"

He rolled away from her, jumped up and ran a hundred yards down the beach as fast as he could go. He turned into the combers that washed high on the shore and ran back, splashing in an inch of salt water. Panting from the sudden exertion, he sat down on the edge of the blanket beside the nude girl.

"Now, let's get back to reality. We were talking about going swimming. I'll go skinny-dipping if you will."

She sighed. "Goddamn you, Johnny," she said softly without anger. "If that's all I get, I'll take it."

They went swimming. There was no one within a quarter of a mile and they ran into the cool Pacific naked, laughing and splashing. They were out of the water in ten minutes, drying and dressing. Johnny found some driftwood and an old flotsam packing case and made a small fire.

"Hey, that was fun," he said. "It's been years since I've jumped waves bare-assed, and never with a pretty girl."

She smiled. "Johnny, there is something else we could do together that would be really fantastic. Sure you don't want to reconsider now that you've seen the whole package?"

"Why? Why me?"

She was surprised. "Why not? You're cute and I *like* you, Johnny. Besides, it's the nicest thing two people can do."

Johnny poked the fire. Damn it, she was right. He was certain it would be fantastic. But he had Sandy. With Angela sex would be the end product, the purpose. With Sandy sex was just an element of a relationship, important, but just one aspect, one small part of an understanding.

Johnny looked at her. She was perfect. Great figure. He sighed. "Hey, didn't you say something about our having a picnic?"

Angela nodded and reached for the basket.

After they ate they talked for a few minutes, then Johnny said he should be getting back.

Angela dropped him off in front of the Free Legal Aid Center and he raced upstairs to the apartment to change before going downstairs.

For three hours he worked the bars and dives, completing the list Nel had given him. He only heard the Mafia soldier's name once and that was in jest. Somebody had threatened to sic Willy the Peep on someone if he made the next pool shot. The shooter made it and everyone laughed.

From eight to nine he worked at the center. There were more than twenty calls in his stack now, and he plugged away at them. He had begun this project with fervor and a store of energy he thought was inexhaustible. Now he was finding out it was not.

He threw his pencil on the desk and sighed. He was tired. It had been a long day.

14

Angela stepped down hard on the gas pedal as she raced away from Kettner where she had let Johnny off. All afternoon she had been thinking about doing it. Now, damn it, she was going to. Nothing and nobody would stop her. She had always thought that Don Marcello understood strength and action. She would show him one hell of a lot of both.

Last night when she got home after staying at the movie until almost midnight, her father had been furious.

"You coulda called!" he had thundered. "You coulda let us know you were alive. A lot of people have been risking their lives out there in that ocean looking for you!" He had never hit her, but last night she was sure he was close to it.

"Why the hell are you doing this to me?"

"Because I think you are being mean to me. I have a lot of respect for you but it's time you listened to me."

Then Manny "The Mover" Marcello broke up laughing. Angela stood openmouthed as she watched him.

"You are some kinda broad, Angela. A damn chip off the old block. Hell, I probably woulda done the same thing!" Then he put his arms around her, kissed both her cheeks and held her tenderly.

"Hey, I understand. Forget the goddamn car. I got another one just like it in the garage you can have." He fished in his desk and brought out a set of keys. "It's the same make, different color. Enjoy it." He hugged her again. "Jeez, I'm glad I still have you. What a trick to play. Sure as hell reminds me of me. Now go see your mother before she has a heart attack."

Her mother had been much calmer, even hinted that she understood what was going on. "All this women's liberation thing," which was as close as her mother came to understanding the women's movement. But Angela was glad that she had made a point with her father.

Now, as she drove away from Johnny, she found a phone booth and called Mimi, one of her best friends. Mimi was twenty-four, had just finished a degree and was bored out of her mind sitting around home.

"Mimi?" Angela asked.

"What's left of me. Angela?"

"Right. Tonight is the night. We're having a council of war at my place, as soon as you can get there. Plan to stay all night. I'll call the other girls, too. Remember what we talked about a few weeks ago?"

"Sure. But is this a good time?" Mimi asked.

"When the hell can we do it any quicker?"

"You're right, I guess. Be at your place in an hour."

Angela made two more calls with the same message. Felicia said she could come right away. Gemma said she had a date for that night, but she could break it without too much explanation.

Angela grinned as she came out of the phone booth. In her hand was a coin with smooth edges on it. She had tried to use it as a quarter in the phone booth. It was a "Susie," a Susan B. Anthony silver dollar Uncle Sam had tried to sell to the public a few years back.

"Susie, you are going to be our good-luck piece, our symbol."

Tingling with anticipation, Angela gunned the Mercedes along the freeway to La Jolla. Then she spotted a San Diego cop coming up on her rear bumper and she eased back on the gas to the legal limit. The expensive German car purred sedately out U.S. 5 north to Ardath turnoff and wound up the hill to her father's mansion.

Angela never thought of it as a big place, but it was. She had always lived there. She was used to a place with forty rooms and four acres of lawns and land, and a high wall all around it. When she was younger she thought everyone lived that way.

Upstairs in her third-floor apartment, she got ready for her guests. She told the cook she would need a special dinner for four served in her apartment at six-thirty, and that it should include champagne. Then she called the gate man to let him know whom she was expecting so he could let them in without a lot of phoning back and forth.

She made sure the three special videotapes were in place in case the girls wanted some sexy male entertainment on her Betamax. Then she found pads of paper and ballpoint pens and began thinking about their plan of attack.

Mimi arrived first. She was the daughter of one of Don Marcello's lieutenants. Mimi was a dark-eyed, tiny girl, only an inch over five feet tall, and constantly fighting a weight problem. She had short dark hair, an olive complexion and a bouncy personality. Angela always enjoyed being around her.

"Hey! I'm the first one here, that means I get to be at least a general in this chickenshit army!" She giggled and tossed her purse on the coffee table in the living room. It hit with a clunk and Angela pounced on it to see what was inside.

She drew out a .45 automatic. She had seen lots of them but never held one before.

"Tomorrow morning I'm going to a shooting range out beyond El Cajon and get in some shooting practice," Mimi said. "To get respect from the Mafia men, we have to show them that we understand their game."

Angela nodded. "I like it!"

There was a knock on the door and the doorman ushered Felicia into the room. She looked at the gun in her friend's hand and frowned. "We've got to whack out somebody already? Hell, we're just getting started."

Felicia was not the fragile type. She was nearly five-ten and had been a rower in college. She was slim, trim and flat chested. She kept her hair just off her shoulders and her face showed the classic Sophia Loren kind of Italian beauty. She had been engaged twice, but broke it off both times. She was the daughter of the *consigliere*, the Family legal brain and top advisor to the Don. Felicia was twenty-two and had wanted to be a nurse, but her father would not permit it.

"I don't know what you two are cooking up, but count me in. I think I can get an Uzi submachine gun when we need it. One of the men has reworked it so it's fully automatic. Makes one hell of a sound and fires 600 rounds per minute."

"We've found our weapons expert," Angela said.

Felicia took the .45, hit the button on it and the magazine popped out. She worked the slide to make sure the chamber was empty, then put the magazine back in.

"Who wants a drink while we wait for Gemma?" Angela asked. She led the way to the small wet bar and they fixed their own drinks.

Gemma came in a moment later, out of breath, hair flying, eyes dancing, and a small overnight case in one hand.

Gemma was the youngest of the group, nineteen, and had the lightest hair, a soft brown. She was waif thin, a music major at UCSD and the smartest of the girls. She was the daughter of the second-in-command to Don Marcello in the Family.

Angela spoke first when the women seated themselves around the coffee table. "I've talked to all of you about the way our parents are treating us. Be good and get married and get pregnant and have six kids, boys preferably. I'm damn sick and tired of it. Last night I told my father I wanted into the action, I wanted to work in one of the legit businesses he owns, and he told me to sit on it. Have the rest of you had similar problems?"

They all talked at once, and the story was the same. Mimi was the most furious. "Last week I told my father I wanted to get a job, anything. I wanted to do something. He laughed at me and said I should take a trip. I told him I've been everywhere, I want a job where I can be useful. He thought I was crazy."

Angela nodded. "If us four had been born with balls instead of breasts we'd be in the Family organization right now. We'd have been moving up in the organization, making good money, big money!"

"And we would have real power," Felicia said. "My brother, Frank, is only a year older than I am, and already he has Family responsibilities, and at work he has a whole department under him."

"I like that idea," Angela said. "Power. We want some power. We all have enough money, but we don't have respect as individuals, and we don't have any power. We are women who want power."

"What we need is a name," Mimi said. She frowned for a minute. "How about the Hard Corps?"

"I love it!" Angela screeched. "It will set the old-line mafiosi on fire with rage." She looked around the table. "Anyone have a better idea?"

"Go," Gemma said. "We've got our name, now what the hell are we going to do?"

"That's why we're here," Angela said. "When I was at Stanford one of our professors taught us how to write good proposals. He said you need to do three things to make a proposal work. You need to figure out your audience. Then when you know that, you aim your purpose at your audience. When you've targeted your audience and your purpose, you figure out what the content must be to do the job."

Gemma was writing. "So our audience is the polarized Family structure management. That part is easy. What exactly is our purpose? To convince the Family management that women can be productive members of the organization, that they must be given worthwhile and satisfying jobs in the business aspects of the Family, taking advantage of the various talents they have developed."

Felicia wailed. "I can see my father screaming right now. He would say for two hundred years *La*

Cosa Nostra has been made up of 'Men of Honor.' Now we want to change that to Men and Women of Honor. We'll get hooted down the first time we try to talk to them about it.''

"Maybe we don't talk with words," Mimi said. She lifted the .45 and aimed at the window. "There are other ways to show them we can function in a man's world.''

Gemma frowned. "I'm not up to being a hit man. It just isn't one of my talents.''

Felicia held up her hands. "No. We don't have to be hit persons. All we have to do is convince the men that we can be effective in the operation, as well as being wives and mothers for the great Mafia.''

"How?" Angela asked.

"That is what we are going to have to figure out before morning," Felicia said. "Now, who wants one more drink before we settle down to a working dinner?''

15

Immediately after work at Killinger's the next day, Johnny went to the hospital to take Karl home. An orderly wheeled a protesting Karl to the curb in a chair, and Johnny was surprised at how well Karl could walk before he climbed into the Bug.

"Hell, I got to get back to my boat. Poke and I need the work. Figure I'll be back out there in two or three days."

"Over my dead body," Johnny said. "Have you tried to lift your arms over your head? Go ahead, do it."

Karl did and groaned in pain.

"That upper chest is going to hurt for another week. You won't be gaffing many fish for a while. Now relax."

Karl stared out the window. At last he spoke. "Hey, could we stop for a six-pack on the way home? I'm out."

"I thought you decided to stay off booze for a while."

"Damn it, boy! Beer ain't drinking! If we don't stop now I'll just have to come out on my own."

Johnny stopped at a market, bought two six-packs of Coors and drove Karl to his apartment. They spent the rest of the afternoon cleaning up the place. Some of the furniture had to be junked. The landlord had been in to make an insurance claim. Both end tables and Karl's TV set were wrecked.

Johnny installed a dead bolt and put up a two-by-four wooden bar to barricade the door. He had just finished when Sandy arrived, lugging three dinner boxes of fried chicken.

While they ate, Johnny sensed that Karl was a little bit scared.

"I don't know what else they want me to do," he said at last. "Hell, I denied ever being south of the channel, told them I was north all day and never saw a thing." Then he looked at Sandy. "Hey, lady. Am I ever going to have any grand-children?"

Sandy laughed. "Dad, we're not even married." She looked quickly at Johnny.

"Have you asked anybody to marry you lately?" Karl said, enjoying the teasing.

"Not lately," Sandy said. "Now can we change the subject?"

"Might as well."

"The first day you decide to go fishing, Karl, make it a tourist run," Johnny said. "I want to come along and help crew. Poke and I can let you play captain."

"Deal. I take on free crew whenever I can get one."

Johnny picked up the remains of the dinner and threw the boxes in the trash, then cleaned off the table. He watched Karl wince when he tried to stand. Johnny figured it should be another week before Karl took the boat out, but he knew Karl would do it before then.

Johnny and Sandy left half an hour later, just as Poke came up the steps carrying a bottle of Canadian Club. Johnny wished he had not brought it, but there was no polite way he could ask Poke to take it back to the car.

Poke promised to keep Karl quiet, and they parted.

The center was dark when he drove past, and no one stood at the outside door, so Johnny turned into the alley, parked and went upstairs. Sandy came up a minute later, after parking her Honda on the street. She stood near the door and stared at Johnny, then grinned and walked toward him slowly.

"I'm sorry if your father embarrassed you," Johnny said.

"He didn't embarrass me. It's just that we've never talked about it."

"About what?"

"About having children."

"Hey, we're getting ahead of ourselves. There's something we should do first." He put his arms around her and held her close. "I was thinking about it today. Maybe, sometime, we should talk about getting married."

"Talk about it, maybe, sometime," Sandy said. "That's not a lot of reassurance for a girl, is it?"

"Not one hell of a lot." He kissed her nose. "Look, let's sit on the couch and talk about it now."

"You don't have to. I hate to be pushy."

"You're not."

"I moved in without asking you."

"Wrong. You asked, I just never answered. As I remember, we found something else to do just then."

"Yeah!"

"So let's talk."

It was well past TV sign-off time when they finally decided they would get married. They were officially engaged. They set the date for September when Sandy had her vacation scheduled.

THE NEXT MORNING AT WORK in the Killinger law office, Johnny called one of his boss's contacts at the San Diego Police Department. He identified himself and asked the woman who answered to run a license-plate check for him. Johnny gave her the letters and numbers of the tag on the car Angela had driven the day before.

"That's registered to Hobart Enterprises Inc., 1919 Sixth Street, San Diego 92101," the woman told Johnny.

"Thank you," Johnny said and hung up.

He wrote the name down in a small notebook and went back to work on his official Killinger business. That morning he told Mr. Killinger he had made no further progress in his investigation of a tie-in with Willie the Peep.

"He's either keeping a low profile right now, or everyone is afraid to mention his name. What about some of the street informers we use? Could they get something for us on this?"

Killinger said it was an outside chance, but he would make some phone calls.

Now Johnny was back to his usual schedule, which meant he had all afternoon free. The first thing he did when he got back to the center was look up Hobart Enterprises in the phone book and call them.

"Good afternoon, this is Hobart Enterprises."

"Can you folks come out and fix my blocked sink?"

There was a cultured laugh on the other end of the wire. "No, I'm sorry, you must have a wrong number."

"Isn't this Hobart Plumbing?"

"No, this is Hobart Enterprises, we're an international, large-project, construction firm."

"Oh, sorry. Thanks." He hung up. International construction. Big money, that figured. He pushed the idea aside, but Angela kept filtering back into his thoughts. Soon her features began to merge with those of someone else. Then the mental image came into focus and he realized he was thinking of Sandy.

Damn, he had done it at last. Engaged! He felt

no different, but there was a new sparkle in Sandy's eye. She would burst when he finally gave her a ring. He looked at his checkbook balance, then went downtown and found the best solitaire diamond he could afford. It came in a matched set and he wrote down the rest of the numbers so later they could get the wedding ring that went with it. Then he drove to Sandy's office and gave her the small plush velvet-lined box. She cried right there in front of her boss and the rest of the women.

She hugged him shyly and he turned and hurried out, knowing that he had barely escaped being hugged to death by the rest of Sandy's co-workers.

Back at the office he called Karl. There was no answer. Johnny frowned. Maybe Karl went down to get the paper, or to the convenience store for some milk.

Just after five-thirty Sandy came in and pulled him away from his desk.

"We're going out to dinner to celebrate!" she said. "I don't get an engagement ring every day."

Johnny blew fifty dollars on dinner at Le Château, and they made some plans for the future. They decided they would have only two kids and they would start saving for the down payment on a condo or a small house.

To cap the early evening they went past Karl's place to tell him the good news—that he might be a grandfather someday, after all.

Karl was not home.

They peered in the small window on the door,

but could see little. They were just going down the steps when Karl came reeling off the sidewalk and up the path to his stairs.

"Hi, Karl," Johnny said.

"Hey, baby girl, and John! *¿Qué pasó?*"

"Not one hell of a lot, Karl. Need some help?"

"Course not!" He stumbled on the first step and fell to the wooden risers. "Damn."

Five minutes later they had Karl in his apartment. Sandy cleaned up the kitchen and washed the dishes.

"Karl, we talked about this, remember?"

"Just had a couple of beers, Johnny, honest."

"How long have you been over at Lewy's bar?"

"Ten, fifteen minutes, tops."

"You had breakfast here, Karl, but no lunch, no dinner. Have you been over there most of the day?"

"Well, got to go to bed," Karl mumbled. Johnny helped him into the bedroom.

"We have to get you sober enough to take out the boat tomorrow," Johnny said.

"Can't do it."

"Sure you can. Poke and I will do the work, you just sit up there in the cabin and play skipper."

"Can't do it. I won't be sober by tomorrow morning."

"You can try, Karl. We can't have you trolling in the bars anymore. You might catch a Mafia ear somewhere."

"Can't go out. Poke is crewing on a six-day long range down to San Benitos on the *Qualifier 105*."

"Damn, you're right. I don't know how to run your boat well enough." Johnny scowled. He thought a moment and shrugged. "So, no sweat. I'll meet you here at one-thirty and we'll go down and do a little painting on that scow of yours. It can always use some new paint, somewhere."

Karl looked up. There were tears in his eyes.

"Thanks, Johnny. I got this little problem when I'm on shore too long. I'll be near sober by noon."

When they left they took all but two bottles of beer, and all the whiskey bottles they could find in the cupboards. Johnny felt helpless. Every time Karl had a drink now he was like walking dynamite. All he had to do was say the wrong thing about spotting that smuggling offshore and the Mafia hit men would light his fuse.

·16

Mack Bolan had called Carlo Genovese right on schedule the previous evening and set up the meet. It would be in either of their cars at Jackson Park Beach, just off 57th Street on the lakeshore. Bolan had said he would be standing by the taco stand at the far end of the parking lot at precisely 10:00 A.M.

The Executioner had agreed to the meet and said they could go from there to one of the vehicles to test the goods. Bolan had been up at six as usual, made a purchase at a grocery store and drove to the park off 57th Street to check the lay of the land. "Any tactical maneuver depends on the situation and the terrain." Bolan had used that bit of Army training again and again in his private wars. Now he studied the taco stand and the surrounding area. It was the type with drive-through service and two concrete table-bench combinations in front.

The stand was actually outside the playground, but served the parking lot and the street on the other side. Bolan decided the best position for his car would be in the street near the taco stand for an easier withdrawal.

He circled and found a spot two cars down from

the taco stand. The Tempo was pointing away from the street's dead end.

Quickly he put together the rest of his plan. He was certain that Carlo Genovese would have heard about Jake Spanno's wipeout, but would Genovese connect it with a coke seller? He might. Mario Montessi was supposed to attend the meet as well, but he could be hiding out somewhere.

Bolan guessed Montessi would let Genovese take the risks. Bolan was not ready to waste Genovese yet. The small man with the big smile was his ticket upstairs to the czar of the Chicago drug trade. The czar was Bolan's main target in Chicago. All the rest were warm-ups for him. In a week of digging he had found no name of the top man. He was protected a dozen ways. Somehow the Executioner had to break through the secrecy.

Bolan stood at the taco stand sipping cola as he waited. He wore the same open-throated shirt and sport coat as the day before for recognition value. A brown paper sack sat on the concrete table beside him. It was five after ten and he knew they were watching him, discussing whether to blow him away. But they wouldn't if they felt he could produce the stopgap supply they needed. He knew Genovese decided on a meet in the open, just in case this "Vito" character had set up some kind of trap. The Mob took no chances.

Montessi himself sauntered up five minutes later, bought a drink at the stand, then sat beside Bolan.

"That the shit in the sack?"

"Could be. Where's Carlo?"

"Waiting. I give him a sign or you get your socks blown off. Is that the goods?"

Bolan picked up the sack. "Yeah, a sealed sample. Let's go."

"Trusting son of a bitch."

"About the way you trust me. It's good business. This a deal?"

"Deal. But I already voted to waste you, bastard."

They walked side by side across the parking lot to the street. They stopped two cars in front of Bolan's Ford near a big blue Caddy that had not been there before.

The left rear door swung open but nobody got out.

"Get in, we go for a ride and test," Montessi said.

Bolan leaned over and peered into the Caddy. The usual glass partition halfway down, a jump seat where a small man with glasses sat and Genovese on the far side of the big seat.

Bolan began to bend over to get in. His right hand snaked under his jacket and when it came out he turned and shot Montessi twice in the chest. Then he tracked the 93-R on Genovese, stepped into the car and slammed the door shut.

"Drive!" Bolan snapped.

The wheelman looked at Genovese, whose forehead was now covered with a thin line of sweat. He nodded and the car moved forward.

"Keep this rig moving or all three of you are dead. Driver, toss your hardware in back."

The driver did as he was told. Bolan's advantage was that he had walked right into the devil's lair, cancelling his enemies' plans to eliminate him should he behave unusually. Indeed he was behaving unusually, sure, but to such a degree that he had just blown away his target's ability to act.

"Who is this?" Bolan asked, motioning with the Beretta at the man wearing the glasses.

"A chemist, he's not a made man," Genovese said. "He works for us sometimes."

Bolan held out his hand. Slowly Genovese took a short-barreled .38 from his shoulder holster and gave it to Bolan.

"Your hideout!" the Executioner demanded.

Carefully Genovese lifted a .25-caliber automatic from an ankle holster and pushed it across the seat to Bolan.

Bolan poked the silenced Beretta 93-R into the chemist's chin. He forced it upward painfully until the man lifted off his jump seat.

"Do you want to stay alive?"

The chemist nodded.

"I want your word that you won't breathe any of this for twenty-four hours. Agreed?"

"Yes, sir!" Raw fear owned the small man.

"Driver, get onto 63rd. I want to go straight west."

The wheelman nodded. Bolan watched the

street signs, and when he saw they were on 63rd, he ordered the driver to stop. Then the Executioner turned to the small man again.

"What's your name?"

"Orville."

"Okay, Orville. This is a chance for you to go legit. Now get out of here."

Bolan reached in front of Genovese and opened the door. The small man with the leather case scrambled out of the car and ran as fast as he could up the street.

"You're Bolan," Genovese said.

"And you're dead, Genovese."

The Mafia hotshot smiled. "That's been tried before."

"*I* haven't tried before."

"No. But you want something from me, or else I'd be dead already, like Mario back there, and Jake Spanno yesterday. It *was* you, wasn't it?"

"You're right, Carlo. I want something, and you're going to give it to me, sooner or later. I have all the time in the world." Bolan tapped the driver on the shoulder.

"Keep on going until you come to Bedford Park."

"What do you want, Bolan?" Genovese asked.

"Don Spanno, the old man. You were with him for years. You know everything about his operation. Take me to him."

"We'd both be blown away."

"I'll take my chances."

Genovese shook his head. "Not so, Bolan. You're not that straight line. I know as much about you as anybody in the world. Made you a kind of private study. You're here to fuck up our drug business."

"If you know so much about me, you'd know you're living on borrowed time."

"Park's coming up," the driver said.

"Good, find a deserted spot and shut it down."

"A hit in the park? Not terribly original for the Executioner," Genovese sneered.

When the big car stopped Bolan told the driver to get out, walk away fifty yards up a slight rise and lie facedown with his arms and legs spread out wide. The driver did it without a word.

"Now, how do I find Spanno?"

Genovese laughed. "You don't want Spanno. You killed his son, the drug boss. You wasted Montessi, another Family's drug man. Now you only have two to go. Spanno is a bluff."

But the first tinges of doubt, of growing fear began to show around Genovese's eyes. Quick nervous glances out the window. His hands suddenly became an obligation, a nuisance. There was nowhere to put them.

"Get out of the car, Carlo. Step back slowly from the door six feet so I can see you. You blink sideways and you get three slugs in your head."

Genovese did as he was told. Bolan followed him and patted him down with one hand, keeping the Beretta ready. The mafioso was clean.

"Back in the car, the front passenger seat. And get in from this side."

The Executioner called out to the driver. "You use a phone in the next three hours and you're dead."

"Yes, sir," the guy called back.

The keys were in the ignition; a wheelman would always leave them there, unless it was a long park situation. Bolan started the big engine, then drove out of Bedford Park to 63rd and headed back toward town. He pulled in to the first motel he saw and rented a room.

Ten minutes later Bolan had Carlo Genovese tied to the bed. His mouth was taped shut, and his hands and ankles bound together.

Outside, Bolan hung the Do Not Disturb sign on the door knob, then left.

The address was in Cicero, a small community close to downtown Chicago. He would go there to continue his campaign in progress, and also to give Genovese time to reflect on things as he lay immobilized on the motel bed. But first he dumped the crew wagon and took a taxi back to Jackson Park. He figured the cops would have given up watching the street around where Montessi had been shot that morning. He was right. He walked a block to his Ford, got in and drove away.

The street the Executioner wanted was half a dozen blocks off Roosevelt, with single-family houses that had been built around the turn of the century. He found the address and parked a few hundred yards away. From the bottom of his suitcase he extracted three small oblongs and placed them in a carrying pouch clipped to his belt.

He changed back to combat black, strapped on his battle harness and snugged the Beretta in a shoulder holster. Around his neck he slung an Uzi submachine gun with double magazines of 9mm parabellum rounds. The second magazine was welded at right angles to the first at the bottom. The extra clip extended toward the muzzle and acted as a second front hand grip that helped stop muzzle-climb on full auto.

Bolan watched as two men entered the front door. He slid around the side of the house and slipped through a back entrance that led to the basement. Lights were on but the windows had been painted black.

As Bolan crossed the threshold, a man dropped the girlie magazine he was reading and clawed for hardware. He was too slow. Bolan put a silenced Beretta round through his head.

The Executioner tried the basement-door handle and it came unlatched. He pulled it toward him half an inch and looked inside.

It was a cutting and packaging room, and two men were working at a long table. At the far end lay three wrapped bricklike packages. On the table was a finely calibrated scale and boxes filled with small plastic envelopes. Beyond them was a heat-sealer machine to close the packets. At the other side of the room a man sat on a high stool watching the procedure. A shotgun rested across his knees.

Bolan nudged the door open another inch and took out the armed guard with one silenced head shot. One of the men opened his mouth in surprise when a red drizzle dotted the white powder. Any scream from him was stillborn as a second slug filled the toothy gap, the impact hurling him off his seat. His flailing hands scattered the white dust that settled on his face, filling his nostrils as the man enjoyed his final high without knowing it.

The second worker broke for a side door, but the Executioner used up a 3-round burst on him, dropping him before he could reach the door handle.

The nightraider listened. Footsteps on the wooden floor over his head, but nothing that sounded unusual. He checked the powder on the table. Cocaine and heroine. He took the split-open packages and dumped the contents in the toilet. He opened the taps in the sink and emptied the other three-pound bags of coke, watching it dissolve and run down the drain.

Back in the cutting room he planted two chunks of the C-4 plastic explosive that he had brought. He placed a charge on each side of the basement ceiling where he found supporting beams, priming the puttylike plastic with a five-minute pencil timer/detonator.

Then Bolan opened the side door and saw a set of steps. Sounds of music floated down the stairway. He started up quietly and as he gained the top tread, he met a black man coming through the door. The man started to shout, but flashing steel stilled the screams as the Executioner's knife slid across the man's throat. His eyes went wide and only a gurgling sound escaped his lips as he tumbled into Bolan's arms. The big man in black let the body down on the steps quietly and looked into the room.

Four men were standing around laughing. Two women passed on the way to the kitchen and returned with fresh drinks. What was it, a convention?

As Bolan hesitated a woman came to the door and pushed it open. Bolan slapped one hand over her mouth, the other around her waist and pulled her into the stairwell. She saw the body on the stairs and stiffened. Bolan could feel her mouth trying to work up a scream.

When she got over the first panic, Bolan whispered to her.

"You won't get hurt if you remain silent. Understand?"

Her head bobbed up and down.

"What's going on in there, a party?" Again she nodded.

"How many people?" He moved his hand off her mouth. She swallowed twice and took some deep breaths.

"Maybe a dozen. They keep coming and going. They're picking up their shit here. All dealers. Who are you? What happened to Wilbur?"

"He got hurt. Are you a dealer?"

"I'm a hooker. I work for the outfit. They say come out here and decorate, pop a few johns."

"How many party girls?"

"Three of us."

"You have a minute to get them out of here. The whole place is going to blow sky-high."

"A bomb? Please don't hurt the girls. I don't care what happens to the other pigs."

"Move it. Get your friends and run."

Bolan gave them sixty seconds, then he cracked the door. He saw someone heading for him. Bolan slammed the Uzi on the side of the guy's head and pushed him down the steps.

"Freeze!" the Executioner shouted.

All heads spun to look at the dark-clad stranger.

Bolan saw somebody clawing for a handgun. The Uzi stuttered off five rounds before the man cleared leather. He slammed backward against the wall, dead before he slumped to the floor. The sound of the unsilenced Uzi was thunderous. Other dealers fanned out, heading for doorways.

For a moment there was only the sound of rushing feet.

One brave soul came around a corner of the living room with a 12-gauge. Before he could aim, the Uzi chattered again. The shotgun shattered in the hoodlum's hands as lead tore into it. More 9mm whizzers perforated the gunman's chest, leaving the soul to rest in pieces.

The sound of the SMG in the confined room

was overpowering. Two men scurried out the front door and Bolan rushed out behind them, not sure how much time was left on the five minutes. He got to the street and blended into the growing dusk.

He was barely across the street when a thunderous roar split the evening. The whole side of the two-story house ripped apart with a blinding explosion. The basement wall blew out. Timber, siding and shattered glass shot skyward. The second eruption came fifteen seconds after the first, demolishing what was left of the house. Windows in buildings on both sides of the cutting factory cracked from the concussive effect.

Somewhere a siren wailed. Fire crackled from the basement. A gas pipe split and the escaping vapor fueled the fire in the fading daylight.

Bolan walked away from the ruined house.

17

Bolan drove back to the motel and parked outside the building. He did not leave the vehicle immediately, but opened the suitcase and rummaged around until he found a small brown leather case. Inside nothing was damaged or broken. There were two throwaway syringes and two plastic vials filled with liquid. It would be the only method the Executioner would use: he would not stoop to turkey-meat torture, nor could he kill Genovese. Right now the man was Bolan's single lead.

He entered the motel room and ripped the tape off the mobster's mouth.

"I thought you were going to let me rot here, Bolan."

"Too simple. Who is the Mafia drug czar of Chicago?"

"I'll be damn near dead before I tell you that."

"You ready to die, Carlo?"

Genovese snorted.

"I hear you used to do some turkey work, Carlo."

"No way, not my style. But it's not your style either, Bolan. Kill, yes. But no torture, no shooting at cops, and you have a soft spot for the civilians. That's your kind of play. Turkey meat? Never."

"Don't bet on that, Genovese."

"What are my options?"

"Damn few." Bolan growled.

"After my wheelman tells them you have me, my word will be shit," Genovese said bitterly.

"So even the score. You don't believe that crap about Men of Honor, do you?"

"It's kept me alive up to now."

"Up to now." Bolan took out the leather case, opened it and took out the syringe, then one of the two vials.

"What's that?" A look of fear crossed Genovese's face.

"Heard about death by injection? Decided to try it."

"Just like that? In cold blood?"

"You're no good to me. I need the name and location of your boss. If you clam up, I'll get it someplace else. In any case, you lose."

The Mafia big shot stared fixedly as Bolan pulled the liquid from the vial into the syringe, then pumped the air out of the barrel.

"L-look, there's no rush. You want names? I've got some. How about the biggest madam in town who also uses girl addicts and hooks every man on drugs who comes into the place. She's also a big supplier to a bunch of dealers."

"Keep talking."

Genovese gave him the woman's name and address.

"You need the drug bosses of the other Families, right?" He gave the names and addresses and Bolan made a mental note.

"That's enough, right? That should get me off the hook. I'll say I escaped after you tied me up, and I can still stay straight with the Families."

"No, Carlo. I want the czar's name. I won't leave without his head."

"Go ahead then! I might as well die right here." Tears rolled down his cheeks. "I figured I might buy it some day, but not like this."

Bolan brought the needle down and drove the point into the savage's arm. Genovese screamed in terror.

"Happy hell, Carlo."

Bolan put his hand over the mobster's mouth as he tried to scream again.

Bolan waited for three minutes, then checked on Genovese. His eyes were open.

"Good morning, Carlo. How do you feel?"

"Feel? Yeah, okay." His words were slow, a little slurred. Bolan knew that was normal for a sodium pentathol injection taking effect.

Bolan began with easy questions, the standard method in interrogating a person under the effects of truth serum.

"What is your wife's name, Carlo?"

"Beth."

"You have two children?"

"Three."

He asked the names of the key drug men of the other Families and Genovese answered as he had before.

"Does the four-family drug czar live in Chicago?"

There was a slight hesitation, then he said yes.

"Where were you born, Carlo?"

"Chicago."

"How old are you?"

"Forty."

"What's the drug czar's first name?"

"Jay." No hesitation.

"How old is your daughter?"

"Twelve."

"What is Jay's last name?"

Hesitation. And a scowl. "Lupo, Jay Lupo."

"Where does Lupo live?"

"In Chicago."

"What's the address?"

"Towers Street, 1814."

"What apartment number?"

Hesitation. "Thirty-four-oh-one."

"Can you get me into Jay's quarters?"

"Yes."

Bolan smiled. The drug would wear off in an hour. Carlo would sleep for another three or four. By that time The Executioner would be back, and he and Carlo would visit the drug czar.

His next appointment was with a madam in Oak Park just off Lake Street. It was a fancier place than he had expected. A quick recon showed it must be party night. Perhaps a big shipment had just arrived and all of the "team" members were on hand for distribution.

Bolan wore his blacksuit with the Beretta in shoulder leather under a dark sport jacket. Over his shoulder hung a small utility bag that contained four white phosphorus grenades.

The Executioner timed his arrival at the door with a group of six other visitors. They did not knock, just opened the door and walked in and Bolan hung behind the group. Inside he found a short hall that led to a huge reception area. A man came into the room holding a drinking straw and a small folded paper packet filled with white powder. The guy laughed and pointed to the room beyond.

To the left a stairway rose to the second floor. Bolan took the steps two at a time, then climbed another flight to the third floor. There were doors on both sides of the corridor. Two of them were open. He peered in the first and found a young woman, engrossed in a card game, sitting cross-legged on a bed, wearing only bikini panties. She looked up and smiled at the big stranger.

"You here for the freebie?"

"No, but I'll give you a tip. Get dressed, you're going to be out in the dark in five minutes."

"Why?"

Bolan let his jacket swing back so she could see the gun. He took a smooth-bodied WP grenade from the utility bag and showed it to her.

"No questions, miss. Just do as I say."

She jumped off the bed and turned around, suddenly becoming shy. Quickly she pulled on a blouse and faded blue jeans and pushed her feet into sandals.

"Collect your other girl who isn't working. I'll talk to the rest."

"The men could get nasty."

"Leave them to me."

The girl grinned as she left the room ahead of him. Bolan tried the door that was closed. It was not locked. He pushed it in and stood there with the Beretta up and trained on the bed. A blonde, straddling an obese man, turned when she heard the door open.

"What the—"

"You have one minute to move downstairs, dressed or not." He spun and left the room, kicked in the next closed door and found two girls entertaining a thin blond man.

"This is a raid!" Bolan shouted. The girls jumped off the bed and scrambled for clothes. The man sat there swearing. When he stood up, Bolan pushed him into the hall. The five hookers stood there waiting.

Bolan popped the safety pin on one of the WP grenades and tossed the phosphorus bomb into the closest room. Five seconds later the device exploded and smoke gushed from the room as well as a thin spray of the white, sticky, burning material. It stuck on the opposite wall and kept on smoldering.

"Everyone on the second floor, out," the Executioner said. The girls scampered down the hall, pushing open doors, screaming at the people inside. Bolan waited at the second open door until a black girl slid into tight pants and pulled on a jacket. Her john jammed himself into slacks and a shirt but didn't have time for shoes. Bolan motioned him out with the Beretta, then tossed in a WP smoke grenade and closed the door.

Smoke began to seep down the stairs. People on the first floor smelled the smoke and everyone began to yell.

One woman in a long red dress with diamonds at her throat was bustling around in the confused throng, shouting orders and screaming. A stream of people poured out the front door to the sidewalk.

Bolan saw someone hurrying back in against the flow.

"Whole damn top floor is burning!" the man said. "We better get out with what we can!"

They dashed to a room at the rear of the building, and Bolan followed them. A box on a large table held bundles of "papers" of heroin and coke. The papers had been folded from magazine pages.

"Who the hell are you?" the woman asked when she noticed Bolan.

"Someone you don't want to know," Bolan replied, palming the Beretta.

Her face lost some of its angry flush and she blanched with fear.

"Well, if it isn't a good cop," she moaned. "But I've paid my dues for the month."

The man beside her whirled with a gun in his hand. Bolan triggered a round from the Beretta. The bodyguard wailed in pain and sank to the floor. The woman pulled a six-inch blade and rushed the Executioner. Bolan sidestepped her and kicked the knife out of her hand.

"I'll kill you!" the woman shrieked.

"You're through ma'am," Bolan said.

He took a WP grenade from his utility bag, pulled the safety pin and caught both her hands. He let the arming handle pop off the grenade, then thrust the grenade into her hands.

She was still staring at it as Bolan surged away from her and through a door. He was barely behind the protective wall when the bomb went off with a whump, spewing bits of the thin shell in every direction, splattering the furiously burning phosphorus in a circle.

The blobs of white puttylike substance blasted into the drug supplier's body and face. She screamed in agony as the sticky substance burned furiously, eating holes into her flesh, tracing a fiery path of destruction past her ribs and on through her heart.

She had slumped to the floor unconscious within seconds after the WP grenade exploded. Fire was already consuming the ceiling from the second-floor blaze.

Bolan had bolted for the back door, slid out

through the opening and vaulted over a six-foot-high fence across the back of the lot and into the alley. He jogged to his car as neighbors came out to look at the growing fire.

Only then did he hear the sirens as two police cruisers ripped past him, skidded around the corner and raced up to the burning house. Then he heard the fire engine.

The Executioner settled back and drove to the motel where he'd left Carlo Genovese. It would soon be time to make his move on the kingpin of Chicago's drug trade.

Time was a commodity in Bolan's favor. He looked at it this way: he had the rest of his life.

18

The small chiming clock in Angela Marcello's living room struck three musical notes. Angela stood up and stared at the three young women lounging around the table. All were awake, in various stages of undress because they simply felt more comfortable that way. Angela had discarded her blouse an hour before and her pink sculptured bra almost matched her skin tone.

"I think we have reached the point of no return," she announced. "It's good management practice to push for a decision, but we have made several, and we'll all think about our main objective. Recap: We will henceforth be known as the Hard Corps." She giggled and the others joined in. "But this is damn serious business," she added. "We have all pledged not to get married for a year, and we will not make the mistake of getting pregnant."

Angela looked around. Gemma nodded seriously. Felicia yawned, but smiled her approval. Mimi whispered, "Damn right!"

"We will all do some thinking tomorrow and meet at Mimi's house in two nights to battle out a money-making scheme that will impress our parents. We've agreed that to be effective this venture must be illegal, something down and dirty.''

"Now can we go to bed?" Gemma asked.

"Right. The couch folds into a bed for two and somebody bunks with me."

Felicia stared at Angela as she unhooked her bra.

"Boy, you've got big tits!" Felicia said.

Angela frowned at her. "No more of this 'boy' and 'tits' sexist crap. From now on we're going to have to act like we have balls, so let's start thinking like goddamn Mafia soldiers.''

NONE OF THE GIRLS got up before eleven the next day, and after breakfast each scurried home. The rest of the day Angela tried to come up with a good racket to make a lot of money fast, the good old Mafia way.

Outside of selling her body by the hour she was stumped. She decided to make one more attack on her father when he came home. She would suggest he let her take over one of the Leisure Lady boutiques.

Manny "The Mover" Marcello did not get home that day until dinner was ready to be served, so Angela could not waylay him until he was in his library watching the all-news TV station. She walked to the set, turned it off and stood in front of it.

"Daddy, I'm going to be like a bad migraine

headache until you see my side of things. I want a job in one of your companies. I just want an ordinary management job where I can use all of those business practices I learned at Stanford."

Don Marcello had been through a tough day. "Angela, we talked that out already," he grunted.

"You might have, I didn't. I'm just getting started. You sent me to get my M.B.A., so I could learn how to make money. I have. I can. Why won't you let me show you? How about letting me run the Leisure Lady outlet in La Jolla? I can have it making more money in two months."

Don Marcello lit a cigar, put his hands behind his head and leaned back in his big chair.

"Making money? How much profit do you think those dress sellers make in a year? Sometimes it's not enough to take care of the overhead. But we don't care. We use them to launder some of our other money, the kind we can't just run to a bank and deposit. Do you realize that any cash deposit of over $5,000 must be reported to the federal government? But when we put the money through several of our business firms no report is made, and there are no problems. Did they teach you that in your fancy business school?"

"Then what difference does it make how the shops are run or who runs them? Let me have one to play with, please!"

"Maybe I should teach you a lesson," Don Marcello said half to himself. "Maybe I should let you know where all those fancy clothes, cars, schools and trips come from. Yeah, why not? You think you've got balls enough to be a soldier, do you? You think you should be a capo just because you wear my last name? All right. At eight o'clock tonight I have a job to do. I want you to come. Wear some pants that aren't skintight and cover up your boobs so you don't look like a bimbo, and wear dark glasses. You got all that?''

"Right. I'll be ready!" Angela whirled and ran out the door.

Once in her room she leaned against the door and hugged herself. At last! She was going to get to see the inside of the workings of a real operation!

Angela quivered with excitement. She put on one of her old bras and tightened the straps. She wore a heavy blouse that was full and loose, and a dark poplin jacket. It was hard to tell she was a girl. From the back of her closet she found some slacks she had used four or five years before. They were the loose, baggy style and she slid into them. Now, not a curve showed. She found sunglasses, the kind with reflective lenses, and tucked her hair under a mannish-style hat. Great! She wiped off all her lipstick and eye shadow and the rest of her makeup.

She was waiting outside her father's study at five minutes to eight when he came out. Don Marcello looked at her, nodded his approval and motioned for her to follow him. He went through the front door first. It was the first time she could think of that he did not hold the door for her. Then she remembered: tonight she was just one of the men, and he was Don Marcello.

They took one of the big Cadillac crew wagons. Her father rode in front and she sat between four soldiers in the back seat. The men looked at her suspiciously but they made no protests.

The limo headed out of La Jolla and down the freeway to National City, where it turned off into an industrial section near San Diego bay. A moment later they stopped inside a yard with the name Warner Trucking over a big warehouse door.

Two of the men faded to the front of the building. One went to the dispatcher's office, which was empty and dark. Two more checked the back door, before signalling to the car.

Only then did Manny the Mover come out of the crew wagon and hurry inside the building. Angela ran to keep pace with him. The two pistoleros led the way to an upstairs office. The first goon kicked the door open, smashing the panel, almost knocking it off its hinges.

"What the hell?" said Bob Warner, the owner of the trucking company, looking up from his desk where he was engrossed in a stack of invoices.

"Just a little chat, Warner," Manny grunted, looking down at the other man. Warner was average height, about fifty years old, with a modest belly, tired-looking eyes behind glasses and a fringe of graying hair around a balding head.

"And your goons ruin my door so we can talk?"

"Nothing personal, you understand. Just business. You're cutting into my trade in the south bay, Warner. I don't like it. I want that Farmington account back."

Warner laughed. One of the soldiers stepped forward and backhanded him in the face. Warner jolted to one side but did not tip over in the swivel chair.

"Now, as I was about to say, you will default on that account. It's for thirty semis a day and you just can't spare the rigs. Do I make myself clear?"

"Fuck you, Marcello!"

The goon began to move ahead but Manny held up his hand.

"Warner, with me it ain't personal. But my boys like to kick ass a bit. I ain't never liked that. Why can't you just take it as a business loss and forget it?"

"I don't like to be pushed around by the Mob, by anyone," Warner snarled. "I just don't like that kind of pressure."

"You're a stubborn bastard. How the hell can I convince you?"

Manny turned and walked around the office. Warner stood up and took a step toward his desk. The soldier who hit Warner pushed him back.

The truck company boss moved so fast, he took the Mafia goon completely by surprise. Warner clamped his forearm over the opened hand on his chest and leaned forward, bending the soldier's fingers backward. The guncock screamed and fell to his knees to relieve the pressure. Warner's right knee raced upward into the man's jaw, and knocked him to the floor unconscious.

The second soldier fisted a huge .45 and pushed off the safety.

"Don't move!" he snarled.

Angela stood at the back of the room, watching it all. She felt a touch of fear, but it quickly dissolved as she watched the drama unfold. She was fascinated.

"This is your last chance, Warner. Tell me you'll forget the Farmington account."

"That's half my business! I just bought twelve new trucks to handle it."

"Better to lose a little money than to die. Think about it."

Manny motioned to the goon with the .45.

"The left knee," Manny ordered.

The sound of the handgun cracked in the confines of the room and Warner fell to the floor as the slug shattered his kneecap. He lay writhing in agony, blood leaking through his fingers.

"Bastard!" he screamed.

"Nothing personal, Warner. Just business. You ready to give up that account now?"

A film of sweat covered Warner's forehead. He spoke slowly, his eyes beginning to glaze as the blood loss sapped his strength.

"I swear you'll pay for this, Marcello."

Manny motioned to his thug again. The man who had shot Warner stepped forward and let fly a kick at the wounded knee.

Warner's eyes rolled upward, and spittle drooled out of his mouth. The unbearable pain sent his body into shock and his head lolled from side to side, the motion gradually diminishing until the man lay still.

Angela could swear she saw a smile on Warner's face. Torture! It was wild, but fascinating, too.

Her father's voice broke into her reverie.

"Downstairs," Don Marcello said. The first soldier, who had been out cold, staggered up and the group exited through a rear door.

Two big semi highway tractor rigs were parked in the center of the large yard. From the trunk of the crew wagon a soldier brought two gasoline cans. He emptied one in each of the two truck cabs, removed the diesel fuel-tank caps and then threw a lighted book of matches into each cab.

The gasoline fumes erupted with a whump as they burst into flames.

Manny watched for a moment, then walked to his car and sat in the back seat. He motioned to Angela, who joined him in the vehicle and soon the car drove out the gate toward San Diego.

Manny flicked on the limo's rear dome light. He was surprised by the expression on her face. Her face was animated, her eyes bright and glistening with excitement. Her fingernails dug into his arm.

Manny "The Mover" Marcello, Don of the San Diego Family, sighed. What kind of a daughter had he sired? She had reacted differently than he expected. He had been sure she would be screaming and begging him to stop the lesson.

"I still wish you were my son," he said.

If he gave her the store he could transfer the manager to another outlet. When Angie tired of the job he would put the manager back. Yes. That would work, and keep Angie busy for a while. In the meantime he was going to pick out a husband for her. That would be his ultimate weapon to keep Angie out of his business for good.

Manny picked up his daughter's hand and kissed it. "Little princess, tomorrow morning you become the manager of the boutique in La Jolla. Will that make you happy?"

"As a start, daddy, as a start." She reached over and kissed his cheek, and as she did she thought of balding truck owner, Warner, screaming in pain. It gave her a throb of sexual pleasure.

19

As soon as Angela returned to the Marcello mansion, she called her three friends and told them the news. She spoke to Mimi first, explaining how she had broken through her father's reluctance.

"It's not exactly what we want, but it's a toehold. A base we can use to build into something else. And our meeting is still on for tomorrow night."

After she had called all three, she sat at her desk with a pad and pencil and jotted down every idea she could come up with. The first on the list was prostitution, then she kept writing.

When she had eleven ideas down she stared at the paper. Most of the ideas were already in use by the Family. Drugs, women and gambling were the keystones of almost every Mafia family.

Angela was stumped. Which plan? All the Hard Corps needed was one good idea. Then they would have some heavy ammunition to throw at the Men of Honor.

She took a long shower, thinking about the trucking company man bleeding on his office floor. She shivered with excitement just remembering it. Once out of the bathroom, she draped on her robe and pondered her new status as manager of the Leisure Lady shop.

All she had to do was double the profits in the first month. How could she do that? She thought through all of the business management methods she had learned and decided to use many of them, but they would only increase profits and sales by two to ten percent. She needed something dramatic.

"What about getting rid of any competition?" she said aloud.

Angela smiled. Perfect. There were other small stores that specialized in clothing for the wealthy of La Jolla. If they were to have unexpected setbacks, it would give her store a big jump in sales.

She checked her watch. It was only a little after ten. She dressed quickly in the same outfit she had worn when she accompanied her father earlier that evening.

In the garage she found two full gasoline cans. She stored them in the trunk of her new 380SL and drove back out of the garage. There was no problem about her going or coming at odd hours. The guard made sure who she was, then opened the heavy metal gate.

Her destination was the Chic Salon, a high-class ladies' wear shop wedged between a department store and a beauty parlor. The store was the best of its kind in town. She parked across from the building for a moment, studying the layout. The rear would be easier, but she could do the most damage in front. She finally decided on the back, hoping it would get a good fire started.

She parked a block from the store, at the end of the alley. When she was certain there were no passersby, she took the two gas cans and walked quickly to the delivery door of the Chic Salon. She poured out the fluid and watched as it ran under the door and inside the store. Quickly she emptied both containers.

Angela's fingers trembled as she struck the first match from the book, then lit the remaining paper matches as she had seen the guncock do earlier. She stepped back a few paces and tossed the matchbook on the puddle of gasoline at the base of the door. The flames raced forward and under the door and Angela turned and ran.

She made it just past the first building when she heard the explosion. It was more powerful than any she had ever imagined. Half the sky seemed to light up, and the sound of the huge conflagration crackled around her. She hurried out of the alley. Then she slowed her pace to avoid suspicion and casually walked the half block to her car. Angela stepped into her Mercedes, started it and drove slowly away from the raging fire behind her.

Her hands were shaking as she parked three blocks down on Prospect. She could see the glow of the fire but no actual flames. Sirens screamed as firetrucks plowed past her. A pair of San Diego police cars roared by. The sight of the city cops startled her.

There was no chance of driving past the burning store. By now the street would be barricaded two blocks each way and crisscrossed with fire hoses.

Angela tried to relax. The first hint of a smile broke through the stiffness of her face and she giggled. The Chic Salon was no longer quite so chic. The gasoline vapors must have blown to the front of the store when they exploded. Now, Manny Marcello, that was the way a member of the Hard Corps made sure that her business made money!

She drove back up the hill to her father's fortresslike mansion. One thought plagued her. Fingerprints on the cans? No, the fire would have burned both cans into twisted hulks. There would be no evidence, no way anyone could tie her to the fire.

Back home, inside her rooms, Angela sat crosslegged on her bed watching the late show. There was a news flash about the incident, but reporters were unable to provide any details other than that the fire damage had been confined to the Chic Salon, which was a total loss. Firemen were unable to determine how the fire had started or spread so quickly. One man across the street said the front windows blew out and suddenly the whole store was a sheet of flames.

"Looked as if somebody napalmed the place," the witness said.

Angela grinned as she prepared for bed. It had

been quite an awakening for her. The trip with her father, the breakthrough with the store and wiping out her toughest competitor even before she took over management! She wished she had someone to share her bed tonight.

Angela fell asleep dreaming about Johnny Gray.

THE NEXT MORNING, Johnny whizzed through his paralegal work for Killinger. The lawyer was going to spend all day in court. Johnny took off an hour early and hurried to Karl Darlow's place. He was pleased to find him sober.

"Ready to chip paint, swabby?" Karl asked. Johnny nodded and half an hour later they were on board the *Flying Fool*. Johnny stripped off his shirt and began to sand down the rear section of the mahogany rail.

Johnny could tell Karl was feeling better. His chest slashes were healing and he was humming tunelessly as he painted the forward bait tank on the bow, out of the way of the dust. Johnny finished the rail section and applied a coat of the special marine varnish.

"Anyone else visited you?" Johnny asked.

Karl shook his head. "Nope. Just as soon never see any of them again. Got me a boat to run. Damn, I sure hate missing this week of catches. The fish count has been way up on the sport boats. I could have made a bundle this week."

They worked the afternoon away. Johnny

topped up his tan and Karl managed to do a few maintenance chores that he usually never had time for. At four o'clock Johnny said he had to leave. Karl never asked why. Johnny took the sea captain home and made him promise not to go out boozing.

At four-thirty Johnny parked his VW near the exit ramp of the Security Pacific Bank Plaza building. There was a good chance he might spot that light blue Pontiac driven by the thug who carved Karl.

He hunched down behind the wheel of the Bug and waited. If the car did not show up by five-thirty he would call off the watch.

At precisely 4:45 P.M. the blue Pontiac slid down the ramp, paused to clear traffic and turned toward him. Johnny confirmed the license plate. The driver was a big guy wearing a blue suit and vest. The VW fired on the first try and Johnny rolled into traffic two cars behind the Pontiac. It was rush hour, a bad time to try to tail a car.

Johnny's quarry appeared to be in no hurry. He cruised up to the freeway, took U.S. 5 north to the Grand Avenue off ramp, made a half dozen turns and parked in front of a small white house a block back from the surf at Pacific Beach. It was not a high-rent district, except in the summer. Johnny stopped half a block back and wrote down the number of the house. So far, so good.

Johnny drove to a filling-station phone booth and called his real-estate friend. Pete had a telephone directory that listed the city by streets. It took him about a minute to find the address in his directory.

"Yeah, Johnny, phone number there is 543-4545. Last known resident was Ted Young, and that was only about three months ago. Could be the same one."

"Thanks, Pete. I owe you one."

Johnny got back into his car and drummed fingers on the wheel. What now? He had an address, a possible name and a telephone number.

He went back to the phone and tried the police ID section again. Nancy Carter was just coming on the evening shift.

"Boy, when it rains. . . ."

"Nancy, I've got a name. Could you check him for wants and warrants?"

"Johnny, you know—" She stopped. "Hell, what's the name?"

He held the line and in three minutes she returned with the information. "Ted Young, a real sweetheart. He's had six arrests, no convictions. Last arrest was for assault and battery. His lawyer got him off due to insufficient evidence. All charges were dropped. Two witnesses failed to testify. Oh, his lawyer is an interesting guy, too. Artie 'The Flake' Dancini. You should know all about him. He's the local mafiosi's favorite mouthpiece."

"That fits in nicely, Nancy. That's two lunches I owe you."

"Story of my life, promises."

"Maybe I'll keep them."

"Maybe. Got to go. Bye."

She hung up and Johnny called a florist he knew. He ordered an arrangement of cut flowers delivered to Nancy Carter in the ID section of the SDPD the next day after five. That should take care of one lunch.

Johnny stared at the phone after he hung it up. Should he call Mr. Killinger and ask him about Dancini? He decided against it. Dancini was Mafia, so his client was Mafia, which meant for sure it was a Mob attack on Karl.

Johnny felt frustrated. Here was a hoodlum who deserved some payback and there was no way Johnny could do it, not without endangering Karl even more. He fumed all the way back to the Free Legal Aid Center. Someday things would be different. Someday he was going to have the method and the opportunity to strike back at these people. There had to be a way to stop them, or at least slow them down.

For just a fleeting second Johnny knew how Mack must have felt, must still feel. The thought gave him renewed strength as he drove back to the legal aid center. He had time to talk to three people there before the center closed.

When he reached his apartment, a little past nine that evening, Johnny found dinner ready.

"I had a call from daddy," Sandy said. "He was tired out and growling. He sounded great!"

"He worked me too hard. I've got dust in my hair." Johnny kissed Sandy and returned her hug. "Did he sound like he'd been drinking?"

"Nope. I told him not to touch a drop. I just hope he doesn't."

As they ate Sandy watched him. "You mad about something? You've got that strange look."

"Sorry, I'm not mad at you, or Karl."

"What then?"

He told her about finding the man he was sure had slashed Karl.

"And we can't do a damn thing about it, can we?" Sandy asked.

"Right," Johnny said. "So we just grin and bear it and hope the Mafia forgets all about Karl Darlow."

Sandy put down her fork and stared at Johnny. "If they hurt daddy again, I'll find out who they are and kill them myself."

Johnny reached across the table and held her hand. "Hey, it's all going to work out fine. Karl is staying home and holding down the boozing, and the Mafia are going to realize he didn't see enough to matter." He became pensive for a moment and finally blurted out what was really on his mind. "I want to know what other businesses the Mafia own in this town."

"I bet Ira would know," Sandy offered. She could feel the urgency of his concern.

"You mean your old boyfriend who was a crime writer on the newspaper?"

Sandy nodded. "If we really want to know we could call him at the paper. He works the morning edition. He'd probably still be there." She left the table and walked over to the phone. "In fact I think I'll ask him."

She dialed the number.

"Ira Blake, please."

A moment later she smiled. "Ira, Sandy Darlow. It's good to hear your voice again. How are you?" After the amenities were over, she turned and winked at Johnny.

"Ira, I need a favor. I've got a friend who is interested in the Mafia in San Diego. Could you answer a few questions for him?" She paused. "Great. His name is Johnny. Here he is."

Johnny took the phone. "Ira. I understand you're the Mafia expert in town."

"Thanks, some might say that."

"I hear they've gone legit. Is that true?"

"They had to, to stay alive. The climate wasn't right for hoodlum warfare."

"What about Philmore Industries, a holding company? Is that one of them?"

"You're well informed."

"Do you have anything else?"

"Sure, Marcello Trucking, Big M Bowlero, Hobart Enterprises, one of the biggest international construction firms in the world, even Leisure Lady shops, twenty-six of them up and down the coast."

"Go on."

"We keep turning up more and more of them all the time. Sometimes we tumble by the lawyer they use on their really important stuff."

"Like a guy called Arturo Dancini?"

"Uh-huh. You know a lot about these hoods. You writing a book?"

"Not really. Thanks for the help."

"Anytime. You take good care of Sandy."

"I plan to."

They hung up. Johnny had written down the names that Ira told him, and he concentrated on Hobart Enterprises. That was the registered owner of the Mercedes that Angela drove. He remembered she had said it was her father's car.

Johnny was puzzled.

"Johnny, what's the matter? What did Ira tell you?"

"Oh, I was just thinking how a Mafia hoodlum could run a dress shop. Those Leisure Lady shops, did you know the Mafia owns them? The whole chain may be a money-laundering setup."

Johnny frowned. Angela whatever-her-name-was had said that the car belonged to her father. For a company to give an executive one car was normal enough, but two, one for his daughter? That would mean Angela's father had to be a big shot in the firm.

He was glad she had refused to give him her phone number. Now he could ignore her, or be busy the next time she called.

He wished that he had never followed up on her license number.

It might have been better not to know.

20

Mack Bolan drove back to the motel to check on his captive. Carlo Genovese was still sleeping. Bolan walked over to the bed, shook the Mafia coordinator awake and removed the bandage from his mouth.

Genovese looked up, groggy and confused by his surroundings. His glazed eyes wandered around the room for a few moments, then came to rest on the granite-etched face of the Executioner.

"Welcome back from the dead, Carlo," Bolan said. "Ready to take me to your boss?"

"No way. You can't make me talk."

"I know everything, Carlo. You told me earlier."

"I told you where my boss is? Not a chance." Then it became clear to Genovese that he had been drugged.

"That damn needle! I still won't go with you. The boys'll cut you down before you get halfway up."

"Uh-uh." Bolan shook his head. "Because you're going to be right beside me."

Genovese snorted. "Why do you need me if you've got the info?"

"Insurance, Carlo. Now move."

Bolan removed the tape from Genovese's arms and legs. The Mafia hoodlum stood up to stretch his legs, rubbing his wrists.

Bolan swung up the weapons case that he had brought from the car onto the night table. Now he flipped it open and Genovese looked inside.

"You going to start a war?"

"It's already started." Bolan looked at the handguns, the Uzi, the .44 AutoMag, boxes of rounds and six fragmentation hand grenades nestled in pockets cut out of urethane-foam padding.

Bolan worked out his plan. The approaches to the high-rise residence would be patrolled and under surveillance by TV monitors. So it had to look natural.

Bolan ordered the mobster to sit, picked up one of the grenades and pulled the safety pin.

"You know how these work, Carlo? All that's keeping this thing from exploding is the arming handle. You're going to hold it down, or we die. Understand?"

The Executioner grabbed the mafioso's left hand and gave him the grenade, making sure his fingers closed around the arming handle.

Sweat broke out on Genovese's forehead as he stared at the explosive. His knuckles were white from the pressure he exerted on the handle.

Bolan ripped up the bed sheet and fashioned a sling, which he tied around Genovese's neck, slipping his right arm into it. Then the Executioner taped the right fist closed so Genovese could not use it. Afterward he bound the arm tightly to the mobster's chest.

Genovese was trembling. Bolan grabbed his left hand, and pushed the cotter pin back in place to make the bomb safe again. Genovese collapsed in the chair. He shook as if he was having a seizure.

"Stand up, Carlo. We're going out to the car."

Bolan wore the blue sport coat that hid a variety of weapons. Big Thunder was on his hip, the silenced Beretta 93-R nestled in shoulder leather. The Uzi was a little harder to conceal, but with the plan he had in mind he figured he might be able to get away with it. He attached a cord to the weapon and slung it around his neck, the machine pistol covered by his jacket.

In his pockets he stuffed two more standard U.S. Army-issue hand grenades. Bolan wished he could wear his combat webbing, but for this job he had to look the part of a normal civilian.

Satisfied with his arsenal, Bolan growled, "Let's go. Any sudden moves and I drop you where you stand."

Half an hour later Bolan parked in a loading zone outside the Towers building, which was away from the main downtown area.

"Which entrance?"

"The one on this side. We're in the north tower."

"Do we have to sign in?"

"No, the guard knows me. I often come at odd hours."

"Good. Out of the car."

Bolan took the grenade from his pocket and pulled the pin.

Genovese shivered when Bolan raised the mafioso's arm and placed the grenade under it. There was no way to fake it. Bolan made sure Genovese saw the arming spoon was free and ready to pop. He placed the handle directly against the mobster's side, then eased his arm down until the pressure held the grenade and its triggering spoon in place.

"Now you're the original walking bomb, Carlo. You get me up to the apartment and I take the bomb out and you live."

"Oh, shit!"

"Try to act cool, Carlo, or the guard might become suspicious. Here's the pitch. You had a car wreck and you're giving me a cash reward because I helped you."

They went up the steps and through an electronically opened door. The guard was stationed directly ahead, staring at the pair, the big dude walking half a pace back from Genovese, whose body almost concealed the tall guy's.

"Mr. Genovese! What happened to your arm?"

"Car crash," Genovese snapped.

"Anything I can do?"

Genovese shook his head.

They walked past the guard to the bank of elevators and entered in the one marked floors 30 to 40.

"What's the layout upstairs?" Bolan asked as he punched the thirty-fourth-floor button.

"Long hall. L-shape. We're at the far end, corner suite. We have twelve rooms. Only entrance is last door 3401. Inside the front door is a desk manned by one of our boys. The guard downstairs has already buzzed the room that we're coming up. The hallways have closed-circuit TV with a monitor in the sentry's office down below and also at the guard station upstairs."

"How's the grenade? You holding it nice and tight?"

"I think my arm is getting numb. What happens then?"

"You die, I guess."

The elevator stopped and the door opened. The hall extended a hundred feet ahead, then turned left. No one was in sight. They walked to the corner and when they went around it a man with a .45 pointed it at Bolan and looked over at Genovese.

"Whimp, what the hell you doing?" Genovese bellowed, sounding tired and angry.

"Tony downstairs said you didn't look right, and that you had company. We don't take no chances, you know that. What happened to you?"

"Totaled my car. Broke my arm and bruised my leg. How the hell you want me to look after that?"

"Who's your buddy? I ain't never seen him before. I thought we better...."

"Whimp, you ain't paid to think. This man helped get me out of my smashed car and took me to the hospital. Probably saved my life. I said I'd give him five hundred, but I don't have that much on me. We came back here to get the rest."

"Fine, but I better pat him down, you know the rules."

"Whimp, right now I'm making the rules!" Genovese's voice went up several notes. "I want a bottle of bourbon and some ice. But open the door first. Then get four hundred from the cash drawer. Now move!"

Whimp nodded, turned and walked down the hall.

At the door, Whimp knocked twice, then opened the panel when it unlocked.

Bolan held the door as Whimp went in, followed by Genovese. They were in a reception room. A heavyset man sat at a desk directly across from the door. He had a .38 in his hand but put it down when he saw Genovese.

Bolan used the mobster as cover to draw the Beretta. He shot the desk guard in the head and whirled, pumping three silenced rounds at Whimp. He staggered backward and hit the floor.

Genovese was cowering against a wall afraid to move in case he triggered the grenade. Bolan motioned him forward.

"Now, your boss's apartment. No funny moves and keep quiet. Any more guards on duty this time of night?"

"One man will come on at 4:00 A.M."

"Good. Move it."

Genovese walked along the hall, turned down a corridor that led toward the outside of the building. He came to a door with the numeral one stenciled on it.

"This is it," Genovese said.

Bolan took out a pick, positioned Genovese where he could see him and quietly worked on the lock. In twenty seconds he had the tumblers positioned correctly. He turned the knob and peered in the dark room.

"How many hardmen inside?"

"None. The boss is alone."

"Come on, you're first."

Bolan caught Genovese's arm and pushed him into the room. It was partly lit by soft night lamps. As soon as Genovese stepped on the carpet an alarm went off. A strobe light pulsed, brilliant flashes stabbing into the large living room.

The drug coordinator huddled against the wall next to the door, his face wild with fear.

A black streak hurtled out of the darkness, bypassed the quivering man cringing against the wall and sprang directly at Bolan's throat. Slavering white fangs were bared as the living missile streaked toward its target.

Bolan got off two shots before the sixty-pound Doberman plowed into him.

Strong jaws clamped around his forearm, but as Bolan rolled with the animal, he felt the jaws relax and the animal fall away. The lead messengers had found their mark. To kill a killer dog triggered no crisis of compassion in Bolan.

A light snapped on down a short hall to the left and a man in pajama bottoms rushed out, staring into the dimness of the living room. He was not much more than twenty, blond, with wide shoulders and a narrow waist.

"One move and you're dead," Bolan called. The man froze, then dropped to his knees.

"Please, don't shoot! I'm a visitor. I don't live here!"

"Flat on your face!" Bolan ordered. He saw Genovese straighten and move out from the wall. "Carlo, walk down the hall ahead of me."

Genovese moved slowly, holding his left arm tightly to his side.

A door opened at the end of the hall and in the subdued light Bolan could see the glinting snout of a weapon. He dived to the side, pulled up the Uzi and triggered a burst.

The resounding gunfire in the confined hallway deafened everyone there. The weapon in the doorway spit flame, and Genovese screamed. The Executioner's arm snaked out to encircle the Mafia man's body before he fell, at the same time using the mobster as a shield. Carefully Bolan pulled him around a corner and slowly extracted the grenade. He pushed the pin back in, making the explosive safe.

Then he looked at Genovese.

The man was dead.

The young blond man on the floor quivered with fear and remained facedown.

Bolan darted for the first door, the one the kid had left. He flattened against the wall and peered around the doorway. The room seemed empty. He jumped inside, the Uzi panning the gloom. A connecting door clicked and the Uzi muzzle tracked upward.

A woman stepped into the room quickly. She was tall and attractive with shoulder-length dark hair. A short black nightie half covered her crotch. Heavy, brown-tipped breasts strained against the see-through thinness of the sheer nylon fabric.

"Where's the gun?" Bolan growled.

"It's empty, on the bed. I thought you were a burglar."

Bolan reached around the door and found a wall switch. The room was another bedroom; the king-size water bed had rumpled sheets. He could see no one else. He picked up the handgun and checked it. She was telling the truth.

Bolan looked more closely at her. The lady was about forty-five, and he could tell her face had been lifted. She had a young woman's figure with long, shapely, tapered legs.

"Who are you?" Bolan asked.

"I'm Jay Lupo."

"Where's the boss?"

"What do you mean?"

"The czar, the top drug man for the four Families?"

"You must be joking. I've only been here a week but he said nothing. . . ." She smiled. "He does let me have my little friends like Alec."

"Where is this broad-minded friend of yours?"

"Out. Some kind of shipment or something. I don't bother with that." She walked toward Bolan, her arms out, her breasts jiggling. "Mmm, you are a hunk."

Bolan caught her arm, spun her around and pushed her ahead of him.

"First, lady, we check out every room in this place, then we have our long talk. Move it!"

The trip took them through two more bedrooms, an office and into the dining room. The suite was empty. The only other person alive in the place was Alec, who was still shivering facedown on the floor.

"Get your pants on and get out of here," Bolan snapped. The young man leaped to his feet and vanished into the bedroom. He was back in a minute, pushing a shirt into slacks and then putting on his shoes as he hurried out. The door locked behind him.

At first Bolan didn't get it, then suddenly everything became clear. The name that Carlo Genovese had given him had thrown him. Jay could have been a man or a woman. Bolan shook his head.

She had moved to the bed and sat down. She stared up at Bolan.

"What do you want from me?"

"I know who you are and I intend to find out all your pipeline connections."

"The Mob will kill me if I tell you."

"You have no choice. If you don't, *I'll* kill you."

She whimpered, suddenly weak and spineless. Her smudged mascara and smeared lipstick gave her face a grotesque look in the harsh light as she began to speak. She gave Bolan the next major link in the pipeline: Denver. They had more shit coming in from Texas, but that line was temporarily out of service. The only other big shipments came in through Hoboken, New Jersey. Bolan memorized the names and addresses.

Moments later he stood at the bathroom door as she leaned over the sink repairing her makeup.

Her right hand snaked under a folded towel on the toilet tank.

The aging moll whirled, a .32 automatic in her hand spitting hot lead.

Bolan's Uzi shattered at point-blank range. A 5-round burst drilled through her right cheek.

Bolan felt a fire in his side as a .32 automatic round grazed his ribs.

The woman was screaming in fury and pain. She sank back on the toilet seat, blood dripping from her left cheek where tooth fragments had torn through her flesh.

"Kill me!" she shrieked through bloody lips.

She stood, looked at her face in the bathroom mirror and flew at him, her right hand a claw that tried to rake his face.

"Kill me!" The words came slower this time.

Bolan pulled a fragger out of his pocket. He stood at the door and tossed the grenade back into the room. He was already in the hall while the explosive was still airborne. He reached the corridor when the grenade went off with a tremendous, contained explosion that sounded ten times as loud inside the building. Bolan covered his ears but still the sound hurt. When he looked back he saw the door of the suite barely hanging on its hinges.

The Executioner rode down the elevator and waved as he went past the guard into the Chicago suburb.

21

After two days in Denver, Mack Bolan had checked out Fairway Ford, "The Workingman's Friend."

The Executioner parked a block from the big dealership, watching the activity. He knew everything he needed to, including the time of the "special shipment" of parts coming in tonight at ten o'clock. The boss, Darrell Hudson, arrived at tenthirty each morning and worked until seven in the evening. He oversaw every department and took special pride in handling most of his own paperwork. The boss ran a tight ship and productivity was high.

Darrell Hudson was a self-made man. He had come up the hard way, lifting himself out of the Depression as a mechanic and later opening his own garage.

A dozen slogans peppered the walls of the dealership, all suggesting that if God drove a Ford, this was where He'd come for fine service.

Darrell Hudson was a leader in a large Baptist church, a member of a Boy Scout committee and a volunteer in the United Fund and half a dozen other civic organizations and nonprofit groups.

He was also the biggest cocaine supplier to the mile-high city.

He was dirty as hell.

Bolan put down the binoculars. The dealership owner had gone to lunch. Tuesday was Rotary. Bolan had found out that Hudson had a perfect record with the Rotarians: he had not missed a weekly meeting for more than twenty-five years.

He would miss the meeting next Tuesday.

Hudson was a tall, thin man in his late fifties, who never drank or smoked, never ran around with other women and had three sons. The youngest was in line to take over the business when his father retired.

Bolan gunned the rented Thunderbird and pulled in at the service entrance. He had been waiting for a line to build up and now his was the sixth car, giving him more time to look around the dealership. He got out of the Thunderbird and leaned on the front fender in the sunshine as he waited.

Three service advisors were working the cars as fast as they could. Bolan decided it was a standard enough dealership for a cold-weather climate: large round showroom with attached business offices and closing rooms. Open service lanes with two wings of barnlike sheds for service bays, and a large warehouse for parts and supplies.

He did not see a likely place where the hot goods could be stashed while they were waiting for reshipment. Maybe inside the service stalls. The paint booth would be ideal, unless a car was in there being spray-painted.

In the line Bolan saw a man he had identified only a few hours before. His name was Carmine Ricco, lately of Chicago, moved to Denver to work for Hudson, overseeing the flow through the pipeline and selling used cars on the side.

Carmine was dark, with a thin face and deadly eyes. He was the Mafia man, on the scene to make sure everything went off on schedule, and he answered to the former czar in Chicago for foul-ups. Consequently everything went down as it was supposed to in Denver.

Until tonight, that is.

When Bolan's turn for service came, he asked if he could have his rental Thunderbird looked at for engine trouble. The service writer suggested he should return it to the agency for an exchange. Bolan thanked him, drove through the dealership and back to his motel.

In his room he checked his weapons case. He was running low on ammo. That meant a pit stop somewhere right after Denver.

Once more he reviewed his plans for that evening. With everything clear in his mind, the Executioner stretched out on the bed to catch some badly needed sleep. He might not be getting any for a while.

Just after nine-thirty that night, Bolan scaled a six-foot-high block wall at the back of Fairway Ford and picked his way silently through wrecked cars waiting their turn in the body shop. He found the spot he wanted midway between the service entrance and the new-car showroom and sat down behind a smashed Tempo.

Twenty minutes later he saw two dark figures emerge from the showroom and station themselves out of sight on both sides of the service drive. That could be the point of entry. Why did Hudson think he needed protection in his own dealership?

Two lights snapped on in the building, then a man walked out a dark doorway into the back lot area and leaned against the Coke machine. It was the Mafia contact from Chicago, Carmine Ricco. The guy pulled a handgun from his belt, checked the cylinder and snapped it shut. A revolver, six rounds. No contest.

Five minutes later another figure came from the office. He was taller than Ricco. Hudson himself.

At exactly one minute to ten, a white Ford maxivan drove up the open service lane and stopped just outside the rolling metal gate. The headlights died and the driver turned off the engine. No one moved, then Ricco walked to the gate and rolled it open. The van's engine fired up at once and the rig rolled inside, then stopped in the open area between the service stall sheds and the new car rotunda.

Delivery time!

A man stepped from the van. He wore white coveralls and a white cap.

"Joker," a voice said from the darkness. The voice was Ricco's.

"Right on time with the goods," Joker said. "You have protection?"

"Of course. Your load as advertised?"

"Two hundred pounds pure. The truck is yours, too."

Bolan's first shot took Joker in the heart and killed him instantly.

Bolan rolled silently to a better vantage point. He could see the black shadow against a dark Ford where one of the protection gunmen crouched.

The nightfighter fired twice at the shadow, and moved again.

The garage had erupted with shouts. He heard Ricco's voice above the din. The door on the far side of the van opened. Bolan turned and sent a 3-shot burst through the rolled-down window of the driver's-side door and heard a scream of pain.

The silenced Beretta 93-R continued to confuse the locals.

"Get the son of a bitch!" Ricco shouted. "What are you bastards waiting for?"

Two whispering slugs from the Beretta slammed into the wall where the Mob overseer was kneeling. He had his own .38 out but no target. He swore and crawled behind a parked car.

Bolan waited for the second armed guard to show himself.

A man rose from behind a Mustang convertible with the top up, which was parked in the center of the area. The figure stared in Bolan's direction.

One 9mm hornet punctured the ragtop of the

Mustang and plowed into the second hardman's skull.

The Executioner jumped up and ran for the white maxivan. The driver's door still hung open. He had almost gained the driver's seat when a volley of handgun rounds peppered the side of the van. Bolan crouched lower as he ran, then leaped into the van. The keys had been left in it as he suspected. He fired the engine.

He rammed the gearshift into reverse and tromped on the gas pedal. The rolling gate had not been closed. The maxivan hurtled backward along the painted lines of the service lanes. Bolan swung the wheel to make a sharp rear turn so he could head out of the dealership.

Ricco swore and ran for his rig. The Windy City overseer slid into his Ranger pickup as the van completed its turn. Bolan found a string of six new cars blocking all but one small exit lane. The Ranger's engine fired to life and raced forward.

Bolan's vehicle hunted the exit. Ricco raced his engine in low, then shifted to second. He was doing almost thirty miles an hour when he rammed into the van from the side. Metal screeched and tore. The smaller pickup pushed the heavier van sideways for six feet. It teetered upward on two wheels before it dropped back down.

Ricco plowed into the back of the van, driving it forward into a brand-new Thunderbird, mating the two rigs into a solid mass of twisted steel. The Chicago connection opened the pickup's door and crawled out, seeking cover. It was not good enough.

Bolan had exited the van a second before Ricco slammed into the back of it. He had rolled away from the impact and gotten to his feet. The Executioner was watching as the small pickup's door opened and Ricco came out.

"Forget it, Carmine," Bolan shouted from ten feet away to the rear of the small truck. The Mafia guncock suddenly swung around, his .38 snarling.

The 93-R coughed once and Carmine Ricco paid his final dues with a lethal 9mm slug ripping through his neck, smashing his spinal column.

Behind Bolan, near the new car rotunda, a new player entered the game. Three shots hit the concrete near Bolan and whined into the cars beyond. The sound was familiar, an M-16 on single shot. It could be a civilian model so it would fire only single rounds.

The Executioner rolled away, sprinted behind the small pickup, the rear wheel protecting his feet and legs. He could not see the sniper. Watching carefully for a reaction over the box of the pickup, Bolan pounded his hand on the rig's sheet metal.

Two muzzle-flashes winked from the other side of the area. Bolan flicked the Beretta's selection lever to automatic and drilled two 3-round bursts in the direction of the ambusher.

No reaction. The Executioner crouched and moved to the front wheels, keeping his eyes on the showroom rotunda. No return fire.

Suddenly floodlights snapped on overhead, and Bolan took in the entire scene, the dead man on the concrete, the wrecked cars, the gate, the rotunda and the tall figure of Darrell Hudson frozen beside the Coke machine.

He saw the last gunman with the black M-16 disappearing behind a car outside the service stalls.

A minute later a bull horn blasted at them.

"Attention, this is the police. Put down your weapons and lie flat on the concrete. The area is surrounded."

The big guy cursed. Things should have happened faster than this; he should have been gone before the police arrived. Now it would be harder. He saw the man with the M-16 rush across an open space. Bolan fired at the fleeing figure, but the man dived behind a wrecked Mercury.

The attacker was moving toward him. Let the police wait a while. Bolan pulled a hand grenade from his pocket. Worth a try.

The gutsy Mob rifleman was working his way forward between parked cars along the front of the service-stall building. He was forty yards away now. Bolan saw a police searchlight stabbing into the compound. No problem, yet.

The rifleman paused, then rushed to the next car. Bolan let him come in range. The Executioner pulled the pin and tossed the explosive. He kept the throw low so it would hit and roll on the concrete. The grenade bounced once, then rolled past the second car and under the third. It exploded six feet from the rifleman, ripping into his ankles and felling him.

A second later the gasoline in the car's tank blew up in a gushing, fiery roar. The flaming fuel flowed to the next new model car and in seconds it, too, exploded. Bolan moved from his position near the pickup and rushed to the van. He jumped into the cab and cranked the ignition. The motor of the partially wrecked maxivan spluttered to life and Bolan slammed into reverse and hit the pedal. The rig screeched as it pulled loose from the T-Bird.

Another new car exploded, and he could hear more sirens. In the firelight he saw Hudson running one way and then the other.

Bolan jerked the wheel, aiming the battered front end of the white van at the drug dealer. Hudson ran across the lot, but saw only the locked doors of the service bays. He turned and ran toward the opening at the end of the row of new cars that had blocked Bolan's first dash for freedom. As Hudson approached it a Tempo exploded, showering burning gasoline for fifty feet.

Hudson stumbled into the deadly rain. His clothes caught fire and he tripped and fell into a raging pool of gasoline. His hair ignited and burned away in seconds. His shoulder hit the concrete where the burning gasoline flamed up, and his scream was choked off as the superheated air seared his lungs, snuffing out his life.

Bolan turned the van toward the narrow exit hole in the line of demonstrator cars. More cars exploded as the newly filled gasoline tanks blossomed like exotic flowers.

A cop stood in the opening between the cars holding up his hand. Bolan gunned the motor and raced for the opening. He beat the explosions there and the cop had second thoughts as he leaped out of the way.

The Executioner penetrated the row of cars and bumped over a curb. He heard police bullets hitting the van. Bolan twisted the wheel sharply to the right, racing down the street. He had no lights. In his rearview mirror he saw two police cars pull out and give chase.

He tore around a corner and through an alley. At the end of th alley he swerved to the right and up a dimly lit street. Suddenly he braked hard and turned into a driveway between two residential buildings. He killed the engine. A moment later both police cruisers screeched into the street and roared past his hiding place.

Bolan started the engine, backed out and drove the opposite way to the police. As he drove into the night, he realized he was carrying a six-million-dollar cargo.

It took him half an hour to find a public park with a fountain that was running full force. He walked to the back of the van and looked for the cocaine. Inside two cardboard apple boxes he found two-pound packages of the white powder.

Carefully he slit open each container and dumped the powder into the fountain, watching it dissolve. Fresh water kept flowing, washing away the saturated solution.

After twenty minutes he had dissolved all of it. He shook some from one plastic wrapper and left a trail of the coke on the fountain's cement wall. Bolan used a nearby pay phone and told the police where they could find the wrappers on six million dollars' worth of coke, and the highest fountain in the world. Then he caught a taxi back to the Fairway Ford dealership and joined the crowd watching the fire. The blaze had spread to two of the buildings and enveloped half the new and used cars on the three lots.

Mack had one more call to make. The second half of the pipeline in Denver was one Oliver Smith. Smith called himself a lawyer, and had a practice of sorts, but primarily he was the drug man for Denver where there was little real Mafia organization.

Smith lived in a luxury downtown condo.

Bolan walked away from the crowd to his rented car. It was just after midnight when he got to the high rise. After waiting a few minutes, he slipped through the self-locking front door with a pair of slightly drunk residents and took the elevator to the tenth floor.

The suite was easy to find and Bolan made short work of the high-security lock.

Inside, the apartment was modern and expensive. The bedroom was on the far side of the five-room setup.

Bolan sensed someone to his left and started to reach for the Beretta when a slender, well-built brunette came toward him. She was naked.

"Hi, thought I heard someone come in. Is Oli expecting you?"

"It's a surprise. But you're a nicer surprise."

She smiled. "Thanks. Oli is in here."

Oli was also naked, lying on the bed reading. He jumped up quickly when he saw Mack.

"Who are you?"

"Boys from Chicago are not happy, Oli. Things went bad tonight. You heard about Hudson?"

"How could I miss it. It's all over the TV news."

"You're the tab on the six mill, Oli."

"No way! I never guarantee. Who the fuck are you?"

"Miss," Bolan said to the girl, "why don't you—" Bolan checked himself. He was about to say "take a powder." But he figured with all this cocaine business going down, she just might take him literally. "Why don't you fix your face or something."

She pouted, then shrugged. Her breasts danced delightfully. "If I have to."

Oli nodded quickly.

When she was gone, Bolan flipped back his jacket, took out the Beretta and checked it, then put it away.

"Oli, it's not important who I am. I need the

latest upstream contact on the pipeline. The quicker you lay out the route for me, the better."

"Hell, we haven't had trouble here in two, three years. Why now?" He got off the bed and pulled on a pair of slacks. He seemed compliant. He went out to a small desk in the living room and took out a notebook and nervously leafed through it.

"The hard hop is getting the goods here to Denver. We do that by car or truck because the private planes are watched carefully at the airports around San Diego. Now it's a straight run. Lots of shit goes through to Salt Lake. It's another pipeline branch. They truck it there, and then fly it out in private jets."

"Who's the major connection in San Diego?"

"Anyone bringing stuff over the border deals with Manny "The Mover" Marcello. Or else they're in deep trouble."

"What's your delivery schedule like? Any problems?"

"I told you. No trouble for three years now. Twice a month like clockwork. The boys in Chicago always keep carping on being regular."

"Thanks, Oli. Who's the bird, yours?"

"Hell, no. Some fancy hooker. Five hundred for the night, if you can believe that."

"Looks like she's worth it."

"She's yours. I'm shot for the night, anyway."

"Such a waste."

"Who, her?"

"No, you, Oli. The Outfit wonders if you've

been dealing on the side. You know they don't appreciate that.''

Sweat beaded Smith's forehead and a wild look crossed his face. He had suddenly realized the big dude he'd just spilled his guts to had nothing to do with the Outfit.

Oliver Smith rushed Bolan, who was standing in front of the open sliding door of the balcony. The Executioner anticipated the wild charge and sidestepped neatly, hammering the back of Smith's head as he raced past. The impact of the blow hurled the Denver drug dealer over the balcony railing.

In the darkness the screaming, tumbling figure was soon lost from view and a few moments later Bolan heard a dull thud that cut off the chilling cry as Smith's body hit the concrete apron ten floors below.

Bolan advised the girl to get dressed as there could be some cops there before long. He stepped out of the apartment and toward the stairway exit. No one saw the big man leave by the side door.

Salt Lake City was his next stop.

22

Angela Marcello and her three conspirators had discussed their plan in great detail, examining the potential pitfalls and the benefits. They had agreed that it would work, make a lot of money, and they could do it on their own.

To research the project they spent four days in Acapulco. The hotel where they stayed was well connected with the Mafia, and the four were treated like princesses.

The cost of the rooms, cabs, food and shopping in the hotel store were all complimentary to San Diego's Don Marcello. Angela realized this meant her father owned part of the hotel or had something to do with the operation. The conspirators moved cautiously and laid out trails of stories about how hard it was to get into the U.S. legally, and how to do it any other way was dangerous.

Slowly they found sympathetic ears and made contact with a high-powered coyote, a man called Juan Morales, who needed transportation for well-paying border crashers.

The girls had figured their costs and expenses and set the price at a minimum of ten thousand dollars per person. This meant they would be catering to the wealthy who for some reason could not get legal entry, and who would pay the price for a jet trip from Acapulco to San Diego without the formality of immigration or customs.

By the end of the four days Juan Morales said he already had two customers lined up, and within a week he could have two more.

On the Aeromexico flight returning to San Diego the four members of the Hard Corps talked softly.

"It's easy," Angela said. "We can use daddy's plane for the first couple of trips at least. We may want to lease a jet after that. The critical part is the pilot."

"Your father has a pilot, I've met him," Mimi said.

"Yes, and a good one," Angela continued. "His name is Dale Ingles, and he's kind of a friend. I'll talk to Dale. Remember that he's hungry, he's in debt, he's an excellent pilot and he's good looking."

"The only problem will be crossing the border and getting that far down and back without some air controller wondering what happened to us," Gemma said. "I've taken some flying lessons, they get sticky about going across the border."

"That's why we have to do it under the radar."

"And we'll have to file a flight plan, maybe somewhere along the border," Gemma said.

They discussed other money-making ideas, even

starting a fancy call-girl operation, but decided it was too risky, because so many people became involved.

They arrived at San Diego's Lindbergh Field in the afternoon and that night Angela phoned Dale Ingles. She told him she was on a hush-hush project and had to talk to him immediately. They met in the parking lot near the croquet courts in Balboa Park. As soon as she parked beside his yellow Corvette, he got into her car.

Dale was six feet tall, thirty-four, single and the athletic type. Angela thought he was gorgeous. He had soft brown hair and a good-looking face with wide-set blue eyes and a firm chin.

"Now, princess, what's all this cloak-and-dagger stuff?"

She reached over and planted a long, hot kiss on his lips. When she pulled away, she giggled in the darkness. "Now you can't tell daddy or I'll say you tried to rape me."

"No sweat. I work for the construction company. Still, I don't want your old man mad at me."

"Good, snuggle up so if anybody sees us they'll think we're making out. We have to talk."

He put his arm around her and she did the snuggling. She outlined the plan for him, and right away he was shaking his head.

"First, you're planning too big. The jet just could not dip under radar far enough to be safe. Acapulco is too far down for good security." She frowned, then turned and kissed him again, probing with her tongue. After a while he pushed her gently away from him.

"Border crossings happen all the time," he said. "but with small planes. They fly about twenty feet off the sagebrush. The only way you can pull the same scam is to have your buddy in Acapulco fly them to Tijuana just across the border here from San Diego. Then they take a ride in a limo on a 'sight-seeing' trip along the international boundary toward Tecate. We'll pick them up on a strip of dirt road, and clip the cactus flying them back across. Land on another dirt road on the U.S. side to meet another car and they are in free and clear."

"Why is your plan better?" she asked.

"We don't risk a million-dollar plane. We have a shorter trip, and we can fly lower, slower and safer with a four-place puddle jumper. I also could get a cover by saying I was teaching you to fly."

She traced her fingers along his thigh.

"Dale, you're right, we'll make some adjustments. We can move only two persons at a time, right? We'll set up our landing sites on both sides of the border."

"Now tell me what the hell all this is about. You certainly don't need the bread."

"Daddy and all the old Mafiosi are so down on us it stinks. We want to show them that we're more than their little princesses."

"Sounds like fun."

"Great. You'll be paid well, Dale, a percentage." She smiled and kissed him again. "And there's a bonus for each trip."

She took his hand and pushed it inside her blouse. His hand fondled her bare breasts.

"This is payment in advance." She found his mouth and opened hers against his, sliding sideways in the seat and hiking up her skirt.

"Right here?" he said when their lips parted.

"You think of a better place where daddy won't know about it?"

"Cops come around."

"We don't have to undress."

"You're wild, you know that?"

"So let's get to the fun part," she said.

THE NEXT MORNING Angela flew to Acapulco. She made the arrangements there with Juan Morales and flew back so she was home in the big house before dark. Juan would bring the first two customers the next day. On a map she sketched the route the dirt road took on the Mexican side of the border between the California towns of Potrero and Campo.

That night in Angela's apartment in the Marcello house, the girls gathered for champagne.

Felicia lifted her glass. "To our leader, who got the first shot at Dale our pilot and scored!"

They kept toasting one another and soon they were giggling and planning other ventures. Juan would call one of them when he had two passengers. If he had more than a pair, then additional trips would be made in one day. The price was cut to five thousand dollars per person, with Juan charging the customer for his end of the transport.

As Angela thought of it, defying her father, risking prison for committing a felony, she sensed the same sharp sexual thrill pound through her that she'd felt when the trucker had been tortured.

DALE INGLES WAS WAITING at the Brown Field airport at the southernmost part of San Diego near the border. Hartson's Flying Service had the four-seater Cessna ready. Angela had never flown in a small plane before.

They rumbled down the runway and took off into the unclouded sky.

"The car on our side of the border—is it waiting on that dirt road we found?" Dale asked.

"Yes. Felicia and I drove down here this morning. She knows exactly where it is."

He pushed a cloth-wrapped item at her where she sat beside him at the dual controls. "You wanted this."

She unwrapped the heavy package and saw the gun.

"Be careful, it's loaded. It's a Wilkinson 'Diane' .25-caliber automatic pistol. Six shots in the magazine and you can carry one in the chamber. Only has a two-inch barrel, which means don't try to hit anything over three or four feet away."

"I've never fired a gun."

"I figured that. After we send our passengers off in the car on the U.S. side, we'll do some practice shooting. It's not too heavy. It's only four inches long and weighs just three-quarters of a pound."

"Sure you're not a gun salesman?"

"Nope, but you owe me a hundred dollars for it."

"I'll pay. Where are we?"

"Crawling up the Sweetwater River above Otay Reservoir giving the radar guys an idea we're sightseeing. In a while we'll slip into a few canyons, scare some rabbits and wind up across the border, sight unseen."

"Won't the border patrol be watching?"

"They can't watch everyone. The few planes they have are used to track big spenders who hire DC-3s to pack in five tons of marijuana, or a business jet loaded with twenty million dollars' worth of coke."

"Where's the border?"

"It's down there somewhere. It's a three-strand, barbed-wire fence. Most of the fence is forty to fifty years old."

"This looks easy."

"It's easier if you don't get caught."

After a few minutes of very low flying through canyon country, they climbed slightly and then saw a black car parked on a dirt road with a man sitting on the front fender. It was the signal. The road ran straight for half a mile. The pilot checked the wind, cut his speed and prepared to land.

He brought the Cessna down in the middle of the dirt road and rolled to a stop. The black car sat fifty feet ahead of them.

Morales came running up, then waved and a man and a woman got out of the car and came toward the plane. Each carried an expensive folding suitcase. Both were dressed well. They were Arabs.

Angela held out her hand and the man handed her ten bank-wrapped bundles of hundred-dollar bills.

"Ten one-hundred dollar bills in each packet," the Arab said in a deep, cultured voice with a slight British accent.

Angela riffled through the stacks to be sure they were all hundreds.

"Do you have weapons?" she said.

"No, of course not," the woman replied.

Dale helped them stow their suitcases behind the seat and assisted them through the door.

A moment later they were all inside. Juan smiled.

"Maybe something in two or three days. I call." He turned and ran back to his car.

The pilot steered the plane into the wind and they took off. There was no conversation. They kept extremely low as they flew back over the border, then slanted inland to Highway 94 and followed it for several miles.

"To the right," Angela said. "I remember that ridge line."

Just over a small hill they found a dark blue car sitting in the shade of a tree. It was parked beside a straight dirt road with a strong but reasonably flat surface. A cross wind buffeted the plane off course for a moment, then Ingles corrected the problem with a side slip and put the wheels on the dirt road.

Felicia was up to the plane almost before it stopped rolling.

"You crazy broad! We did it!" Felicia was jumping and yelling, her shoulder-length hair flying in every direction.

"Naturally," Angela said. The transfer was made with the couple safely into the car. Felicia came back to the plane.

"Hey, what a handsome man. Arab, isn't he? They want to go to the airport in San Diego, which is fine by me. See you guys at our assembly point. Get Mimi and Gemma there, too."

Felicia ran for the car. She set out on the drive back to the hard-surfaced Highway 94 that led to San Diego.

Dale Ingles came around the plane with a box of shells.

"Let's see if you can fire that thing." He showed her where the safety was. She closed her eyes, pointed the automatic at a tree, held it at arm's length and pulled the trigger. It went off with a crack. She missed.

Ingles took over and gave her basic training on firearms and the use of a pistol. He made her fire three magazines. By the time they were empty, she could hit the tree trunk from twenty feet away.

Then he showed her how to load the weapon and keep the safety in the On position. He had a soft, leather holster bag with a snap top that hid the pistol but made it easy to get at in her purse.

Ingles looked at his watch.

"We ought to move out of here."

"No time to fool around in the back seat?"

"No time and no room."

"Next time I'll bring a blanket."

They had an uneventful flight back through the canyons and took a loop around the Otay Reservoir. Then they landed at Brown Field.

Angela handed the pilot two packages of bills. "Twenty percent for you and you pay for the plane rent, right? And here's a hundred for the automatic."

"Pleasure working with you," he said. They taxied back to the agency and both got out. He went to the office. She walked to her car, got in and drove away.

She sang all the way back to town. She called Mimi. The celebration was at her place.

23

Just before 11:00 A.M., Johnny picked up his extension phone at the Killinger law offices.

"Hello."

"And a good morning to you, too, Johnny Gray. This is Angela. I still owe you that dinner. How about lunch instead, right now?"

"You sound excited."

"Is it that obvious? I am feeling good, and I want to pay my debt."

"You don't owe me anything."

"Please, Johnny. We'll do what you want. How about a sail in the bay on our twenty-seven footer?"

"Sailboat? No motor?"

"You sail it home or you swim and push it."

"I have all this work piled up."

"Sailor, the work will be there forever. You miss this day, you can never get it back!"

"There's something else. I know that your last name is Marcello."

"So?"

"So your father is Manny 'The Mover' Marcello."

"What's that got to do with anything?"

He was quiet.

"You can at least have the courtesy to insult me to my face. Don't be a coward, Johnny. Let's have lunch and we'll get this all talked out. I'll be there in ten minutes. Meet me in front of your office, okay?"

Johnny hung up the phone. He had sworn he would not see her again. She was Mafia. What in hell was he doing? He would talk and ride around a little, tell her he was not going to see her anymore and get out of the car. Quick and simple.

A half hour later, they sat on a blanket on the grass at Harbor Island watching the sailboats skimming over the big San Diego bay. A Navy destroyer powered silently down channel toward the sea two miles away.

It had not been simple.

She had on a low-cut white blouse and a billowing Hawaiian print skirt and she looked like an angel. As soon as he got in the car she kissed him and told him she could explain everything. Before he knew it he was helping her spread out the picnic lunch.

"Johnny, I am not what my father is. That Mafia crap is nonsense anyway. My father is a businessman. You damn gringos wouldn't know a Mafia hood from a Sicilian olive-oil merchant."

She grinned at him. "Damn, I wish we were alone somewhere!" She reached over and caught his hand.

"No, Angela, I'm only here to talk, to tell you why I'm not going to see you anymore."

"You don't really want to get rid of me, Johnny. You said you liked me, that I was beautiful. And I am rich. Want me to buy you a sailboat, that thirty-seven footer? I could."

"No, I don't want a sailboat. Angela, the Mafia caused three members of my family to die."

He held up his hand when she moved toward him.

"No. No more. I know you're a Mafia princess. Someone who works for your father beat up a friend of mine, almost killed him. Right now I'm caught up in a situation where I can't do anything about it. But at least I don't have to be seen with the daughter of the man who ordered the beating."

She still had a smile on her face, still trying. Johnny Bolan Gray stood up and walked away. He hoped he would never see the girl again.

KARL DARLOW EASED THE *Flying Fool* around the last buoy into the commercial basin and slid her to a gentle landing at his spot off the H & M pier. He and Poke had taken a test run, and he felt good. His chest pains were almost gone. The scars on his chest were not quite healed, but the flesh was firm.

They had done some trolling for big yellows and found a few, but he was not ready yet to pole them over the side. They had the small catch in boxes ready for the dock. Poke would handle that.

Karl wanted to get back to Lewy's bar and tell his friends that he was back in action. Hell, he'd make them all buy a round. Besides, the run had made him thirsty.

Inside the dockside bar, Karl's friends were happy to see him and the drinks were flowing freely. The drunker the men got, the taller the fish stories became.

"You see some damn strange things out fishing. Hey, I tell you about the rust-bucket freighter I saw?" Karl put both hands over his face and peeked through his fingers. "Damn, not suppose to talk about it, but what the hell, you guys my buddies. This damn freighter makes a meet with a powerboat, little twenty-four footer, and they take something on board. Not more than five miles off San Diego here. Got to be smuggling something. Coast Guard can't search every sport boat and private gig that comes into the bay. Hell, think what musta been in them boxes!"

Karl suddenly fell silent. He shook his head and pushed his glass away. "Got to go fellas. If my daughter and her boyfriend find out I've been drinking, I'll be in one heap of trouble."

Karl stood up and with as much dignity as he could, headed for the door. He made it, only hitting one shoulder on the casing as he stepped into the early afternoon sunshine.

Now where did he leave his pickup? He saw it on the street three cars down. When he got there a man was sitting in the driver's seat.

"Boys said I should take you home, Karl. Give me your keys."

"Huh? Oh, yeah, probab...probably right." He finally found the keys in his pocket and dropped them into the big man's hands. Karl stared at the guy, but was not sure who he was. Something about the hulking shoulders seemed familiar but he couldn't pin it down.

Karl leaned back in the seat. "Damn nice... boys do this. They pay you?"

"No, Karl. We're just your buddies, us fishermen got to stick together, right?"

"Damn nice."

The man started the pickup and shifted into gear.

Karl shook his head to clear it. He knew he should have cut off the booze, but he was having a good time with the boys. Maybe he had said too much. Too much about that damned rust-bucket freighter! He stared at the man driving.

The driver looked back at him. "You all right? You look a little sick."

"Need to stop," Karl said, trying to get his brain in gear. "Feeling sick." He looked out the window. "Hey, this ain't the way to my place!"

"No kidding," the driver said.

"Stop!" Karl said. Fear had sobered him up fast.

"Not a chance."

Karl lunged at him. It did not matter now, a car wreck or a slug in the back of the head. This way he would have a chance.

The pickup was on Rosecrans Boulevard, a four-lane road leading to the end of Point Loma. Karl slammed into the driver, who tugged the wheel to the left, narrowly missing a sedan. He steadied the car in the left lane before it crossed the center line.

The Mafia man shoved Karl back with his right forearm, then hit him with a backhanded fist that drove Karl to the far door. A .45 appeared in the driver's hand, the snout pointed at Karl.

"You want to buy it right here, old man? You move once more and I drill you! Now sit still or I'll blow you away."

Karl sat back in the seat. He had to think. He was frightened and confused. He tried his pockets. A penknife with folding blade. Useless. Knife? Slowly he let his hand move to his belt on his right side. The sheath hung there, and the eight-inch filleting knife nestled inside it.

Karl shifted his weight. Keep talking. He loosened the knife with his right hand as the driver turned of Rosecrans and held it beside his leg out of sight.

"Who are you? What do you want of me?"

The man shrugged. He headed up Canon Street, which led to Catalina and out to the end of Point Loma and the old lighthouse and observation area.

Karl waited. There would be a better time.

"Where we going?"

"Where does it look like we're going?"

Karl was quiet. There was not much of an opportunity to surprise the goon. He had the .45 in his right hand, steering with his left. Karl might get halfway across the seat. The blade would have to go through his side and all the way to his heart. Slim chance.

Wait.

Karl watched Point Loma and the land mass he had seen for years from below. He usually did not notice all the white grave markers in the military cemetery. Thousands of them. It was still light. Maybe four o'clock.

The pickup wound up the hill to the end of the road on Point Loma. The driver turned into the lower parking lot near the observation building and parked near some brush where a trail led away to the rim. There were no other cars in this lot and only a few in the lot above, nearer to the center.

"You do exactly as I say, old man. Now get out on this side."

Karl huddled at his side of the seat.

"Come on, grandpa, get over here." The killer had stepped out of the pickup, and Karl began edging across the seat. He moved slowly, keeping the blade under his right thigh and out of sight. At the door, Karl looked up.

"I'm dizzy. Give me a hand or I'll fall."

"Who cares?"

"Hell, you gonna have to carry me." Karl rested on the edge of the seat, his hand gripping the handle of the filleting knife.

The goon took a step toward the car. Karl lunged outward. He thrust the knife ahead of him, locked his wrist and elbow and drove toward the guy's chest. The blade punctured the jacket, grated across a rib and drove inward.

The Mafia snuff man screamed and staggered. Karl pushed off the edge of the seat, driving the big man backward until he stumbled. The thin-bladed, razor-sharp filleting knife sank to the hilt as the two men tumbled to the paved parking lot. The man stared at the knife handle growing from his chest. Blood seeped from his mouth. Then he lifted the .45 and before Karl had time to roll away the Mafia soldier shot Karl Darlow in the belly.

He pitched away from the hoodlum, clutching at the big hole in his bowels.

Karl struggled up to one elbow. His gut hurt, burned like it was on fire. The Mafia goon lifted the .45 again, but Karl used all his remaining strength and kicked the weapon out of the killer's hand. It tumbled out of reach.

At that moment a car drove into the parking lot. Doors slammed and a couple in their twenties laughed and talked as they ran toward the trail leading up to the center.

Karl looked up and for a moment thought he saw Sandy and Johnny. Then he knew it was someone else.

"Holy motha!" the youth said as he saw the two men, a knife handle protruding from the younger man's chest, the old guy gripping his stomach, his fingers dripping blood. The girl hung back but the man edged closer.

"Help me!" Karl said weakly.

The boy knelt beside him.

"Get...help," Karl said.

The young man turned to his girlfriend. "Kathy! Run up to the center and tell them to call the paramedics and the police! Two men are hurt bad, one shot, one stabbed. Run!"

The girl left, eyes wide, terror etching her pretty young face.

The stranger removed his Windbreaker and placed it under Karl's head.

Karl sighed. It did not hurt so much anymore.

"The...Mafia goon?" Karl asked.

"He sure looks dead to me. He's Mafia?"

"Hit man," Karl replied, grimacing. A thin trickle of blood escaped through his lips. "Said he would drive me home in my rig. Then pulled that gun and drove my pickup up here."

"Please don't try to talk. The paramedics will be here soon."

Karl blinked in the sunshine. He felt weak. He was thinking about his boat. How it would be a good season once his chest healed a little more. Felt damn good to be out there on the water again today.

He loved to fish more than anything. Fishing had been his whole life.

A jolting, searing pain slammed through his body and Karl gritted his teeth.

"Steady. Help's on the way," the young man said. "What's your name?"

"Karl."

"Karl, just try to breathe slow and easy. You'll make it."

"Don't think so. That .45 cut a big hole in my gut."

"These paramedics are great," the boy said. His voice broke and tears tracked down his cheeks.

Karl took a big breath. It did not matter anymore. He felt as if he was dreaming. The voices around him kept filtering in and out of his consciousness. He wanted to say hello to the crowd, to smile and wave at them, but he knew he could not.

He heard a siren. Medics coming. Too late. He looked up and realized the sun was still shining. For a moment a dark shadow passed over him. It felt cold. Strange, he had been sweating a moment before.

The shadow came back.

Karl saw two white-coated figures kneeling next to him.

They looked at the boy who held Karl's head.

"Look at Karl first, I think the other one's dead. Karl's got a .45 round in his belly."

Karl heard the anxiety in the medic's voice as someone fumbled to unbutton his shirt and trousers.

There was no hurry. Karl could tell them that.

Only he was not sure he could talk. He could see them, the worried faces. The pretty girl who came first was at the edge of the crowd. She was crying. Karl looked up at the youth who held him.

"Thanks," Karl said, his voice only a whisper. The young man heard and nodded, his youthful tears coming freely now.

The medics checked the hoodlum and put a blanket over him covering his face.

Two police cars rolled into the parking lot. Karl had not heard the sirens. He saw the red lights blinking. Slowly he realized he could not hear anything. Lips moved but he heard nothing. The light faded again, then came back. He blinked and saw the paramedic's lips move.

Briefly Karl thought about Sandy. He hated like hell to leave her, but Johnny would take care of her.

For a moment Karl felt as if he was floating above the scene. He could see it all, a bird's eye view. Somehow he had become detached from his body, hovering in the air. He could still see his body below him on the ground, the paramedics, the blanketed hit man, the cop cars, the white van.

The paramedic looked up at his co-worker as he removed the stethoscope from his ears. Then he shook his head.

As Karl watched, the scene below him faded to total blackness.

24

An hour after Karl Darlow died, the San Diego Police contacted Sandy at her office. Her work number had been listed in his billfold as next of kin. She called Johnny at once and told him what had happened. He said he would come right down and pick her up at the Home Federal Building.

Johnny was so enraged he almost sideswiped a bus on his drive the few blocks downtown. He sceamed at the driver who cut him off and at once steered to the curb and parked for a minute, taking in deep breaths and wiping the tears from his eyes with the back of his hand.

He had thought Karl was out of danger, that the Mafia had decided he either did not see anything incriminating or that he had decided to keep quiet about it. Now what? They could know nothing of Sandy, she was safe.

Johnny wanted to see the police report, talk to any witnesses. Hc would demand to know exactly what had happened. Now there was nothing to stop his investigation. He would dig into it until they came after him. He shook his head. Not that way, they would just kill him and forget about it. He had to make a plan.

First Sandy, she came before anything else.

He saw her standing on the sidewalk in front of the Home Federal Building on Broadway. She saw him and ran to the car. Sandy got in and they drove. Her eyes were red and swollen.

Sandy leaned against him and he turned down Sixth until he found a place to park.

She was crying. He held her tightly and kissed her hair.

"Why?" she asked tremulously.

"They were afraid of what he knew, or thought he knew. And they're going to pay."

"No!" She pushed away from him. "Johnny Gray, you are going to do nothing, do you hear me? We do what the police said and we drop it. They killed one man I loved. I won't stand for them killing the second!"

He put his arms around her and they sat that way for five minutes. Her sobs diminished.

"They said we had to go to the...to identify...."

"Yes. I'll do it."

Johnny knew where to go. He tried to talk Sandy out of the identification. He could do it. She insisted.

"I want to see him once more. Then...then cremation. He always said he wanted his ashes scattered over the Pacific. We can go out on the boat with Poke."

In the morgue Sandy stood weeping silently, looking at her father's relaxed face. Then she nodded, and Johnny helped her out of the room.

Johnny put Sandy down to bed when they arrived home. There would be no dinner that night. When Sandy went to sleep, Johnny called a cop he knew on the night desk at the downtown police station.

The officer read a copy of the report to Johnny before the watch sergeant came back.

"What was the other dead man's name?" Johnny asked.

"Ted Young," the officer replied, and Johnny thanked him and put down the phone.

He sat at the little kitchen table staring at the wall. He knew exactly what he wanted to do. Take a .45 and walk into Manny Marcello's office and blow his brains out. But that would be suicide. Besides, there wasn't a chance that he could even get close to the big man.

What could he do? Sandy said do nothing. Let it lie.

He could not function that way.

He would have to exercise patience.

Somewhere down the road there would be a time and a place.

The Mafia would pay!

25

Two days after the Hard Corps' celebration over their initiation into crime, Angela contacted Dale Ingles for another smuggling job across the border.

She had had a stormy session with her father and had talked him into letting her take flying instructions. Manny had laid down a take-it-or-leave-it requirement: the lessons must be given by his own pilot, Dale Ingles.

Angela had bristled at the suggestion and argued for a moment, then conceded, laughing inside all the time at the neat way she had fooled her father.

Now they landed at another spot along the border. Each pickup was at a different location so locals or border watchers could not establish a pattern. So far they had made four successful trips, and the Hard Corps coffers had grown considerably.

This time when Morales walked up to the plane after it stopped on the dirt road, he looked nervous.

"Only one hombre this time," he said. "When I

tell him the price, he no say nothing. He carry a heavy suitcase."

"Dope?"

"He is Colombian, *señorita*. I think it is co-caine."

Angela set her pretty mouth. "Bring him over and we'll talk." Bargain for a higher price, she thought.

The man was small, and darker than Juan.

"Do you speak English?" she asked.

"No speak," he said.

"Tell him to pick up his suitcase," Angela told Juan.

The dark man did.

She walked up to him and frisked him complete-ly.

She lifted her small automatic and aimed it at the passenger.

"He's got a hideout gun in his shorts, Juan. Take it away from him or no ride."

Juan chattered at the man a moment in Spanish, then the Colombian unzipped his pants and pulled a small revolver from a holster on the inside of his thigh. Dale took the weapon.

"Tell him he'll get it back when we cross the border." Then they haggled, through Juan. At last they established thirty thousand dollars for the price of the crossing. It was a bargain, Angela thought. He probably had two million dollars' street-value worth of cocaine in the heavy suitcase.

The trip went off without a hitch. Mimi had the

car and drove him to the Intercontinental Hotel near the bay. He could afford it.

Juan said he had another client the next day. He guessed it was another dope run.

Dale had frowned. "A little wetback-smuggling don't matter," he said. "But your old man's gonna shit his pants he finds out you're running dope in. That's competition."

"What he doesn't know, won't hurt us. A couple more runs," she said.

THE NEXT DAY Angela and the pilot took off from Brown Field as usual, only this time he made her handle the dual controls.

"We're going to fly straight and level, and then you're going to work on doing S-turns, just like we should be doing if you're getting your money's worth out of lessons. And in case some border-patrol plane is watching. We've been making too many flights lately. I saw a border-patrol plane warming up when we took off. He's faster than we are, and I'm watching for him."

Angela took the controls, excitement showing on her face as she piloted the small plane.

Five minutes later Ingles took over.

"Okay, our watchbird just left us, we can get to work."

They were late arriving at the pickup point, which was farther along the border this time. The same Colombian was there. His name was Nieto. He was nervous and angry. He told Morales he was being overcharged. Juan translated for Angela.

Angela drew her small automatic and waved it at him.

"Tell the jerk he can walk across and then try to get to his hotel!"

Nieto reacted at once, and it was plain he spoke English.

Angela caught it. "Drop the bag and step back."

The South American laughed at her. She fired once into the dirt between his feet. He stopped laughing and did as she said.

"Open it, Juan. Let's see for sure what he has in his bag."

Morales hesitated, shrugged. He knew this contact was blown. The new top-quality suitcase was locked. He held out his hand for the key, which Nieto gave him.

Inside were stacks of clear plastic half-pound bags of white powder.

"Test it, Dale."

The pilot opened a pocket knife, sliced one of the bags, then licked a finger and tasted the powder. He spit quickly.

"Sure as hell ain't sugar. A-grade coke. I've done a few lines from time to time."

"So, Nieto. You still think you're overpaying?"

Angela turned and was almost too late. Nieto had drawn a six-inch knife as they concentrated on the package. He sliced Juan on the arm and lunged at Angela, the blade racing toward her left breast.

The knife was only two feet away. She jerked up the automatic and pulled the trigger four times.

The little gun bucked and the charging Colombian stopped abruptly, as if jerked back by an invisible string. The knife fell from his grasp, a surprised look in his eyes as he fell facedown in the sand.

"What the hell are you doing?" Ingles roared.

"Take out that bag you tested and give it to Juan," Angela ordered the pilot coolly. "Then close up the suitcase and let's get out of here."

She walked to Morales, pulled a scarf off her hair and looked at his arm. It was not a bad cut. She wrapped it tightly with the cloth and tied the ends.

"Gracias."

"Forget it. You know what's in that bag?"

"Sí."

"You know what it's worth?"

Morales shook his head, his eyes gleaming.

"A half pound of coke on the street is worth at least fifteen thousand dollars. Of course you need an outfit to push it and customers who can afford it."

The Mexican coyote smiled. "Do not worry, *señorita*. I shall find the customers."

"This is our last trip with you, Juan. Bury the Colombian in some gully. Welcome to the rich life."

Ingles was waiting in the plane with the suitcase. He looked at her and shook his head.

"Hell, but you are cool," he said as they took off. "You just made your bones!"

Angela shrugged. "You taught me how to use the gun, remember? He was nothing. He made a big mistake." She looked at the bag in the back seat. "About sixty-five pounds?"

"About. You're talking two million dollars on the street."

"And wholesale?" she asked.

"Half."

"That's still a million dollars! Damn, a hundred percent markup." She paused for a moment. "No time for fun today. We make the meet with the car, stash this in the trunk and don't tell Gemma what it is. I've got to come back with you or they might get wise. Is that border-patrol plane around?"

"Haven't seen one since we left Otay."

"Good, I can see Gemma and her blue Lincoln."

They landed and Gemma was more relieved than curious about no passenger.

"I would have been late for my hair appointment anyway. Do I just leave the suitcase in the car?"

"Yes. And drive carefully," Angela said. "No speeding tickets."

"You two...ah...staying here a while?"

"No, Gemma, I have to get back to town."

"Right. See you tonight."

The little plane worked its way carefully along

the gullies and ravines until they climbed higher to get over the last ridge and snake down into the Otay Reservoir area. As they did so, a four-seater plane came up on them from the side, flew even with them a hundred feet away and the pilot picked up his mike and pointed to it.

The radio chattered on the Brown Field frequency.

"Seven-seven-oh-seven, do you read me?"

"Right, I can even see you. What's happening?"

"U.S. Border Patrolman Johnson. I am notifying you of suspicion of illegal activity and request that you proceed directly to Brown Field and land for inspection."

"What if I'm heading for Lindbergh Field?"

"You'll have to divert."

"I don't get it. Just finished a little cross-country with a private student. That against the law?"

"That's what we'll find out."

Ingles hung up the mike and shrugged. "Just hassling us. They can't prove a thing."

"I'm not licensed to carry this .25 auto."

"Yeah. Neither am I."

"I'll crack the door. When our friend is looking the other way, I'll drop the automatic out."

"A small turn toward him should do it. Get ready."

The Cessna turned and the patrol plane veered away from them, heading toward Brown. Angela dropped the murder weapon out the door and relaxed. That one little problem was solved.

When they landed, there were two border-patrol inspectors waiting for them at the taxi strip. The men went over the plane carefully, found the un-eaten picnic lunch and shrugged. It took them a half hour to do the work. They did not take off any sheet metal but they made sure none was loose. At last they stood back and let them taxi the plane on to the rental agency.

After turning in the plane, which Manny was now paying for since it was for lessons, Ingles leaned on Angela's 380SL's door.

"I want half," he said.

"No way, Dale. You're a hired hand, not a partner. I'll forget you said that. And don't think you can make points with dad. Who the hell do you think I'm going to sell this coke to?"

She watched the pilot's surprised expression as he jumped out of the way when she gunned the Mercedes.

For just the briefest of moments she thought of how it had felt to kill that man. Actually there had been little feeling. It came too quickly. She knew in a microsecond that she had to shoot, and she simply brought up the weapon and fired to pre-vent the attacker from killing her. There was no shock, no remorse, no guilt. The bastard had known the odds of three against one. He deserved to die.

She drove up the freeway toward La Jolla. Now the big problem was going to be talking to her father. At first he would not believe them. She had decided all four of the Hard Corps must be there. He would not get so abusive if she had her friends there.

As she drove, Angela fine-tuned her strategy. It had to be done just right, so there could be no way for her father to refuse them. They would split the million four ways. Not bad for a couple of weeks' work.

She stepped on the gas and felt a surge of power as the German roadster responded. She couldn't wait to confront her father with the fruits of her project.

26

The Hard Corps met at the Star of the Sea Room at Anthony's on the wharf, one of the best restaurants in San Diego. Angela had summoned the other Hard Corps members to dinner as her treat at seven. The best corner table had been reserved for them.

Angela wore an elegant black dress, bare over one shoulder and most of the back. It had cost nine hundred dollars and she had worn it only once before tonight. Earlier she had asked Gemma to drive past the main house with the suitcase and Angela had stored it away in a safe place.

Now she lifted the pink champagne in the crystal stemware she had requested.

"A toast!" she said softly, and with feeling. "I propose a toast to the Hard Corps, who are only just beginning!"

They murmured approval and Angela noted that Gemma was not as enthusiastic as she had been. There might be a problem downrange with her.

"Tonight we have an appointment with Mr. Marcello at eight-thirty. I hope none of you has plans because I think you'll want to be in on this. It'll be a fascinating evening for us all."

"What's so hellishly important?" Felicia asked, flipping her shoulder-length hair around so she could see Angela better.

"That's the surprise," Angela said. "And it's good news. We'll reason with Mr. Marcello, and then we'll negotiate with him."

Gemma looked up. "Does this have anything to do with my delivery tonight at your place?"

"Yes, but let's not spoil the surprise."

Only Gemma seemed not to be listening. She stared out the window at the lights across San Diego bay, and at a large sailboat sliding past using the last of the evening breeze. There was definitely a problem with Gemma.

They ate and chattered and talked about trips coming up and trips past, and boyfriends. The dinners came and they ate, and drank more pink champagne.

Promptly at eight o'clock Angela called for the check, gave the waiter two hundred-dollar bills and did not wait for the change.

"Everyone at my place in fifteen minutes," she said, then they all went outside and scattered to their cars. Angela walked down to a no-parking zone, got into her Mercedes and drove home.

She stopped at the Marcello mansion gate and told the guard that she was expecting three girl-friends. She parked and ran to her room to check on the suitcase. It was still there.

She carried it downstairs and hid it in the closet outside of her father's den. Then she walked into the huge living room and stared at the flames in the fireplace. Her father loved a fire. Sometimes she thought he turned up the air-conditioning to make it cool enough to have the fireplace going.

At twenty-five past eight the three girls arrived. Angela met them and they all walked up to the den on the second floor and knocked on the door.

"Come!" a voice called.

Angela let Mimi go in first, then the others and she came in last. She had not told her father there would be four in the group to talk to him. He had expected only her.

"Daddy, you know my three friends." She paused as he said hello to each of them. No kiss on the cheek this time.

"We want to talk to you about something that is extremely important to us, and vital to the operation of the Family business."

"I talk Family business with men, not with four ladies who should be getting themselves married."

Felicia laughed and Manny looked at her coldly.

"Sorry, Mr. Marcello," she said. "It's just that you sound exactly like my own father."

"Daddy," Angela cut in. "We are representing a group within the Family you may not know about. It's been kept a secret from you up to now. We are not competing with you. This group is known as the Hard Corps. That's us. We have decided that since men dominate our lives and the

Family structure, we will prove to you that we can make money as well as any of your boys."

"You all should be sent to a goddamned nunnery!"

"I knew he'd say that!" Gemma said and began crying.

Manny hated to see any woman cry. It tore him to pieces. He left his chair behind the big desk and walked over to Gemma. He patted her head, then he put his arms around her.

"Don't cry, Gemma. I'll listen, even if it bores me to death."

"We've been working," Angela continued. "And in the last two weeks, we've done all right. We've earned this." She emptied her big purse on his desk.

"Mr. Marcello," Mimi said. "I know this might not seem like much to you, but we earned it all by ourselves, and none of us got into trouble."

Manny looked at the girls in surprise.

"How much is here? What did you do to earn this?"

"There's seventy-eight thousand dollars in cash. We earned it by starting an airline," Felicia said.

"An airline?"

"Right, we transported passengers," Angela added.

"That's why you wanted Dale Ingles, those damn flying lessons! Ingles will be sorry he ever got involved in this."

"It's not his fault. We threatened him that we'd tell you. And we paid him for his services."

"You ran illegals over the border, right? Important ones who would pay three or four thousand for the ride."

"Five thousand, with two passengers on each trip," Felicia said. "We know how to make money."

"What happens when you get caught?"

"We won't. Today was our last trip."

"Thank God for that. So divide up the money. Go around the world. Have fun, get married. What do you want from me now? Your little game is all over."

"Not quite, daddy." Angela went to the hall, brought in the suitcase and placed it on the floor beside him.

"We bought something today, we'd like to re-sell it to you. And of course there is room left for you to make a tidy profit."

Manny the Mover, boss of San Diego, snorted contemptuously.

Angela lifted the heavy bag and swung it to the top of her father's desk. She took a key from her purse, unlocked it and swung back the top of the suitcase.

"Sixty-five pounds of high-grade cocaine," she said softly.

"Where in hell did you get—"

Gemma broke in. "That's why we didn't have a passenger today, just his suitcase."

Manny turned to his daughter, his eyes flashing angrily. She had never seen him so furious.

"I don't suppose your passenger just gave you the junk."

"No, I shot him. He's dead."

The other girls gasped. Manny took a step backward. "You killed him?"

"Yes. He came at me with a six-inch blade. Either I died or he did. I made sure it was him."

"Would you let me talk with Angela alone, please," her father said with a chilling calm.

"No!" Angela said vehemently. "This stuff belongs to all four of us. We all talk about it. We're in the coke business for one transaction. The goods are worth two million on the street. We'll sell them to you for one million, cash."

Manny's face was now beet red. He stared at each of them.

Then he sat down in his desk chair and threw his arms wide and roared with laughter.

"You four broads are absolutely the strangest. I worked for ten years to make my first million!"

Angela leaned on the desk in front of him. "Are you buying, or do we distribute this ourselves?"

"Relax, Angelina. You've got a deal. I don't want you rounding up a crew of hustlers for the street. Hell, that could drive me right out of business."

He closed the bag and used the phone to call downstairs.

"I want these goods out of the house. None of that poison is ever to be in this house!"

"First the checks," Angela said. "Four of them at two hundred fifty thousand each."

"I don't write checks. Why don't we handle that tomorrow at Philmore Industries downtown? Or we can transfer the amounts directly, electronically, to your bank accounts."

"My banker would go into hysterics," Mimi said.

"We'll work it out. Is that okay with you businesspersons?"

They left the room, knowing that they had won a vital battle.

"Shit!" Angela said when they were down the hall. "We won!"

But on the way to Angela's rooms, Gemma burst into tears. They got her calmed down, but she was still shaking.

"I don't know for sure, but I think I'm pregnant," she moaned.

27

Mack Bolan had spent two days in Salt Lake City working out his targets and strategy. His hits were always the result of complete reconnaissance and direct assault.

As far as he could tell there was no real Mafia organization in Salt Lake City. It was undeveloped territory for the Mob. It was a way point, a connecting link in the pipeline that ferried the poison into the east and midwest. Salt Lake City was the fly-out center for the goods in an area where the Feds did not check airports as stringently as they did on the coast.

Salt Lake City is a power unto itself. It is the closest thing to a functioning theocracy in any state in the union. To be "well connected" in Utah means you must be an active Mormon, a giver and a worker for the Kingdom. The Mafia was smart when it picked Salt Lake City as a joint in the pipeline; they made sure they used a local man, a good Mormon who could be turned to their way of thinking in one small aspect—drugs.

They found the man they needed in Dick Blanchard, a well-heeled building contractor who had several aircraft of his own. He also had a sexual appetite for young boys. This fact was detailed and Blanchard was quickly blackmailed into using his construction firm as a cover for the pipeline operation. In return he received a generous amount of money and a safehouse where he could enjoy his aberrant sexual disportments.

It was a small matter for him to buy a few more aircraft and to expand into this new venture. He established a department, staffed it with one man who was local, well connected and knew exactly what was going on. The rest of the workers either did not understand what they were doing, or were non-Mormon and were sworn to secrecy with money.

Blanchard Construction Inc. owned and operated a large hangar on the edge of the Salt Lake City International Airport. In the huge building sat a twin-engine cargo plane, two sleek Lear business jets, a twin-wing replica of a Sopwith Camel that Blanchard himself flew for publicity and parades and a four-seater Beechcraft.

Bolan parked his rented Chevy outside the hangar and walked in. A mechanic came up to him at once, a foot-long wrench in one hand.

"Hey, you work here?" Bolan asked before the other man could speak. "I'm the new relief pilot on the Lear. Mr. Blanchard said I should take a look at it this morning, then do a test flight this afternoon with one of the other pilots."

The mechanic shrugged. "You got a name?"

"I'm Pete Barlow."

The mechanic stared at the Executioner for a moment, then shrugged again. "Lear 64 there is open. Take a look, but don't work any of the controls. Got some testing to do on them."

"Right."

Bolan walked over to the sleek jet. Once inside he moved to the rear of the aircraft to one of the storage compartments. Out of sight he planted a quarter-pound block of C-4 plastique. Into the soft substance he pushed a pencillike, radio-controlled detonator. One radio signal from the transmitter in his pocket, and the whole tail section of the plane would be blown off. He worked around the rest of the jet, but could find no trace of drugs of any kind.

Ten minutes later he left the jet, waved at the mechanic and said he had to go into town.

The Executioner knew that cocaine was a high-profit, low-bulk item. It was easy to hide and carry, and a large dollar amount could be shipped in a small space. Business jets were ideal for transportation and cover.

It was time to close the snare. Bolan's first call would be the Mafia connection man in town, Tony Campagna. Campagna had an office in the construction firm's new plant in the suburbs, but was seldom there. Today was his golf day.

Typically Tony liked to play golf by himself. He was a perfectionist who demanded total silence, so he always played alone.

Bolan found him on the fourteenth tee. Campagna had rolled up his golf cart and taken out a two-iron when the Executioner came up the slope behind the tee and spoke.

"Morning, Tony, they said I could find you here."

Tony spun, his hand going automatically to his chest but there was no shoulder rig there. He scowled. "Who the hell are you and whaddaya want?"

"Manners, Tony. Manners. The south side of Chicago was never like this, was it?"

Campagna's eyes flicked to his golf bag by the cart, and Bolan guessed he had a piece. But it was too far away.

"Tony, you might recognize this." Bolan tossed him a marksman's medal. Campagna caught the metal disk and looked at it. This one had a pistol bar hung below it.

Campagna dived toward his bag. Bolan got there first. Tony rolled and came to his feet, looking around wildly, trying to find an escape route, at least a chance. There was none.

"What the hell you want from me? I went straight. I ain't even connected no more."

Campagna swung the golf club and Bolan jumped back quickly. The Executioner recovered and, while the mobster was still off balance, leaped into the air in a flying dropkick. All of the fury and anger Bolan had been building up for two days exploded in the maneuver as his feet connected with the target's head. Bolan heard a snap as Campagna's neck broke and the man slid to the clipped turf.

Bolan checked for a pulse. It was extremely weak, fluttering, then it stopped. The Executioner got Tony's cart, lifted the dead Mafia goon into it, let off the brake and aimed it down the hill at a pond.

There was no one else in sight on the course. A fringe of trees protected the fairway and observation from one side, and the starkly dry desert of Utah showed across the boundary fence on the other side.

Bolan faded into the line of trees as the golf cart bumped down the slope. The cart picked up speed and rolled into the water with a splash. Bolan watched as the rig sank, showing only the tips of Campagna's expensive set of woods sticking out of his bag.

Bolan walked back to the clubhouse parking lot and eased out of there in his rented Chevy.

Next stop, Blanchard Construction corporate offices.

Twenty minutes later he parked next to the brick structure and nodded. It was a big operation that would soon get a lot smaller.

A smiling receptionist said he didn't need an appointment. Mr. Blanchard made it a policy to see anyone who came to talk. His office was two doors down.

Bolan opened the door to an office that held a

desk, secretary and two wooden benches. The lady behind the desk was blond, attractive and smiling.

"You're in luck this morning," she said. "It's a slow day. You can go right in."

She opened a door and Bolan stepped inside.

Dick Blanchard came around his big desk smiling, his hand outstretched.

"Dick Blanchard," he said. "Who do I have the pleasure—"

Bolan ignored the hand.

"Blanchard, tomorrow morning everyone is going to know about you and your games with young boys in the Walnut Avenue house. I have videotapes taken with a special camera. There is only one way your secret remains with me. Tell me everything you know about the cocaine pipeline connection the Mob has with your company."

Blanchard staggered back. It was as if he'd been hit in the head with a two-by-four. He sprawled in his big leather chair, one hand over his heart. He was no more than forty, short and balding with a reddish complexion and a potbelly hanging over his belt.

"I don't know what you're...." He could not finish it.

"You have two trucks of Mexican red tile due in here right now from San Diego by way of Tijuana, Mexico. You and I are going to meet those trucks and wash all that cocaine down the sewer."

"They made me do it," Blanchard said.

"Sure. They could force you to do anything, you slimy bastard."

Blanchard recovered his composure and pushed a button under the desk. A moment later two men came in a side door. One was blond, his T-shirt bulging with muscles. The second man was smaller, darker, and carried a businesslike .45 automatic aimed at Bolan. He grinned and walked into the room, glancing from his target to his boss.

"You ever fired that cannon?" Bolan asked.

"Want to find out?" the gunman said.

Bolan looked at Blanchard. The gunner also looked that way, and the Executioner's right foot pistoned upward. The kick caught the gunman's wrist, broke it and launched the .45 into the air. Before Muscles could catch the weapon, Bolan palmed his Beretta 93-R, covering the three of them.

Bolan squatted to pick up the .45 auto and stuck it in his belt, his eyes never leaving the trio.

He indicated the door with the gun. "You go first, Blanchard. And remember—be cool. I'm ready to kill."

Bolan turned to the other two when he and Blanchard reached the doorway. "No one will follow us. This man will live if you do not follow us."

A new Mercedes diesel sat at the end of the walk outside the side door. Bolan told him to get in the passenger side and slide behind the wheel.

"Warehouse four, I believe it is," the Executioner said.

"How did you find out?"

"Doesn't matter, Blanchard. All you need to know is that Tony Campagna won't be here to help you. He got swamped with some problems of his own and right now he's in over his head."

With Bolan's gun pointed at his crotch, Blanchard drove until they reached the large doors of the warehouse itself, half a mile across the huge storage area and equipment park. A tractor with a flatbed trailer was reversing into the building. Strapped down securely on the forty-foot flatbed were pallets of red Mexican tile.

"Get out and tell them to unload it as usual," Bolan said, concealing the 93-R.

Blanchard nodded and went out to the truck.

Two wooden boxes were taken from inside the stack of tiles. Workers moved the containers to a closed area at the rear of the big warehouse.

After Blanchard ordered the workers out, Bolan opened the crates. Both contained cocaine. The Executioner slashed the plastic bags and set each box under a shower stall in the washroom and turned on the water, sluicing the evil poison down the drain into the Salt Lake City sewer system.

As Bolan checked the last of the boxes he saw Blanchard charging into him. Bolan moved to avoid the tackle and slipped on the wet floor. By the time he was up, Blanchard had rushed out of the washroom and locked the only door.

Bolan used the silenced Beretta 93-R to blast the lock apart. By the time he was out of the building,

he saw Blanchard's car racing toward the highway. Bolan saw a company pickup sitting nearby
with the keys in it. He jumped in and charged after
the fleeing construction man.

The pickup could not match the speed of the
Mercedes, but Bolan kept the hammer down to
keep the car in sight. It was evident Blanchard was
heading for the Salt Lake City International Airport.

They turned into the airport commercial section
and Bolan was only a block behind by the time the
Mercedes slid to a stop at the Blanchard Construction Inc. hangar.

Bolan knew he had Blanchard. It would take
several minutes to get one of the jets warmed up
and ready to roll.

Then he remembered the radio in the Mercedes.
Blanchard had called ahead and the jet was already warmed up and waiting. Just as the Executioner pulled up to the hangar he saw the Lear jet
roll past him on the way to the runway. Bolan
caught a flash of the NC number. It ended in 64,
the same jet he had examined that morning.

The Lear taxied to the end of the runway, so it
could take off toward the main part of the field.
Bolan waited midway along the strip, and as the
Lear lifted off the runway, he snapped the switch
to Fire on the small black box he had taken from
his pocket.

Then he pushed the red button once and the
Lear jet in front of him exploded. The whole tail

assembly blew off, the suddenly nose-heavy jet aimed for the ground.

It exploded again as it splattered into the concrete, fuel bathing the aircraft and turning the sleek plane into a jumble of smoking rubble in seconds. No one could have survived the crash, and any drugs on board would be vaporized in the explosion and the intense heat.

Mack headed the pickup slowly back to the construction outfit. Already there were reporters and TV production trucks on the site. He slid into his rented Chevy and drove quietly out of the parking lot.

The Executioner was on schedule, slowly disabling the Mafia drug monster. The next step was to hit the beast's mouth, where the drugs were brought into the country and sent on their destructive way.

He would fly to San Diego. His target this time was Manny "The Mover" Marcello, the San Diego capo.

28

Mack Bolan stared down at the changing scenery below. The browns and grays of the desert mountains gave way to checkerboard green, then a splotch of bright blue reservoir water behind a canyon dam, and at last the man-made patterns of a few small towns.

Soon the sprawl of the big city came into view and Bolan saw San Diego clinging to the shoreline of the Pacific Ocean.

Bolan had mixed feelings and sad memories about this West Coast metropolis. His thoughts raced back in time to his combat visit to California's oldest city.

He had gone there on a "rescue" mission on behalf of a deceased former commanding officer from his Nam days. Scandal had surrounded Bolan's ex-C.O. in San Diego, and all indicators had pointed to "Howlin'" Harlan Winters's death as suicide. Bolan had been there to rescue his former mentor's name and reputation.

Now the Executioner smiled as he remembered how the men under Howlie's command in Nam had hated him. And loved him. No way could Bolan have swallowed the story of suicide. Not about the Winters he had known. And he had known the man like a second father.

Winters was the man who had tutored and directed a young sergeant in Nam until he had become the original execution specialist. And it was around Bolan's specialized abilities that the first Penetration Team was formed.

"There are no rules of warfare," the colonel used to say to Bolan. "The only rule of warfare is to win."

Bolan acknowledged the fact that his old C.O. had been knowingly involved with the Mafia. But the Executioner had not been ready to bury Winters without military honors, or without learning how much the Mob had coerced the old man into illegal, treasonous activities, before he balked. So they had set up his execution. And that was the way Bolan had read it.

The reverse thrust of the descending plane broke into Bolan's thoughts. He watched the metropolitan center speed past.

The only rule of warfare is to win!

Well, this was war. He had names—he had the biggest name of all, Manny "The Mover" Marcello, the San Diego capo.

It was a little after three in the afternoon when Bolan landed at Lindbergh Field in downtown San Diego, along the bay. He took a cab to the new Intercontinental Hotel, registered as

Mark Hill, then switched to another taxi to Philmore Industries. At the desk just off the elevator he flashed a card at a young receptionist.

"I'd like to see your vice-president in charge of accounting."

The woman studied the card. It looked genuine. Bolan had had it made in Chicago and it identified him by name and picture as Mark Hill, a senior field investigator for the Internal Revenue Service.

"Oh, I'm afraid he's gone for the day. I could let you talk to Sydney McBride, our head bookkeeper."

"Yes, if you please."

She nodded, made a call and led Bolan to the right door. He walked into a room with a bank of computer terminals around the walls and a desk in the middle. Two operators worked at the machines. A small man with red hair, a mustache and half glasses looked over the tops of the specs at Bolan.

"Yes, Mr. Hill, what can I do for you?"

"I'm with the IRS, out of San Francisco. We make spot checks from time to time that our local offices know nothing of. I'd appreciate it if this could be kept confidential."

"Come into my office, Mr. Hill."

Once in the office, Bolan checked to see that no obvious recording devices were in sight or intercoms left on, then he pushed McBride against the wall and shoved the Beretta against the surprised man's forehead.

"McBride, I need certain information from you quickly. If it's accurate you have nothing to worry about. If it isn't, you're dead meat." Bolan took the weapon away, slid it in his shoulder holster and smiled at McBride, whose face was still chalk-white.

"Do I make myself perfectly clear, Mr. McBride?"

Ten minutes later Bolan took the elevator down and out of the building. He had the names, addresses and companies he needed. He had plenty. Nothing like a bookkeeper to know everything about a firm, especially one like Philmore Industries, which was one of the thin covers for the Marcello Family operations in San Diego.

The Executioner found a rental agency and picked out a car, a new Pontiac. He gave the Intercontinental Hotel as his address, room 1804. Then he drove to a posh Italian restaurant in Mission Valley. The catery featured Italian cuisine, but it was not known for the quality of the food or the service. The availability of the waitresses and the rooms upstairs were more of a hit with the general male population.

There was also a move toward equality, and if a lady customer made the right moves she could entice one of the busboys through the beaded curtain to the stairs for a session topside. Despite police raids, the Italian Stallion restaurant flourished. For special customers there was a basement gaming room where only doubly checked-out clients were permitted. The stakes were extremely high. The profits higher.

Bolan wore his traveling clothes, gray slacks, a blue sport shirt and lightweight blue sport jacket. He wore the shirt collar open.

After a beer at the bar, Bolan motioned to the barkeep.

"I need to see Little Joe," Bolan said.

"No one here by that name."

Bolan folded a twenty-dollar bill and palmed it, handing it to the apron. "Friend, Little Joe Calabriese said I should come in tonight. I'm in from Phoenix. First time here. He said you could point me in the right direction."

"Over to the far booth, through the door past the men's room. Knock twice when nobody's looking."

The Executioner followed the bartender's directions and when no one was coming to use the john, he knocked twice. A small panel opened in the door.

"Looking for Little Joe," Bolan said.

The sliding panel closed and the door unlocked. The Executioner walked in and was met by a smiling bear of a man who blocked his further progress.

"Buddy, this is a five-thousand buy-in night."

"I know. When is the tally going up?"

"When we get too crowded at five."

Bolan took a packet of bills from his inside jacket pocket and handed them to the man, who riffled through the hundreds, then gave him a velvet bag filled with chips.

"Good luck." He moved aside and Bolan stepped past him through a soft curtain into a casino room. Nowhere did he see anyone who looked the way Little Joe Calabriese should look.

The Executioner worked the tables, placing a few bets here and there, winning now and then. The place was rigged for the house. He watched a man leave. The guy went to a small window to the rear of the big room, vanished behind a curtain and never came back. Rear exit.

Bolan worked the roulette wheel, lost half of his five thousand and wandered to the back, then went to the window. He said he had to cut out and wanted to cash in.

An Italian-looking face nodded, pointed to the curtain and Bolan went through it. Behind the curtain stood two men with side arms. Both had Mafia soldier written all over them. The glass booth from the inside was now a teller's-type cage window.

Bolan put down his velvet bag and the weasel-faced man behind the window counted the contents. There was $2410 left. The Executioner took the money, shifted it into his billfold and when his hand came out from his jacket, he was holding the Beretta. He put a round into the wall beside the first guard's head. The silent cough alerted both men who stared at the 93-R.

"Dump it out!" the Executioner barked at the cage man. "All your cash! No alarm or you die first, asshole!" Bolan growled the last warning as the teller reached for a silent alarm.

One of the guards clawed for his weapon. Bolan put a 9mm whizzer through his nose, dropping him silently in a froth of blood and brain tissue. The second goon lifted his hands and laced his fingers together on his head.

The teller dug stacks of bills from a drawer and stuffed them in a big bank bag. He repeated the movement several times and looked up.

"The rest of it or you join your friend over there," Bolan growled.

The weasel-faced man dug out more stacks of rubber-banded bills and put them in the bank bag.

"That's all of it, I swear!"

"Good." Bolan turned deliberately, giving the cashier a chance to reach for his piece. He took the bait.

When Bolan spun back, a small-caliber automatic was halfway up from the desk, the man snarling. Bolan drilled two rounds into his heart and watched him slump into the booth. The Executioner turned the knob on the outside door and took the bag of bills. He tossed a marksman's medal to the living guard.

"Tell Manny he's a dead man," Bolan said, looked out the door, then ran to the front of the establishment.

He walked to his car and drove away. Little Joe would not report the theft to the cops. And the two dead soldiers would be handled privately. Little Joe could not afford to scream about a robbery in a gambling room that did not exist.

Bolan turned onto the freeway and headed back to the downtown area. He continued out to Pacific Beach where he stopped half a block from a small outfit that advertised itself as the PB Finance Company. It was one of Manny Marcello's outfits. The Executioner threw the bank bag in the trunk of the Pontiac, and walked past the finance firm. It seemed to be open. Lights blazed from the front office. He stepped inside.

A bell rang as he entered, and feet shuffled in the back room through an open door. A moment later a man in his thirties wearing wire-rimmed glasses came out.

"Yes, sir?"

"Hey, you lend money?"

"That's the whole idea of a finance company."

"Good. I lost my job last week. My damn wife left me and now people are screaming for their money for bills. I tried a bank, but they laughed at me. Can I borrow money on a signature?"

"Maybe. We usually don't need collateral. How much you need?"

"Oh, a thousand. I'm a computer programmer,

see. And I draw down six to seven hundred a week, minimum. I'll get another job in a week or two. But I just need to get the collectors off my back for a while...." Bolan looked up with what he hoped was a confused, worried expression.

"Live here in town?"

"Sure, 1414 Fortieth Street, but I got my wallet swiped in a bar last night."

"No shit? Drive a car?"

"Yeah, Pontiac, brand-new."

"License number?"

"Hell, I don't remember. I'll drive it up here." Bolan jogged to the car, drove back and parked a space down from the store.

The finance man read the license and went back inside.

"Yeah, we can lend you a thou. Pay it back in three months and it costs you $100 for writing up the deal, plus three percent a month, or $30 a month. Total cost $190 for the three months."

"Okay! Where do I sign?"

The man pushed the pen toward Bolan. "Course, you don't pay it back in three months, there are some penalty charges."

"Yes, yeah. Okay, deal. Get the cash."

"Sign here, and here. Press hard."

The man turned to go into the back room. Bolan gave him twenty seconds to get the safe open, then scaled the counter and landed jungle-cat quiet. The Beretta was tracking. He came around the door and saw another man cleaning a revolver. The salesman was just pulling open the door of a safe. He turned, saw Bolan with the Beretta up and fumbled for his belt-holstered revolver.

Bolan shot him in the head, then swept the silenced 93-R toward the second man who had not moved after he saw the Executioner.

"Please, I've got a wife and three kids!"

That's what Pop said, Bolan thought, raw fury consuming him. "Dig out the money in the safe."

The man left his gun on the table, reached over his dead co-worker and brought out the cash. He stuffed it in a paper sack and put it on the table.

Bolan picked up the weapon, then handed him a marksman's medal. He stared at it.

"What is this?" the guard asked.

"You'll soon find out," Bolan replied. "Take that gift to Manny the Mover. But first I want you to set this place on fire. Drag your friend out if you want to."

Bolan waited until the goon torched the finance company. Then the Executioner walked to his car, and drove away as the first people on the street ran to watch the burning building. The Mob soldier slumped on the sidewalk where he had carried the corpse. He was so glad to be alive he could not remember anything but the death of his friend and the terrible talisman he clutched in his hand.

In his rearview mirror Bolan saw the jagged teeth of flames licking the night sky. Tomorrow

Manny the Mover would be damn sure the Executioner was in town. The San Diego capo was running out of time.

By the time Bolan was finished in San Diego, the Mover would be wishing he *had* moved—to another town.

29

Johnny Bolan sat at the breakfast table gazing at the *Union* morning newspaper. "HAS EXECU-TIONER RETURNED HERE?" The two-column headline leaped at Johnny from the bottom of the front page. He read the story intently.

"Law enforcement in San Diego may go on special alert today after the appearance of an Army 'marksman' medal on a murdered man in Pacific Beach last night. A witness to the kill-ing who worked at the small finance company said only that a tall, dark-haired man burst into the firm early last night and gunned down his partner.

"The tall man then forced the survivor to torch the office. San Diego firemen said the building was completely gutted, destroying all loan records and damaging small stores on each side.

"Dead is Malcolm Wilson, 36, of San Diego. His partner, Roland 'Roxie' Valenti, who listed his address as La Jolla, said the man came in ask-ing for a loan. When the safe was open, the stranger pulled a gun, cleaned out the lock box, shot Wilson and ordered Valenti to burn down the building.

"When asked if the marksman's medal meant the return of the Executioner, Valenti said he had never met the man, so he didn't know.

"Several years ago the Executioner came to San Diego and ran roughshod through organized crime figures here, resulting in many still-unsolved crimes and deaths. Some say the Executioner had declared a one-man war against the Mafia, defending those the Mafia take advantage of. He has never been known to attack or fire upon law officers.

"Neither San Diego police nor the District Attorney's office would make any comment about the possibility that the Executioner has returned.

"Reporters who covered the Executioner here before say the story sounds like his vintage work, especially leaving the marksman's medal, his trademark. The medal is an announcement and warning to organized crime members.

"Off the record, police said they were girding for more violence, and that known members of organized crime were being watched."

Johnny read it again. Sandy looked over at him.

"What's so interesting in the paper?"

He showed her. A cold sensation crept into Johnny's bones as he watched his fiancée.

"We have to move out of here, Sandy."

"Why?"

"Because of Karl."

"But...."

"The Mafia might know who we are. They might figure that your dad told you what he saw. I hope it's not too late."

Sandy's big brown eyes seemed to widen. Slowly she nodded.

"Yes, you're right. But where can we go? I know—my friend Paula from work asked if I'd baby-sit her place while she's on vacation."

Johnny and Sandy packed a suitcase and moved to the friend's condo in Mission Valley, then they both went to their jobs. All morning at the office Johnny tried to figure out how he could get in touch with Mack.

There was a break in a project he was working on with Mr. Killinger and Johnny brought up the problem in a roundabout way.

"Mr. Killinger. If the police think that this Executioner guy is fighting the Mafia, why don't they contact him and work together on it?"

Killinger shook his head. "Actually, Mack Bolan is a wanted man, probably even here in San Diego. There is no way the police could find him. He's like a shadow at midnight. I know there's one person who'll try to lure Bolan out into the open—Manny 'The Mover' Marcello."

Johnny decided not to press the point any further, in case his boss wondered why he was so interested. Johnny was stumped. If it *was* his brother wreaking havoc, Johnny would certainly like to meet him.

What about the trucking company and that other place, Philmore Industries, where he had first met Angela? That had to be a front operation. Maybe if he hung around them he could spot Mack.

That afternoon after he left the law offices, Johnny sat in his Bug half a block from the entrance to Marcello Trucking. He slid low in the seat watching every car parked near the place. He saw nothing unusual, only the early evening traffic.

Around five he decided to give it up and head back to the condo in the valley.

"You look worried, John," Sandy said, when her fiancé walked in the door.

"Yeah," Johnny mumbled bleakly. "I want to get in contact with Mack, but I don't know how. And I can't do anything that would allow the Mafia to use us for bait to get their hands on Mack."

He told her about his wasted afternoon.

"Could you logically try to figure out his moves?"

"That's precisely the problem, logic. I'm not sure I know how he thinks. We'll probably hear about it on the news. He'll be busy somewhere. I've got a list of five outfits that Marcello owns. I'm going to be watching some of them tonight. The Free Legal Aid Center will to have to struggle along without me for a while."

"John, please be careful."

"Don't worry. I will. Shall we eat out?"

They ate a light dinner at a Jack in the Box restaurant and returned to the condo.

At seven Johnny left to begin his stakeout on the firms he knew the Family owned, staying from fifteen minutes to an hour, then moving on. Finally he drove out to La Jolla and parked three houses up from the mansion owned by the don of San Diego. He had found out Manny's address from Killinger's office and driven past just after he learned Angela's last name.

He studied the concrete-block wall with the barbed wire on top and he guessed it had intrusion alarms as well. The place was huge and sloped off to the rear. He figured there must be a ravine or a steep drop-off. Another good defensive feature. There were a few trees, but all had been trimmed so they did not overhang the wall from either side of the property line.

Few cars were parked on the street in this land of three- and four-car garages.

As he sat there waiting, Johnny pondered the bizarre way the Mafia slime had contaminated his family. Could it be that the moment Sam Bolan had his first dealings with the Mob, the Bolan kin became a ripe host, ready to be tainted forever? Why was the Bolan clan chosen—or condemned—to be haunted by this evil cancer? And wasn't it enough that his parents and sister had died, victims of Mob violence?

Even now it looked as if Johnny might cross paths with his brother after all these years, the events surrounding their encounter precipitated by that terrible, common link—the Mafia.

It was almost midnight when Johnny sensed rather than saw a car glide to a stop a quarter of a block behind him. The rig's lights were off. Johnny slid lower in the seat and looked in his side mirror. He saw the dome light come on and off quickly as someone got out and closed the door with no noise.

Interesting.

Johnny watched the sidewalk.

Nothing moved.

He stared at the blackness of the shrubs along the walk and just behind a three-foot hedge. There he saw a figure working slowly forward.

A burglar? If so, he must be from out of town. All of these expensive places would have electronic protection.

An owner sneaking in to avoid his wife? Maybe.

Suddenly a car's headlights penetrated the gloom. A vehicle swung around a corner a block down and rolled along the street. The figure froze behind the hedge. Johnny slid even lower in the driver's seat. The car passed.

At once the figure sprinted forward inside the hedge and came to the end of the cover two houses this side of the Marcello mansion.

His concealment gone, the dark shadow stood and walked casually past the Bug and on toward the Marcello place. At the near side of the Mafia fortress, the specter vanished into shrubs that half covered the wall. There were no security lights around either house.

Johnny sat waiting.

Had the man been Mack?

He appeared to be the right size. He wore all black, had black hair. A muscle twitched in Johnny's cheek as he tried to relax. He felt a rising excitement. It could have been Mack. A tremor ran through his shoulders and down his spine. It could be a burglar. He'd make sure.

He timed it on his watch. After five minutes Johnny stepped from the Bug. No light to worry about, the overhead bulb burned out months ago. He closed the door quietly, not latching it fully, then paced up the sidewalk away from the Marcello house, making no noise.

When he came to the intruder's car at the curb Johnny saw it was a late model Pontiac. A small "C" decal was stuck on the right front of the windshield. A rental code.

Johnny decided to wait next to the Pontiac. The instant he saw the black figure returning Johnny would move into the street and hide behind the rig. His hands were shaking, so he folded his arms tightly against his chest.

That could be Mack out there! Johnny shivered and stood, no longer able to remain still. Nervous energy made his teeth chatter for a moment. Johnny took three deep breaths and walked away from the Pontiac, away from his own car.

He walked half a block down, then back, never taking his eyes off the rig. He made the trip again and when he got back to the Pontiac he saw a black shadow moving toward him on the sidewalk. The figure had just left the darkness of the Marcello block wall.

There was no attempt at stealth this time. It was the same man. Johnny could tell by the fluid, easy gait.

He remembered Mack's athletic movements when he walked. Sudden emotion cut off the sound in Johnny's throat as he attempted to shout his brother's name.

The dark-clad figure continued to move toward Johnny. The young man tried to take a step forward, but he was frozen in place behind the car, hidden he hoped.

When he heard the man come to the driver's door, Johnny stood.

"Mack?" Johnny asked.

The man in black caught sight of him in his side vision and his head snapped up.

Then the stern resolve that had been holding Johnny in place left him, and he bolted for his car. He dashed the forty yards, leaped into the Bug, started the engine and raced away.

BEHIND HIM, Mack Bolan paused with his key halfway in the door lock. He heard a tremulous voice call his name, jerked the key out and took two steps toward the sound, but as soon as he did the man ran away.

The shock of hearing his name in this stygian gloom, followed by the strange actions of the caller, caught him off guard.

In a heartbeat the Executioner's combat senses were back to full alert, as he jumped into the Pontiac to give chase.

He saw the taillights flare ahead of him, then headlights as the car raced away.

No problem. The VW's speed was no match for his rental car.

The smaller car ahead charged down the block, took a left and headed down the hill toward La Jolla. Bolan eased in behind him, following at fifty feet, not ready to shoot out a tire, especially not in a quiet residential neighborhood like this. There would be time.

They screeched around a corner and aimed for a larger street, then another and another, until they were in downtown La Jolla. A few blocks later the Bug careened around a corner, heading for a freeway ramp.

Bolan knew the play. Far enough. After they were on the freeway for a short distance, Bolan pulled alongside the Bug, waved Big Thunder and pointed to the highway's wide shoulder.

The shadowy figure of the driver stared straight ahead.

Bolan nudged the Pontiac ahead half a car length, then started moving into the Bug's lane. The driver hit the horn, his frightened face showing through the side window.

Bolan continued to herd the VW and slowly it gave ground, moving into the far right lane. The big guy kept jockeying the Pontiac gradually inward toward the smaller car, not wanting to crush the Bug. He sensed no threat from the other driver, still his finger caressed the trigger of the silver hand cannon that lay on his thigh. The VW's wheelman braked hard, and Bolan stayed with him.

The Volkswagen hit the shoulder and stopped. The Executioner pulled the Pontiac at an angle in front of the Bug, blocking any forward progress.

For a moment neither man moved, both engines still running.

Bolan jumped out of the Pontiac with the AutoMag, aiming it over the roof of the car at the other driver's window.

Slowly the Bug's window rolled down.

"Shut off your engine and step out, slowly!" Bolan thundered.

A pair of cars swept by in the fast lane.

The Bug's engine died and the door opened.

Bolan reached in and turned off his car's engine, pocketing the keys. The snout of the

.44 never wavered its head from the Bug's door.

"Show yourself," the Executioner growled.

"Mack, it's Johnny." The words were emotion-racked as the man in the VW stood up, hands held above his head.

"Johnny?" The nightwarrior peered at the bespectacled youth across from him, trying to get a fix on the face.

The big dude rammed the AutoMag into leather and ran around the Pontiac. Johnny met him halfway and they embraced each other.

After a few moments, Bolan gripped the young man's shoulder firmly and held him at arm's length, studying his face.

"Sorry I drew on you, John-0."

"It's. . . it's okay. You couldn't have known."

Bolan patted his brother on the back, then brushed his hand across his eyes, grateful for the darkness.

"You're a man now, John. Wish Mom and Pop could have been alive to see you."

"Way it goes, I guess," Johnny said, his voice breaking again.

"How is Val?"

"Happy. Still lives in Cheyenne with Jack." He stared at his older brother. "You haven't changed much since I saw you in St. Louis, Mack."

A transport truck roared past, drowning out Johnny's last words.

"Let's get off the freeway and find somewhere

to talk. We have a lot of catching up to do!"

"Follow me. I know a place in Pacific Beach," Johnny said. He stared at his brother. "This is still hard to believe. I've been dreaming about this day for a long time."

"So have I, John."

30

Johnny and Mack Bolan sat in the Pontiac in the diner's parking lot and talked for two hours. Johnny brought Bolan up to date on his Navy career, and the two years since then. He told his big brother about Sandy and their plans to marry in the fall.

Bolan had little to say about himself. Johnny did find out that he had worked for the government, that he had been called Colonel John Phoenix and that he was on his own once more.

"I'm on the run again, Johnny. The Feds, the CIA and the KGB are on my tail. I guess I've been lucky so far. My war has brought me back against my old enemy, the Mafia. I have a fix on one of the biggest narcotics pipelines into the States. The port of entry is San Diego."

Johnny told his brother about Karl Darlow and what happened to him.

"I've been trying to figure out how I can get back at the Mafia. The San Diego Family is run by Manny 'The Mover' Marcello."

"I know. I picked up his name in Denver and Salt Lake City. Perhaps you won't have to do anything. Recall that talk we had in St. Louis some years back?"

"Yes, but I'm not a kid anymore."

"True. But I still feel you should stay out of it. These people are more dangerous than you could ever imagine."

Johnny changed the subject.

"Hey, we don't need to sit here. Let's go back to our place and talk. Sandy will skin me alive if I don't bring you home. She's our family now."

Mack Bolan smiled but shook his head.

"I have a job to do tonight, Johnny. Anyway, no lady I know likes to have visitors at two in the morning, especially when it's a surprise. Give me your phone number and I'll call you tomorrow."

Johnny wrote down the number and passed the paper to Bolan. Then the young man shook his brother's hand, got out of the car and drove away.

Mack Bolan shook a cigarette out of his pack and fired it. He felt strange, a new kind of family closeness that he had forced himself not to think about for years. It was the same kind of warm contented feeling he used to have when the family gathered for Elsa Bolan's Sunday dinner back in Pittsfield. Yeah, family, the right kind of family. What a good feeling. And one that he had to be careful of. He knew exactly what would happen if the Mafia ever found Johnny Bolan again.

The Executioner flicked the smoke out of the window and started toward downtown San Diego. He had one more call to make tonight.

The location of the hit was North Park, that section of San Diego just north of Balboa Park, in the middle of town. The area had long been a conservative, middle-class neighborhood, but had changed dramatically when blacks and Hispanics began moving in.

Referral House was his next target. It was a halfway center for rehabilitating narcotic addicts, with a remarkable rate of success.

The step-into-society center had been funded by one of the shadow Marcello enterprises, and it looked one hundred percent straight.

No one in San Diego realized the true function of Referral House. The rehabilitation center was in fact a drug-pusher training base.

Every former addict who showed that he could stay off drugs became a trusted pusher, with a car of his own and more money than he thought existed. He was on commission. If he performed well, the pusher had it made. If his sales slipped, he was threatened with what happened to those who had bad reports to their parole officers.

Right now there were ten "students" at Referral House, and four instructors. In a special room the pushers did their homework, cutting or diluting the pure cocaine from Colombia with mannitol, a white crystalline powder.

Bolan was ready to declare a recess at this particular drug school.

The Referral House did a lot of night work. Lights were still on when Bolan cruised past the

North Park house at 2:35 A.M. He parked a block away, then came up the alley. There would be protection, Bolan was sure.

He found the first man leaning against a garbage can, smoking a cigarette and humming to himself.

The nightstalker worked from shadow to shadow until he was within ten feet of the guard, whose eyes were closed as he lost himself in the tune.

Bolan tossed a stone against a wooden fence on the other side of the guard. The singing sentry canceled his tune and jumped up, clawing for iron.

Bolan charged silently across the gap as the guard stared down the alley in the other direction. The Executioner's strong right arm clamped around the guard's neck in a steely grip. He lifted the man off the ground and then dropped him, at the same time twisting the victim's neck.

The snap resounded above the scuffling feet and Bolan let the corpse drop to the alley.

The Executioner ran to a garage that abutted the alley. He saw a door leading into what he guessed would be a kitchen or utility room. He tried the knob and the wooden panel swung open to reveal an empty kitchen. The nighthitter nodded. The "training room" must be on the second floor.

Like a silent black ghost Bolan glided through the cooking area, the Beretta's selector set in 3-shot mode.

The warrior came to a living room with a stairway at the far side. He holstered the 93-R and strode confidently to the stairway. Sometimes no concealment is the best camouflage. Someone was descending the steps. Bolan nodded and went past the woman without a second glance. She frowned for a moment, shrugged and went into the kitchen.

At the top of the steps the partition had been removed to form two large meeting rooms. Only load-bearing walls remained. He could look into both rooms. Lights were on in the one to the right and at the far end two blacks and a white man were talking. They looked up, suddenly alert.

"Is Johnson here?" Bolan asked, as he stepped into the glare. "They told me to report to Johnson. This the place?"

One of the blacks took a step toward Bolan.

"Don't know any Johnson. I'm Bill Harris. I run the place. What you looking for?"

"You, Harris, and the rest of the scum in this sewer. I want all your shit!"

Harris's hand darted under a red-and-white print sport shirt. But the Executioner cleared leather and fired before the man could touch his piece.

The 3-round burst caught Harris in the chest, hammering him against the wall. The 9mm parabellums created a new design on the Hawaiian shirt as the man slid lifelessly to the floor.

The white guy dived to one side, seeking cover

behind a heavy wooden desk. He almost made it when three rounds from the Beretta stitched new buttonholes up his shirt.

The other black man fell to his knees, looking up at Bolan.

"Where you coming from, man?"

"Not important. But I know where you're going."

"Please, I'm just looking to score, brother."

"Not this time. Three strikes, you're out. Now beat it," the Executioner growled, ignoring the man, checking the other room and finding nothing.

Downstairs. He took the steps three at a time, saw the front door open where he guessed the woman had gone. On the far side of the house he found a locked room. He had met no other people.

With a pair of well-placed kicks, the door splintered open.

Inside, the Executioner found a cutting room as well as delivery point. Orders were tacked to a wall, and on a long table sat precision scales. Next to it was a box filled with squares of white powder with a label he could read: Mannitol.

From his jacket pocket Bolan took a chunk of C-4 plastique, already rigged with a pencil timer. He set the timer for five minutes and placed the bomb under the middle load-bearing wall of the cutting room.

On the other side of the house he placed a second lump of the puttylike charge. After making sure there were no innocents left in the building, he walked out the front door. Fifty yards away he triggered the detonator.

The first blast tore a ragged hole in the night silence, followed twenty seconds later by the second detonation. The walls of the old frame house bowed outward for a second, then fell into the yard and the upstairs came crashing down to the first floor. Somewhere a small fire began. Electric wires fell and began sparking in a tree in the front yard.

Up and down the block, residents in night-clothes ran out to view the ruins.

"What the hell happened?"

"Those nuts at the halfway house blew themselves up."

"Just a matter of time. I told you they were screwy."

"Anybody called the cops?"

Mack Bolan had placed a marksman's medal on the front steps as he left. He was sure the police would find it with the morning light.

31

It was almost 4:00 A.M. when Johnny arrived at the condo in the valley.

He shook Sandy's shoulder gently. She smiled and mumbled sleepily. He kissed her neck and she rolled over, reaching for him.

"It's morning already?"

"Sandy, wake up. I found Mack. We talked for two hours!"

"Oh, Johnny, that's amazing. Why didn't you bring him here?"

"Long story, but he's going to call later today."

Sandy sat up and rubbed the sleep out of her eyes.

"Look, I'm so excited I think I'll have a shower and stay up," Johnny said.

"Okay, I'll get breakfast."

Johnny nibbled at his poached egg, trying to contain his elation. He pushed back his chair and stood up.

He drove to work and got caught up in the job, waiting for Mack to call. At one o'clock he had a quick sandwich and went to the legal-aid center.

It was almost seven that evening when his phone rang.

"Mr. Gray?"

"Yes."

"This is your brother. No names. Where can we have dinner?"

"My place, the condo."

"No. I don't want to involve your lady. It would be risky. I'm in the San Carlos area, a little restaurant called Coco's, in Lake Murray Boulevard. Can you find it?"

"Sure. I'll be there in twenty minutes."

Johnny brushed past two people waiting to see him, told them he had an emergency, and rushed out to the Bug.

AT THE RESTAURANT, Mack Bolan sipped coffee while he waited. He had spent the day scouting more of the potential locations of the drug pipeline. Now he thought about the freighter and the death of Karl Darlow, and the details surprised him. Most drug transfers took place at night.

Why was a pickup made in daylight?

Bolan decided it must have been an emergency delivery, not routine. They had risked only two men and a small boat.

The Executioner thought about the La Jolla estate owned by Manny Marcello. It would be hard to attack because of its location on the steep bluff. A frontal assault or from one of the sides might work. Time for planning later.

He knew the Marcello trucking company would be involved in the distribution. A carefully concealed package could be hidden in almost any cross-country shipment that only the driver would know about. Highway trucks could stop anywhere these days and make a delivery.

Johnny came in the front door, saw Bolan in the booth and walked over. Several years had made a big difference in the skinny teenager Bolan had known. Johnny now was filled out, about five-ten and determined. He had grown into a fine young man. Bolan rose to greet him.

"Hi, kid."

"Hi, Mack," Johnny said shyly.

They both laughed, then shook hands warmly and sat down. A waitress bustled up with menus and water.

"Give us a few minutes please," Johnny said. The woman smiled and vanished.

"Mack, I've been dreaming about this day for years. I want to help you in your crusade."

Johnny held up his hand when Mack tried to protest.

"No, I don't want to be in the trenches with you. What I have in mind is some kind of support. Last night you told me a little about Stony Man Farm and the backup group you had there. Now you have no one to help you."

"But that's the way it was before Stony Man."

"You had Leo Turrin, and a few others. Just

think about the idea. Now, I told Sandy you were in town and she wants to meet you."

Bolan smiled. "You did well, kid. I want to meet my future sister-in-law. Don't forget, you don't have family approval yet to marry the girl." Then he became serious. "Treat her well, John. For the memory of our sister."

At the mention of Cindy Bolan, Johnny lowered his eyes and quickly changed the subject.

"Tell me what happened behind the Iron Curtain. Did they really frame you for the murder of that labor leader? How did you get away?"

They ordered and Bolan gave him a sketchy account of his trip through Russia and his escape.

"It came at the point when I knew I was not an organization man. I didn't enjoy taking assignments, even from Brognola. I guess I'm too much of a lone wolf. When it all happened I was glad to be on my own again, though the death of my woman was the biggest blow since Pittsfield. April put herself in the line of fire and got hit by a bullet meant for me. She made the supreme sacrifice and I must live with that for the rest of my days. As for my work, it's best that I'm alone. People have hunted me before. I can live with that kind of pressure better than always worrying about 'policy.' I like the President. We got along fine. But he represented all the rest of it."

Johnny Bolan's eyes sparkled. "Don't you see? That's why you need me, right here in town, in a safehouse where you can leave messages, and—"

"Not so fast. Let's talk about it later, Johnny. You said I had some time to think it over."

Their food came and they ate. Johnny saw that Mack was not a lover of fine foods. He ate to stay alive and to keep the machine running.

As they talked, the subdued conversation turned back to Karl Darlow.

"Johnny, Karl saw something he wasn't supposed to. It must have been an emergency shipment of some kind to risk a daylight transfer."

"We've moved to a friend's place," Johnny said, "because I suddenly realized they'd figure Karl would tell his daughter. It wouldn't take much suspicion for them to come after her, would it?"

"You're learning quickly, guy. For them the slightest suspicion is enough for a hit. Yes, you were right to move her. This daughter of Marcello. Could she associate you with me?" Bolan asked.

Johnny scowled. "I don't know. But Angela is a sharp girl. She just might make a connection."

"She could be a problem."

"I don't think so. From what she said, she's in a big fight with her father to get in on part of the Family action. He wants her to get married."

"Sounds like he's the one we need to worry about."

Johnny closed his eyes for a moment. "Mack, I can't shake this terrible feeling that Sandy is in trouble. I'm going to call her. If she doesn't answer or if there's a problem, I want you to come down there with me.''

He dialed the number and the phone was picked up on the first ring.

"Johnny, is that you?"

"Yes. You sound scared. Is something wrong?"

"Somebody tried to get in the door! I had the bolt thrown the way you showed me. But this is the ground floor. I'm not sure I can keep them out if they break a window!"

"Call the police. We're on our way!"

32

The trip from Coco's to Mission Valley took ten minutes with Bolan driving the Pontiac. Johnny watched for cops and gave directions as the speedometer needle crept to eighty-five on the freeway. They zigzagged through the early-evening traffic, hit the off ramp and wound around to the condo complex on the north side of the expensive strip of land through the heart of San Diego.

The huge subdivision was made up of two-story units in attached buildings.

"Last one on the left!" Johnny shouted as they sprang from the car on a run. Bolan palmed the silenced Beretta as they ran, holding it close to his body.

A car lunged away from the curb with the black snout of a pistol poking out the window. The two men hit the turf. The Executioner came up and triggered two 3-shot bursts into the rear of the fleeing vehicle, but it kept going through the parking lot and into the street beyond.

"Inside!" Bolan yelled to Johnny.

They ran to the apartment on the ground floor.

The front door was unlatched. Bolan kicked it open, then jumped back, leaning against the outside wall. He waited a few moments, the 93-R pointed skyward, his left hand gripping his right wrist. Nothing happened. Slowly he edged into the condo.

The living room was trashed, as if there had been a struggle.

"God, no!" Johnny shouted. He raced through the rooms. No one was there. He came back to the living room where his brother was standing.

"We've got to do something!" Johnny yelled.

The Executioner holstered the Beretta, then grabbed Johnny by the shoulders.

"Easy, take it easy. She's alive. They want her alive, or they would have killed her here."

Johnny took deep breaths, trying to control himself. He was pale, panic in his eyes.

He shook his head. "I should never have left her alone. I should have sent her to San Francisco. It's all my fault!"

"Calm down, John. They might have left a message. Let's look."

After three minutes, Johnny found the note taped to the telephone in the kitchen. He read it, then brought it to Mack.

"John Gray. Sandy is with us. She is unharmed. How long she stays that way is up to you. Call the phone number below at nine o'clock."

Bolan looked at his watch. It was 8:50 P.M. "Call. Is there an extension?"

Johnny pointed to the bedroom.

"Okay, find out what they want. But tell them they get nothing until you're certain that Sandy is alive."

Johnny slumped on the couch, torment racking his body. "They better not hurt her."

"We wait until nine. It'll work out," Bolan said. But he felt a chill. He had to keep Johnny's hopes high, that was vital right now.

"They probably want some assurance about what Karl told you. Legally you couldn't testify against them. It's only hearsay now."

Johnny watched the digital kitchen clock flicker to 9:00. He dialed. The phone on the other end rang twice, then someone picked it up.

"Yes?"

"This is John Gray."

"Good, right on time. We have a package you want, is that right?"

"You son of a bitch! You hurt her, it'll be the last person you ever hurt."

"You want to see the lady again, shut up and listen. We need to talk to you. Take down these instructions."

Bolan was listening on the extension with his hand over the mouthpiece.

Johnny wiped a line of sweat off his forehead, a pencil in his right hand, poised over a pad of paper.

"At ten tonight, come to the upper circle road in Presidio Park. Come alone, unarmed, and do not contact the police."

"Sandy remains, unharmed, or you get nothing. You threatened Karl and then killed him."

"Relax, kid. I don't know anything about anybody killing Karl. Now be there!" The man on the phone hung up.

Bolan came in from the bedroom. "We don't have much time. You make the meet. I'll be waiting there. I need something from the car."

Moments later Bolan brought in a suitcase from the trunk of the rented Pontiac. He changed into the skintight blacksuit, then strapped on combat webbing. The big silver flesh-shredder hung on his hip, and the Beretta 93-R in shoulder leather.

"I need a weapon," Johnny said. He picked up an Ingram Model 10 submachine gun from the suitcase and hefted it. "This will do." He picked up one of the magazines and slammed it into the handle. Loaded with the 30-round clip, the Ingram weighed almost eight pounds.

Johnny stuffed another 30-round magazine into his pocket. "I'm ready," he said.

The Executioner slid some surprises on his webbing and they headed for the door.

"Careful how you use that thing," Bolan said.

Johnny glanced up at his big brother. "Don't worry, I've killed men before."

Johnny drove into the park from the bottom, coming down Highway 8 through the valley, then taking the Taylor Street off ramp and turning left into Presidio Park. He wound up the hill past the museum to the one-way lane on the left with picnic tables.

The Executioner checked the cover and conceal-ment. There was a downhill stretch to the south, a clump of bushes at the far end, and less than a block to the north were residences across the street.

He found a big pine tree and some brush that would offer the most protection. Bolan showed Johnny where to park when he came back. They had driven the Pontiac because Johnny's Bug was waiting at Coco's restaurant in San Carlos. Johnny drove down the hill and out of sight.

The nightwarrior found some better cover just below the picnic area on the other side of the road. He settled in and waited.

Promptly at ten o'clock, Johnny drove along the one-way road and parked near the large pine tree, the Pontiac pointed out of the park for a quick exit.

The Executioner figured the Mafia would have a lookout to the north.

At ten minutes past ten, a dark-colored car cruised down the dark lane with its lights off. It came in the lane the wrong way and nosed up to the rental car. For a moment no one moved. Then the Executioner saw Johnny look over the top of the Pontiac. He had been standing behind it waiting. Now he exposed himself only for a sec-ond.

A door on the Lincoln opened and three men got out.

Gunners, Bolan thought.

One walked to the rear of the crew wagon. The second soldier jogged to the far side of the Pontiac and waited. The last man was smaller, better dressed. He walked around the car and approached Johnny.

"Where is Sandy?" Johnny asked.

"You didn't expect me to bring her here," the smaller man said. "She's okay. I need information."

"Not until I see Sandy."

"Afraid you might think that way." An automatic appeared in the man's right fist. "So I brought along a persuader."

Johnny could not reach the Ingram. He had forgotten to unzip his jacket as he waited. From the shadows along the laneway came a cough, and the gunman holding the automatic yelped in pain as his wrist developed a hole and his weapon dropped to the ground.

Johnny dodged behind the car again, unzipping his jacket and bringing up the Ingram. The gunman at the far end of the Pontiac began to move. The Model 10 spit fire as a 5-round burst razored the night.

The gunman was tracking on Johnny when the leaden hail ripped through his chest, jolting him backward into a palm trunk before his lifeless body tumbled to the grass.

Johnny was swinging the SMG on the second guard when a muted cough from the Beretta pinned the second guy against the grille of the car.

"Coming in!" Bolan said, running toward Johnny.

"This one is alive," Johnny said. "Let's get out of here."

They threw the wounded Mafia lieutenant into the rear of the Pontiac. Johnny picked up the hood's .45 and slid in beside him, the automatic aimed at the Mafia negotiator's belly.

"Your turn, bastard!" Johnny spit at him. "Is Sandy okay?"

"I don't know. My orders were to get you, bring you back, alive or dead."

Johnny brought the butt of the .45 down across the hoodlum's face, breaking his nose, gouging a big flap of flesh off his cheek. The man screamed and cowered in the far corner of the back seat.

Bolan wheeled the Pontiac north into the maze of streets in Mission Hills, merging with the other traffic in the area. Behind them they heard sirens.

"Okay, hotshot," Johnny said to the goon. "Start talking, unless you enjoy pain."

The mobster looked up in the darkness. He saw only the crazed eyes of the young man holding the automatic.

"Where's the girl?"

"Safehouse. Best one is in the San Carlos area."

"Good," Johnny said. He jammed the .45's muzzle into the man's kidney. The hoodlum bellowed in agony. "What's the address?" Johnny demanded.

"Don't know the address, but I can show you."

The battered face shook in the dim light as the car came out of the hills toward the freeway.

33

Bolan gunned the Pontiac along the freeway, watching for the California Highway Patrol. Ten minutes later the gray-faced Mafia hostage whispered, "This is it."

The street was only a block long and dead-ended into Beaver Lake Drive.

"Turn right, it's the second house on the left."

Bolan eased past the house and slid to the curb two houses down. Lights showed in the front rooms.

"How many guns there?" Bolan asked.

"Usually two, one outside, one inside."

"John, you stay here and watch him. I'll nail the outside man."

The nighthitter slipped out of the car and moved across the street, fading into the shadow of a large tree in front of the house next to the target. A redwood fence surrounded the building. Bolan crept up to the wooden barricade and peered over it into the front yard.

A shadow moved on a small porch near the door. The silhouette moved again and Bolan saw the guard where he sat in a lawn chair, his feet propped on a low iron railing. A pinpoint red glow brightened for a moment as the man took a drag on a cigarette.

The Executioner waited until he saw a red arc as the sentry flicked the butt into the yard. The guy stood and looked around, then lifted his arms to stretch his muscles, looking like a cardboard cutout in a police shooting gallery.

The Beretta 93-R sneezed once as the 9mm parabellum caught him dead center. There was an audible sigh and the man sat back dead in the chair.

The Executioner ran to the Pontiac.

"Out, hero," he said to the Mafia leadman. "You're going to run interference for us. Your big chance."

Bolan held the man by his good arm as they left the car. The warrior in black turned to his brother.

"Cover us from the fence about ten feet away. Don't shoot unless you have to."

He propelled the prisoner forward, across the street and up the driveway. "Knock on the door the way you're supposed to," Bolan growled. He jammed the Beretta in the man's kidney and left it there as a deadly reminder.

The hostage glanced briefly at the body slumped in the chair on the porch. He groaned under his breath, then looked at the white painted door. He rapped twice, once, twice again.

Nothing happened.

"Again, harder," Bolan prompted.

The second knock brought the sound of footsteps. Bolan heard the sound of three locks being turned inside, then the door swung open.

"Henry, what the hell you want this time?" a short, thickset man asked.

Bolan never saw the enemy weapon. He heard a gun go off and felt his hostage shudder. The Executioner pushed the dying man forward, slamming him against the gunman and they both went down in a tangle on the floor.

Bolan stepped hard on the gunner's weapon arm and brought his left boot heel down on the man's skull.

Johnny had rushed to the door, the Ingram up and ready. He took one look at the bodies on the floor, then ran into the living room.

No Sandy.

Johnny charged down the hall, checking each bedroom. Nobody. He rushed back to the kitchen, spotted another door and started to open it when Bolan came up near him.

"Be ready. There could be guns in there."

Johnny jerked the door open, dropped to a crouch, the Ingram SMG sweeping the room. A light burned brightly inside.

In the middle of the ten-foot-square room stood a metal table. Something was lying on the table.

Bolan also saw it and rushed in front of Johnny, trying to block his view.

"Don't look, kid."

Johnny shook free and walked into the grisly

room. Blood was splattered everywhere. Johnny trembled and dropped the Ingram on the floor as he stared at the bloody mass of bone and tissue on the metal table.

It was Sandy Darlow.

She was still alive.

Her waist-length hair had been burned away. She lay naked. Her arms and legs had been broken, the limbs askew at impossible angles. Her entire torso was slashed and still bleeding. There was not a square inch of flesh that had not been cut, leaving red bleeding gashes.

Johnny screamed and leaned over, staring at her face.

One eyeball had been gouged from the socket and dangled on her cheek, held there only by white tendons. Only splinters of teeth were left sticking out of shattered gums.

"Please. . . ." Sandy whispered. Johnny sobbed. He knew what she meant. She had only misery and unspeakable agony left for an hour, perhaps two. The Mafia turkeymeat specialists had struck again. Johnny shook with a terrible, agonizing fury.

Sandy pleaded with him silently for a quick and merciful death.

Johnny bent and touched her bloody lips with his own.

"Johnny. . . don't let me live," she whispered hoarsely, as blood flowed from her mouth.

Tears tracked down his cheeks.

"We can save you!" he cried. "The Lifeflight helicopter! I'll have them here in fifteen minutes!"

"I'm hurt too bad." She stiffened and her scream of pain came out garbled, and more blood gushed from her lips.

Mack Bolan stood grimly behind Johnny, watching the horror. He had seen it before, sure. And with hideous inevitability the sadness enveloped him. Johnny had witnessed it firsthand, after all Bolan had tried to do to protect him.

The big guy felt a burning behind his eyes. He blinked back the tears.

Johnny looked at his brother, holding out his hand for the 93-R.

"Darling Sandy," the young man whimpered, chocking back the sobs, "maybe someday we'll meet again."

Sandy twisted in pain. Her body shuddered, a stream of blood trickled from her mouth.

John Bolan Gray took the Beretta from his brother and raised it. He moved the weapon so Sandy could not see it, aimed it over her heart and fired once....

34

The final battle had begun!

The Pontiac hit the freeway and the Executioner looked over at his brother. He knew that Johnny's blind anger would result in the kid's quick death.

"This can't be a wild vengeance trip," the Executioner said. "The Mafia in San Diego can be blown away, but we'll have to do it by careful planning and with cool detachment."

The Executioner kept talking. It was two hours before Johnny said a word. Then he looked at his elder brother and nodded, accepting the terms of war. He took a deep breath.

"They must all die, Mack," he said.

They rode in silence a while, through downtown, along Harbor Drive toward Point Loma.

"Johnny, this is a one-time blowout, you have to understand that. I'm not taking you on as a full-time field partner. This time you can work with me, but that's the end of it. Revenge can go only so far if you value your health."

"I understand. I never thought I'd kill another human being again. I did in Lebanon. I was scared to death. That was enough combat for me. I don't know how you guys did it day after day in Nam."

"It was a job that had to be done," Bolan said.

"Mack, after this I won't fire a weapon again in anger, I promise you that."

They drove around the edge of the bay, onto Point Loma and down to the man-made Shelter Island off Scott Street. The island was covered with parks, restaurants, marinas and several private clubs.

Bolan drove into the parking lot of the Kona Kai Klub.

"The Marcello yacht is not in its slip," he said. "She was supposed to go out tonight on a supervising run. From what I heard there's going to be a sizable drug pickup at sea tonight. I've made some arrangements."

They drove back to a small shipyard repair facility between Shelter Island and the shore. Bolan used a key on a gate and they both slid through. Johnny still carried the Ingram.

Bolan walked to a dock and checked out a thirty-two foot powerboat. "This is our transport."

It was a Stamas 32 with plenty of power and range.

"Hey, swabbie, remember how to cast off mooring lines?"

Johnny nodded and let off the bow line. When

the motors started he let off the stern line and stepped on board.

"I have some surprises inside," Bolan said.

Johnny looked at the arsenal and whistled. There were six large magnetic limpet mines. Each weighed about twenty pounds. Three had been fixed with flotation collars of Styrofoam. Beside them was a weapon Johnny knew well, an Armbrust disposable antitank weapon and three extra tubed rounds.

"Where in hell did you get these?" Johnny asked.

"Old friends," the Executioner said. He guided the little boat out of the dock area into the bay and headed for the channel that led to the open sea. He had all running lights on.

"Another freighter?" Johnny asked.

"As near as I can figure, or maybe a large fishing boat. Around midnight there's going to be a drop."

A short time later they cleared the channel buoys and headed in a more southerly direction.

"The transfer point was supposed to be somewhere around the border area between U.S. and Mexican waters," Bolan said. "So we've got a ten- to twelve-mile run. It should take us half an hour at twenty knots. What time is it?"

"Eleven-fifteen."

"Take the wheel. Point her at those Tijuana lights."

Bolan entered the small cabin and came out

with scuba mask and tanks. It was warm enough
not to need a wet suit.

"The small boats will be hardest to find if they
get away," he said. "I expect them to use a fishing
boat and the Marcello yacht. He calls it the *Angela
II*. We better turn the running lights off. No sense
advertising our arrival."

They cruised south for a half hour. Bolan lifted
a Startron nightscope and scanned the water.

The black hulk materialized out of the night.
The freighter had to be at least four hundred feet.
The Executioner made a quiet circle to the right.
On the seaward side of the big vessel they saw a
smaller ship.

Bolan lifted the nightscope again and studied
the craft. "It's a fishing boat, a forty-footer,
rigged for commercial trolling. They're moving
packages down ropes."

Bolan turned the Stamas quietly and cruised in
a circle a mile wide outside the tanker. Nothing.
He nosed the sleek powerboat back toward the
freighter, which was doing ten knots even during
the transfer.

"No yacht. He must be in radio contact, but I
don't know what channel they're using. We hit the
fisher, then the freighter. We'll look for the yacht
later. They have the hot goods all on the small
boat now."

The cruiser was idling five hundred yards off
the fishing boat. Three minutes later she let go the
lines and pulled away.

Bolan had been edging north as he waited, and now the fishing boat turned toward him to clear the freighter, aiming for the San Diego harbor entrance.

Johnny checked out the Armbrust weapon. It was in perfect condition and ready to fire. Johnny himself was hardly in such good shape. He ws still in shock, still reacting to events like an automaton. But he was an automaton ready to explode. He aimed through the scope and found if he concentrated he could keep the sights on the bobbing boat.

"We'll swing around her and come in from dead ahead," Bolan said. He was all too aware of his young brother's drastic state; he had to keep the kid involved, constantly, with no letup.

He negotiated a wide turn and opened up the 340 HP MerCruiser power plant to twenty-five knots. The thirty-two-footer tried to stand on her tail as they slammed through the calm seas.

Bolan eased back on the throttle, swinging the Stamas around, waiting for the fishing boat to come within hailing distance. The boat seemed to change course for a moment, then came back on the run for San Diego.

When the vessel was within a hundred yards, Mack took out the bullhorn.

"You are ordered to cut power and go dead in the water for inspection! Cut your engines now!"

A rifle shot cracked the soft night air, followed by a stuttering machine gun. None of the rounds came anywhere near the blacked out attacking boat.

"You have one more chance. You will be blown out of the water if you do not come about and cut your engines."

Again the rifles and machine gun fired.

Bolan looked down at Johnny who had his eye on the sight of the Armbrust rocket launcher.

"Do it, Johnny."

The young man fired. He sensed that he had missed. The upward surge of the Stamas on a swell lifted the round over the target. It exploded harmlessly, just past the fisher, and the shouts came from the craft.

Johnny flipped off the empty tube and slapped a new one on, going into his firing position, seated, knees spread supporting his elbows.

He judged the regular movements of the boat this time and fired. The rocket launcher, with no back blast, sounded like a pistol shot. Johnny kept the fishing craft in his sights.

The commercial fishing boat erupted into a fireball, lighting up the sea.

A secondary explosion ripped the fuel tanks on board.

Ten seconds later the forty-footer was going down.

Johnny lowered the Armbrust, picked up his In-

gram as his brother nosed the Stamas toward the sinking boat.

A lone figure on the stern waved for help. Johnny brought up the Ingram and fired a 5-round burst at him. The volley pinned the man to the deck, then dumped him into the swirling water as the bow slid slowly into the Pacific.

Johnny looked at Bolan. "No survivors, no prisoners," he said grimly.

The Executioner nodded.

The Stamas 32 nosed ahead. Johnny moved to the bow, and sat astride the anchor board. Each time he heard splashing and cries for help, he turned the spitting Ingram on the position, hosing down the floundering crewmen.

"Die you bastards!" Johnny screamed as they circled the area for five minutes.

"Now the freighter," Bolan said.

They turned south again, found the big ship chugging along at ten knots. The Stamas slid in quietly with lights out beside the rusty freighter. Bolan would not need the scuba gear. He set three of the limpet mine detonators for ten minutes and waited as Johnny nosed the little craft within two feet of the black plates on the big vessel.

The Executioner hung over the side of the steel rail of the Stamas and reached down as far as he could. He placed the limpet three feet off the waterline and saw it cling to the freighter's steel plates. There was no noise. He motioned Johnny to work forward a little more.

Bolan was about to push the second mine toward the hull when a rifle cracked from above. The lead slug hit the railing two feet from him and ricocheted off into the night.

He drew the Beretta and fired at the rail above where the rifleman had been. Then he grabbed the limpet mine again and motioned for Johnny to edge in closer. At two feet, Bolan leaned down and placed the mine only a yard from the slapping waterline. The strong magnets held it in place.

"Now let's get out of here!" he muttered. They raced into the night, pursued by rifle shots, then Johnny circled a quarter of a mile away, watching the big ship.

It was five miles off the coast and somewhere west of Imperial Beach when the first mine exploded, lighting up the side of the ship like a billboard. The mine shattered plates and opened a ten foot split in the outer skin, extending two feet below the waterline.

A siren began to wail on board the freighter.

In reply the second limpet exploded. The big freighter listed to port almost at once. More sirens wailed. Men scrambled across the slanted decks. Lifeboats swung out from davits.

Deep in the bowels of the big ship the cold saltwater hit the boilers.

A roaring, muffled thunder shook the whole ocean. Nothing showed above water.

"Blew the whole bottom out of her!" Johnny said.

Two minutes later half the ship was under water and she was going down quickly.

"We have to find the yacht," Bolan said. "That freighter has enough lifeboats in the water. Most of the men are probably innocents, but we don't have time."

The Stamas raced for the San Diego harbor. Bolan took the wheel and made large "S" turns across a bearing for the harbor entrance, but found no yacht.

"They could have been listening to the radio reports from the fishing boat," Johnny said. "When it went sour they might have headed south at flank speed."

He slid both used Armbrust tubes over the stern and watched them sink. Then he and Mack climbed the ladder to the little flying bridge. Johnny sat in one of the soft cushioned chairs behind the console. He was still pale, like death had kissed him.

"We hurt them tonight," Bolan said. "They must have been moving thirty to forty million dollars' worth of cocaine off that freighter."

"What's the next target?" Johnny stared at his brother.

"We must get back on dry land. Bring the Armbrust. We'll need it."

Johnny Bolan Gray took a deep breath. He nodded. Round one was over, round two coming up. He closed his eyes and thought of Sandy, not as he had last seen her, but as he remembered her laughing and running along the beach.

He would always remember her hair blowing in the wind, her smile, her concern for other people. That was the Sandy he would always remember. Johnny knuckled wetness from his eyes. He would never see her again. He turned away in the seat, looked aft and let the tears come.

35

It was a little past 2:30 A.M. when Bolan and his young brother parked the Pontiac half a block from the fence that surrounded Marcello Trucking. They had moored the sleek powerboat at the dock where they'd found it. The Executioner had taken out a heavy barracks bag and put it in the car. Now he opened the bag and showed Johnny the contents.

There was an M-16/M-203 grenade launcher-rifle combination and a sack filled with 30 grenades for the tube. He also pulled out a compact hand-held M-60 Army machine gun that fired 7.62mm rounds at 550 a minute, no tripod needed. There was a variety of other weapons and ammunition.

"First we take out a warehouse in here. My intel points to it as the major terminal for incoming dope." He referred to the police data supplied to him by the crippled, fiercely loyal Bolanist he called The Bear—Stony Man Farm's Aaron Kurtzman.

They left the car and faded into the shadows along the eight-foot-high chain link fence. Three strands of barbed wire ran along the top, angled outward.

They walked to the main gate. It was spot-lighted and wide open, waiting for late-night trucks arriving from all over the country. A guard with a clipboard and a .38 on his hip came toward them.

"What can I do for you guys?"

"Manny said to come right down," Bolan said. "He here?"

"Mr. Marcello? No. What's that tube thing your friend's carrying?"

"Special nightscope for seeing in the dark," the Executioner replied. "We're looking for those sneak thieves who been ripping off the merchandise."

"You'll need authorization to come in at night," the guard said. "Besides, I didn't hear about no sneak—"

"This enough authorization?" Bolan asked, drawing the Beretta from his shoulder holster. Johnny came around behind the guard and pulled the guy's revolver from his belt. "Down this way, man, and you won't get hurt," Mack said.

They left the guard tied up fifty yards away behind some parked trucks. The two Bolans walked toward the far warehouse. It was half the size of the other huge storage barns. This building was made of concrete block, with security lights around it and only one door.

"There must be a backup guard somewhere,"

Bolan whispered. They were crouched in the shadows beside an International highway diesel tractor. Bolan pointed to the left and Johnny began scanning the darkness and shadows that way.

"Got one," Johnny whispered. Bolan's gaze followed Johnny's pointing finger.

"Yeah, he's no civilian. Wait here."

Johnny crouched on the macadam as Bolan vanished into the night. Two minutes later Johnny saw a black shadow hurtle toward the man, a soft rustle and then silence. A minute later the Executioner knelt beside Johnny.

They came around the far end of the big truck talking in normal tones. Another guard appeared at the single door in front of them, wielding a double-barreled shotgun. Security was edgy; the marksman's medals of the last few days had fanned day-to-day fear into paranoia of epic proportions. But inevitably, not every sector had told the truth about the Bolan visits, in order to protect certain individuals from the wrath of the head honchos. So security everywhere was *too* jumpy—misinformed, underorganized, and when it came right down to it, based on nothing more than each man for himself.

They stopped in front of the guard.

"Stow that scattergun or I'll ram it up your ass," Bolan said quietly.

The guard started to pull up the shotgun.

The Executioner fired twice with the Beretta.

The slugs slammed the man against the chair, the shotgun flying out of his hands. He slid to sitting position. It looked like he was stealing a nap.

Bolan checked out the door. There was a padlock on it.

Two more silenced rounds from the Beretta destroyed the lock with little noise. Johnny pulled the door open and they entered the building.

Bolan felt along the wall just inside the entrance until he found a switch. He flicked it on. There were no windows.

Two long tables in the center of the room were stacked with neat bundles of plastic-wrapped cocaine and heroin.

To one side were precision scales protected with dust covers, ounce sized plastic bags and sealing machines. In a big bin behind the table lay labeled blocks of mannitol for cutting.

Bolan looked around and saw a fire hose neatly coiled around a hanger on the wall.

"Slash the bags open," Bolan said. He unwound the hose and turned on the valve. An inch-wide jet of water gushed out the nozzle, and Bolan directed the spray on the slashed bags of white powder. In five minutes several million dollars' worth of drugs dissolved into a chalky liquid.

The Executioner shut off the water and motioned to the door. Outside he pointed to Johnny's Armbrust, then at the concrete wall.

They walked fifty yards away and Johnny lifted the Armbrust. He pushed off the safety and sent the AP round slamming through the block wall.

For a silent moment nothing happened. The explosion, when it came, was sharp and rumbling. The roof lifted several inches off its supports, the wall crumbled, and the whole structure sagged, then collapsed inward. Johnny shouldered the Armbrust and they walked back toward the front gate.

A fire siren wailed. A dozen men ran around in confusion, not certain what to do. Fire crackled at the far side of the building that was now some of the most expensive rubble in the world. Security had gone all to hell. This was not a hardsite but a lab and storage facility, so manpower was at a minimum. Lies and false estimates about Bolan's return would continue to stymie the guncocks as they attempted to close ranks against the new Bolan onslaught. Tonight, at the warehouse, it was a lost cause. The wandering, confused rifleman didn't even catch a glimpse of the two brothers as they slipped back to their car with unnecessary stealth.

As they drove away Johnny looked at Bolan. "Now we go for Marcello himself, right?"

Bolan nodded. "Before he has a chance to bring in more soldiers."

"The La Jolla hardsite?"

"That's the target."

Half an hour later they had infiltrated the backyard of the house next door to the Marcello mansion. They were still an immense distance from the house. The rear lawn of the Mafia chief looked like a golf course.

An all-night party was in progress. The Executioner advanced, finally looked through binoculars over the top of a six-foot-high brick wall and checked the pool, which was covered by a "floating" type roof, and patio area.

A dozen men sat around the pool with drinks in hand. Several charts on easels stood nearby.

"Conference of some kind," Bolan reported back to Johnny. "They wouldn't have a party this late without women.

Johnny had the Armbrust over one shoulder with the last tube-round locked on the firing mechanism. Over the other shoulder he carried the M-16/M-203 hybrid. At his feet sat an olive drab bag filled with thirty of the 40mm grenades.

The .44 AutoMag rode the big guy's hip, with the Beretta 93-R in shoulder leather and the M-60 machine gun in his hands.

Quickly they retreated to the darkness of the trees that edged the huge lawn and laid out the attack plan and synchronized their watches. Bolan faded back through the trees and around toward the direction of the street.

Three minutes later Johnny loaded the grenade launcher and dropped the first 40mm round into the patio area.

The first hit the pool itself and went off with a subdued blast.

The second landed a few feet from a patio table.

The head of an obese Mafia hit man disintegrated in a puff of smoke as the round exploded.

The dozen men fanned out in all directions, one falling into the pool. They stormed into the house and raced to the sides of the estate, wildly seeking safety.

Johnny followed three men with rounds into trees at the far side. An air burst riddled two of the men, the third raced for the front of the house. Shortly Johnny heard the M-60 chattering its death message to any who tried to escape by the street entrance.

Johnny loaded and fired. Quickly he was out of targets, so he moved his grenading to the patio and under it, trying to get rounds inside the house. He leveled the barrel, hoping to bounce a grenade through the open door.

His hand scraped the bag for the last round, which he sent into the far corner of the estate, wounding a man who dived behind a tree.

Johnny dropped the M-16 hybrid and picked up the Armbrust. He aimed at the ground floor beside the patio and fired the AP round. It ripped through a picture window into what he guessed was the living room. The shot leaped from the tube and exploded with a roar, the concussion shattering all the windows in the rear of the house.

Time to move. Johnny scaled the wall, taking the M-16 with him. He had four 30-round magazines of the high-velocity 5.56 hailstones of death.

He pushed the safety off on the M-16 and

sprinted through the edge of the shrubs to the lawn. One man left the protection of an overturned table and ran for the house.

Johnny lifted the M-16 and sprayed six rounds at him, dumping the Mafia hoodlum's lifeless body in the grass. He checked the others in the patio. All of them were dead. He ran to the back of the house where the door had been. Now a gaping hole opened to the living room.

Furniture littered the room, walls shattered, mirrors on the floor, plaster still falling from the sagging ceiling. A fire burned in the far end of the living room. Johnny checked the room carefully. No one there.

Smoke and cordite hung in the air like an omen. He charged through the room into a hallway leading toward the front of the house.

Someone looked out a door, then fisted a .45 and sent a wild shot into the floor in front of Johnny. He triggered a 4-round burst through the door, heard the man groan and fall facedown into the hallway, blood pouring from his chest into the thick carpet.

Johnny could hear the stuttering M-60 at the front of the house. Mack was taking care of business there.

Johnny remembered Angela saying something about her father's office being on the second floor. He ran down the hall, saw a man on the floor look up at him in anger and terror. The left side of the man's face had been seared by an explosion, his left arm hung in broken tatters.

Johnny lifted the M-16 and sent a mercy round through the man's forehead, then ran forward to the stairway.

Mack Bolan came through the door to the left, the M-60 tracking. He realized it was Johnny just in time and the machine gun wavered off target. Johnny led the way up the steps, peered over the top step and saw two men standing guard outside a pair of double oak doors ahead, their guns level and ready to fire.

Johnny cut both of them down with 5-round bursts from the M-16 and charged ahead. Just as he reached for the door he heard machine-gun fire behind him. He spun around as one of the guards jolted backward, a big .45 falling from his hand. Johnny looked at his brother in blood, offered a quick, silent thanks for saving his life, and then kicked in the big doors.

It was Manny the Mover's inner sanctum, his den and home office. Marcello stood behind the big desk, holding an old-fashioned Army grenade in one hand. He held the safety pin and its ring in the other, showing them to Johnny. Only Marcello's fingers kept the arming spoon in place to prevent the grenade from exploding.

Mack Bolan ran into the room and stopped beside Johnny, who had lifted the muzzle of his M-16, centering it on Marcello's chest.

"You ordered Karl Darlow killed, you piece of human-shaped shit," Bolan said.

"Yes, it had to be done."

"Did you order them to torture Sandy Darlow?" Johnny said, his voice quavering.

Manny smiled evilly. He knew who these two men were. "Sometimes, little boy, a man's got to do things he doesn't especially like."

Johnny took a threatening step forward.

Marcello lifted the grenade. "I drop this, we all die."

"I'm ready, Marcello. After what they did to Sandy I want you to die slowly."

Johnny put a 5-round burst into Marcello's knees. He screamed and fell to the floor.

"Honest, kid," the mobster cried. "It was nothing personal. It was just business."

Thunk!

The metal spoon sprang away from the grenade, arming it as it rolled over the rug toward Johnny.

In 4.2 seconds it would explode.

36

The two men dived to the right as soon as they heard the arming spoon fly off the grenade. They hit the floor and rolled away from the death ball moving across the carpet. They ended up behind the heavy cherrywood desk just as the bomb went off.

The noise was almost unbearably painful. Johnny shook his head to clear it and felt his left leg throbbing. He looked down and saw a slash in his pantleg and a bloody stain where a piece of shrapnel had sliced a half inch through his calf. Somehow it hurt very little.

Bolan was on his feet staring down at the battered corpse of the Mafia capo.

As Johnny rose to his feet he saw a door inching open on the far side of the room. A hand holding a .38 revolver probed into the room.

Before either man could shoot, the person holding the weapon stepped forward.

"Angela!" Johnny said.

Her shoulder-length dark hair was matted with blood. An ugly gash on her forehead extended upward into her hairline. She held one hand over her left eye. Her white dress was splotched with dark red stains.

Johnny rammed a new magazine into the M-16 and waited.

The girl looked at the Executioner. Her mouth tightened. The weapon was not pointing at either man. Her gaze moved to Johnny, then tears spilled from her right eye.

She took a step and they saw that she was wounded seriously. She staggered, then lifted the gun toward Johnny. She could not raise it high enough to point at him. Angela tried again and fired into the floor.

The brothers remained in place, both watching her, weapons ready.

She looked up at Johnny again "I loved you, Johnny."

She tried to smile but could manage only a grimace of pain.

"Say...something, Johnny."

"You were born into slime, Angela. And you had a chance to rise above it, but you didn't."

Angela took her left hand from her eye and moved it down to the handle of the .38, trying to lift the weapon.

Johnny gasped when he saw her eye. A piece of shrapnel had caught it from the side, cut into it and jerked the eyeball out of its socket, leaving a mushy mass.

Suddenly the image before him was transformed to another face and raw fury overtook him.

Both her hands lifted the .38 this time and it came up strong and true, almost centering on Johnny's chest.

He did not let it complete the move. From his hip Johnny triggered the M-16. A burst of five 5.56mm slugs dug into Angela's chest, ripping her to shreds.

The leaden hail propelled Angela Marcello backward and she died before she hit the floor, the .38 bouncing once on the carpet.

Johnny walked over to Angela and stared down at her. He shook his head.

"We take the rear entrance," Bolan said.

Johnny gripped the M-16 at port arms and followed Bolan as they raced down the stairs and out to the patio. Fire had eaten into half the mansion.

The two combat-hardened brothers vaulted to the top of the block wall and jumped over the wire into the neighboring yard, went across two more backyards and then worked their way slowly toward the street.

A fire truck had arrived half a block down in front of the burning Marcello mansion. Another was on its way. Three San Diego police cars sat at the curb, red lights blinking. Dozens of people crowded the sidewalks behind the police lines.

Mack held the machine gun at the side of his leg as they walked quickly through the darkness to the Pontiac, which he had parked a block away. They stepped inside, put the weapons on the back seat and drove down the hill as another fire truck raced past them, heading for the blaze.

Johnny sat stiffly in the car seat not sure where Bolan was driving. He took a deep breath. There was work to be done. He knew he had to strike fast or Mack Bolan would be gone, perhaps for years. He had to do it now. He had to convince him tonight.

"Let's go to your hotel," Johnny said. "We have some planning to do."

37

It was after 4:00 A.M. when they parked at the Intercontinental Hotel on San Diego bay. Bolan broke down the M-60 machine gun and stowed it and the other special weapons in the suitcase, which he put in the trunk. He picked up two packages from the trunk and took them upstairs to his room.

They both sat on the edge of one of the twin beds.

"Mack, I have plans, lots of plans. I want to help you in your fight. I want to be a backup, a home base for you right here in San Diego."

"We'll talk, Johnny. But we'll both make more sense if we wait until tomorrow."

"Promise you won't vanish on me the way you did that day when I was fourteen."

"You got it," Bolan said.

Johnny fell back on the bed. He looked at his brother.

"I'll never see her again, Mack."

"I know the feeling," his brother grunted.

Johnny's eyes drifted shut and he slept.

THE SUN WAS AT ITS ZENITH the next day when Bolan and Johnny settled down on the wide strip of warm sand at Del Mar, a small community just north of San Diego. There were no clouds in the sky and the reflection off the sparkling Pacific hurt the eyes.

Johnny brought his hand up to his forehead to shield the glare, trying to get everything worked out just right before he started. Bolan looked away from a pair of bikini-clad girls walking by and nudged Johnny.

"Okay, John-O, what's this big plan you have?"

"Like I told you, I think you need a support base, a place where you can get some R & R now and then."

Bolan smiled. "When I started out fighting the Mafia, I was totally alone. Then Leo Turrin showed up and I had a kind of ally. After a while I got to know Hal Brognola. And they helped. Damned right they helped. But you, Johnny...."

"I was thinking of a permanent base here in Del Mar," Johnny said. "A house I've been looking at. It's perfect. Secluded, with beach access down a twenty-foot cliff."

"Might work," Bolan said, watching the waves. "But I'll have to see some plans."

Johnny's eyes glowed with excitement.

"I thought we could call it Strongbase One," he said. "The ground floor would be just like any house, but we can make the top story into a command center."

"I have one big question," Bolan said. "Is the beer we brought in that little cooler still cold?"

Johnny laughed, dug out two cans and gave one to Bolan.

"Well, what do you think?"

"Beginning to make sense. What about weapons?" the Executioner asked.

"Oh, they're in the basement. Down there we can keep all the small arms, and military-type weapons you'll need. You'll have to teach me how to get my hands on this kind of nonlegal material."

Bolan watched a pretty brunette walk by and then turned to Johnny. "It'll be good to have someone I can trust absolutely."

Bolan looked at his grownup younger brother, so horribly bereaved by the same enemy as his. Johnny was as tough as they come. Damn straight. He was a Bolan.

Maybe Johnny's idea was sound. A place for the Executioner to get some R&R along the hellfire trail. A place where he could cease to worry about every footstep, every shadow. Even though he was at home in the shadows.

"I know only this, little brother," he said finally. "I have always had a great fear, the one overriding fear of my adult life. It's been a fear that has lurked below the surface, hidden, something that springs out at me when I least expect it.

"The fear has been *you*, Johnny. I was afraid that one day my path would cross yours, that somehow you'd be bloodied by my war. I was afraid that your life would echo mine, that you'd feel the same swirl of blood around your ankles, breathe the same goddamn smoke of my battlefield.''

Johnny looked at his brother, so rock hard even in repose. The youth's face was still ashen white from shock and loss, yet his eyes burned bright as he gazed at his own flesh and blood.

"But I no longer have that fear, Johnny. You've cauterized it, burned it out of me. I have just seen you leap into hell and I was glad. I saw you find out what it means to take an eye for an eye—literally, God rest our souls—and I was grateful to God that it should be. Because I am one with you now, Johnny.''

The young man's eyes misted as he stared out to sea.

What a brother this was. . . .

No, the hurt within him would never leave, could not ever leave him, but he had found the one true way to healing.

He had found Mack Bolan.

The Executioner.

His brother.

He had found, at last, his life.

**Choose from the titles
on the following pages
and join the world's
most daring men and women
in the hottest adventure books
on the market today.**

From the publishers of Gold Eagle Books.

Mack Bolan's
PHOENIX FORCE
by Gar Wilson

Schooled in guerrilla warfare, equipped with all the
latest lethal hardware, Phoenix Force battles the powers
of darkness in an endless crusade for freedom, justice
and the rights of the individual. Follow the adventures
of one of the legends of the genre. Phoenix Force is the
free world's foreign legion!

"Gar Wilson is excellent! Raw action attacks the reader
on every page."

—*Don Pendleton*

Phoenix Force titles are available
wherever paperbacks are sold.

**GOLD
EAGLE**

HE'S EXPLOSIVE.
E'S MACK BOLA ...

He learned his deadly skills in Vietnam...then put them to good use by destroying the Mafia in a blazing one-man war. Now **Mack Bolan** ventures further into the cold to take on his deadliest challenge yet—the KGB's worldwide terror machine.

Follow the lone warrior on his exciting new missions... and get ready for more nonstop action from his high-powered combat teams: **Able Team**—Bolan's famous Death Squad—battling urban savagery too brutal and volatile for regular law enforcement. And **Phoenix Force**—five extraordinary warriors handpicked by Bolan to fight the dirtiest of antiterrorist wars, blazing into even greater danger.

Fight alongside these three courageous forces for freedom in all-new action-packed novels! Travel to the gloomy depths of the cold Atlantic, the scorching sands of the Sahara, and the desolate Russian plains. You'll feel the pressure and excitement building page after page, with nonstop action that keeps you enthralled until the explosive conclusion!

Now you can have all the new Gold Eagle novels delivered right to your home!

You won't want to miss a single one of these exciting new action-adventures. And you don't have to! Just fill out and mail the card at right and we'll enter your name in the Gold Eagle home subscription plan. You'll then receive six brand-new action-packed Gold Eagle books every other month, delivered right to your home! You'll get two Mack Bolan novels, one Able Team and one Phoenix Force, plus one book each from two thrilling, new Gold Eagle libraries, **SOBs** and **Track**. In **SOBs** you'll meet the legendary team of mercenary warriors who fight for justice and win. **Track** is a rugged, compassionate, highly-skilled adventurer. He's a good man in a bad world, a world in which desperate affairs require desperate remedies, and he's got just the prescription.

FREE! The New War Book and Mack Bolan bumper sticker.
FREE AUTOMAG the Magazine of Action-Adventure. This informative newsletter is filled with previews of upcoming books, inside news about your favorite Gold Eagle characters and much, much more about the world of action-adventure.

As soon as we receive your card we'll rush you the long-awaited New War Book and Mack Bolan bumper sticker—both ABSOLUTELY FREE. Then under separate cover, you'll receive your six Gold Eagle novels and your copy of Automag.

The New War Book is *packed* with exciting information for Bolan fans: a revealing look at the hero's life...two new short stories...book character biographies...even a combat catalog describing weapons used in the novels! The New War Book is a special collector's item you'll want to read again and again. And it's yours FREE when you mail your card!

Of course, you're under no obligation to buy anything. Your first six books come on a 10-day free trial—if you're not thrilled with them, just return them and owe nothing. The New War Book, and Automag and bumper sticker are yours to keep, FREE!

Don't miss a single one of these thrilling novels...mail the card now, while you're thinking about it.

HE'S UNSTOPPABLE.
AND HE'LL FIGHT
AGAINST ALL ODDS
TO DEFEND FREEDOM!
Mail this coupon today!